Readers love
the Moonlight Prophecies series
by AMANDA MEUWISSEN

By the Red Moonlight

"...trust and keeping an open mind can lead to unique relationships and something different yet no less extraordinary."

—Love Bytes

Blue Moon Rising

"The mystery and suspense was very twisty and hard to figure out."

—TTC Books and More

Wane On Harvest Moon

"*Wane On Harvest Moon* is a splendid read... I always love Amanda Meuwissen's ability to get the world-building spot on for my taste, and her characters are superbly different."

—Love Bytes

By Amanda Meuwissen

Coming Up for Air
Their Dark Reflections

DREAMSPUN DESIRES
A Model Escort
Interpretive Hearts

MOONLIGHT PROPHECIES
By the Red Moonlight
Blue Moon Rising
Wane on Harvest Moon
By Cold Moon's Night

TALES FROM THE GEMSTONE KINGDOM
The Prince and the Ice King
Stitches
The Bard and the Fairy Prince
Void Dancer

Published by DSP Publications
After Vertigo

Published by DREAMSPINNER PRESS
www.dreamspinnerpress.com

BY COLD MOON'S

Night

AMANDA MEUWISSEN

DREAMSPINNER
PRESS

Published by
DREAMSPINNER PRESS

5032 Capital Circle SW, Suite 2, PMB# 279, Tallahassee, FL 32305-7886 USA
www.dreamspinnerpress.com

By Cold Moon's Night
© 2023 Amanda Meuwissen

Cover Art
© 2023 Kris Norris
https://krisnorris.com
coverrequest@krisnorris.com
Cover content is for illustrative purposes only and any person depicted on the cover is a model.

Trade Paperback ISBN: 978-1-64108-578-6
Digital ISBN: 978-1-64108-577-9
Trade Paperback published August 2023
v. 1.0

Printed in the United States of America
∞
This paper meets the requirements of
ANSI/NISO Z39.48-1992 (Permanence of Paper).

Chapter 1

ON SECOND thought, Bash was certain he loved Halloween again, because anything was better than mid-December and having a strand of tinsel fall onto him while trying to grope his boyfriend in the wee hours of the morning.

"Why did you let Preston decorate in here?" Bashir "Bash" Bain grumbled, plucking the sparkly red cousin to glitter from the back of his head. He'd be finding little pieces of the stuff for months, even after washing the bedsheets.

The ceiling fan was not an appropriate place for garland, even when turned off for the colder months.

"I didn't." His lover, Ethan Lambert, giggled beneath him, green eyes glittering far more hypnotically than tinsel ever could. "I decorated. I like being festive."

"And I like a morning fuck without obstacles." Bash snapped his teeth at Ethan's jawline, prompting another giggle, and tossed the piece of garland to the floor.

There were also snowflake cutouts taped to the windows, creating interesting shadows across Ethan's pale, pretty face with the emergence of the sun. Too much sun might annoy Ethan or make him squint, but real vampires didn't burn in daylight.

Bash groped farther down Ethan's long, lean body, finding a responding bulge beneath the stretch of tight boxer briefs. He'd persistently told Ethan not to bother with underwear in bed—or any other coverings for that matter. Not that Ethan needed to sleep, but he still could and did so wrapped in Bash's arms each night until one or the other roused and inevitably started to rut. It was remarkably…

Domestic.

Ethan nipped back at Bash as Bash nosed the crook of his neck. Bash palmed him through his underwear, thrusting his own leaking, naked cock against Ethan's hip. The next nip from Ethan was a graze of actual fangs, and Bash jerked downward with a sharper thrust. He let his multitude of larger fangs grow in answer, offering a firm, playful bite. Ethan groaned and nosed Bash too.

"If someone had told me, even two months ago, that with my next lover, I'd look forward to nuzzling the tufts of *fur* behind his ear, I never would have believed them."

Bash was indeed sprouting some of his silvery wolf fur, teetering between Stages One and Two. Being with Ethan always stirred his shifter side, just as Bash's attentions brought out Ethan's fangs and made the young vampire's green eyes glow gold.

Yellowish in color was good. It meant Ethan was well-fed, whereas turning amber, or worse, red, meant he might frenzy and seek out the blood he craved like a feral beast.

Like this, though, Bash didn't mind if Ethan drank from him and often longed for that forthcoming prick.

"Next lover?" Bash licked and nipped below Ethan's ear again, slipping his fingers beneath Ethan's waistband to palm him bare. "Planning for another after me?"

"Not at the moment," Ethan said.

He had his hands up around Bash's neck and traced his fingertips across the tattoo he'd inked onto Bash's shoulder with his own needle and careful artistry. Gray clouds like watercolor over the expanse of Bash's left shoulder parted to the rising of a bloodred moon. There were stars mimicking a night sky that even seemed to sparkle on Bash's dark skin. Along the bottom it read:

By the red moonlight.

Those words had been part of a prophecy Bash experienced the night he killed his father, usurping Baraka Bain as Alpha in Centrus City over a decade ago. Deservedly too, because Baraka had not been a good man or a good leader. Bash never dreamed the riddle he'd waited all those years to decipher would lead him to a vampire in his bed whom he never wanted to let go.

Ethan's hands drifted from the smoother surface of the ink to one of Bash's many scars, courtesy of dear old Dad and countless fights in and out of wolf forms. Ethan was one of the few people allowed to see, let alone touch them.

Bash was more interested in Ethan's skin and his *several* tattoos. Bash couldn't reach Ethan's shoulder, but there was a simple black-lined design there, depicting deconstructed Avengers' symbols combined into one, like a partial star for Captain America, a reactor for Iron Man, an arrow for Hawkeye, and so on.

The tattoos Bash could reach were on Ethan's wrists, and he turned his head from Ethan's neck to draw one to his mouth, kissing the pillar there. That was the left, with a white skull in the center, while the right had a fist holding scales. Very badass-looking, despite being from a tabletop game. In *Warhammer*, the symbols more or less meant police and secret police, which was an in-joke Ethan must have loved, given he'd been a CSI before going to prison.

Bash's favorites of Ethan's tattoos were lower.

After finishing his kiss at Ethan's wrist, he tugged Ethan's hand down to suck a thumb into his mouth and reached with his free hand to one set of the lightning bolts at Ethan's hips. A pair of yellow bolts framed either side of him, right down the grooves zeroing toward his cock that Bash was vigorously stroking. It was sopping in his hand, a slippery mess of eager drippings.

"*Bash.*"

Bash yanked Ethan's underwear down and took the gifted wetness, reaching lower between Ethan's already spread thighs. They parted wider, hips arching upward to admit him. Stretching wasn't necessary, but Bash liked to slick his way inside and finger Ethan a little, coaxing the mewling noises that poured from him so readily.

"Ah… *oh*… mmm…."

Bash thrust in one finger, enough to graze Ethan's walls and make him squirm. Then he paused, holding the finger deep inside Ethan without moving. Ethan's mewling grew whiny, questioning, and he started fucking himself on the patiently immobile digit.

"Come on."

"No."

Ethan groaned, hips jerking wildly, underwear still locked above his knees and cock bobbing beautifully against his taut stomach.

"Keep fucking yourself like that and maybe I'll offer a second finger."

"Fuck you." Ethan laughed.

"Later. This morning I'm fucking you."

"Do it, then!"

"Keep earning it."

Ethan's groans of frustration were beautifully vocal—but he didn't stop rocking his hips. He twisted and pumped to get the finger inside him deeper and at different angles, as if hoping that somehow, this thrust or that one might hit the right spot. The agony on his face made Bash more patient to not give in, despite the throbbing and twitching of his own cock, no longer able to rut against anything with Ethan's hips pulled back.

With his mouth dropping open from his panting and moans, Ethan's fangs caught the morning light. They were smaller than Bash's, shifter fangs being longest on their eyeteeth, with less significant sets beside them, and on their lower teeth too. Bash often had Ethan like this, utterly at his mercy, yet Ethan's delicate tips could do more damage than any shifter's if he used them with purpose.

Bash offered that second finger slowly. Ethan could take so much more and kept rocking his hips in search of it. Keeping the hand inside Ethan free of claws, Bash released them on the other and dragged their points down the back of Ethan's thigh toward his sac.

Ethan's eyes flashed brighter, a predator's stare, like he had his prey right where he wanted. He slowed his momentum, vampire eyes locked on Bash's that had to be glowing too, bronzy-brown and vibrant. Ethan held Bash's gaze as he rocked Bash's fingers in and out of him. Tongued his fangs. Licked his lips. Moaned.

"*Bash.*"

He won.

He always did.

Bash impaled Ethan on his ripe prick with one slam, and the corners of Ethan's lips curled up in a satisfied smile. While pounding into him, Bash let more of his wolf form free, more than he ever had with another, even with other wolves. It bordered on his Stage Three bestial form, enough that he was larger, framed in silver fur, ears starting to point and teeth growing. He raked his claws up and around Ethan's thighs to grip his hips and slammed into him harder as a growl built and rumbled between them.

Ethan growled too, still moaning and panting and putting on a show to drive Bash further into his animal nature. They were both beasts, even if not cut from the same cloth, sewed together like a quilt of fate.

Diving his head back into the crook of Ethan's neck, Bash marked him like a wolf in the wild, grazing fanged teeth and breathing in Ethan's unique scent. Everyone said mates smelled incredible to each other, but Ethan wasn't some comforting scent from childhood or typical aphrodisiac. He was graphite and copper, like he'd just finished a sketch outdoors and came in to escape a storm. He didn't smell like blood, but he did smell like static, like lightning, and it made Bash tingle, as if a storm were brewing in that very room.

Ethan enveloped him with every rut forward, tight hole clenching and retracting on Bash's cock like a challenge to be given more. So, more Bash gave and let himself grow one step closer to a hulking werewolf. His cock thickened with the rest of him, and Ethan roared, latching on to Bash's neck with a piercing bite that this time drew blood.

Bash spilled inside Ethan from the spike of pleasure being fed on caused him. His mind went blank, pure bliss overtaking him from the release and briefest of moments being utterly under Ethan's thrall. The trust Bash had in Ethan was its own strange bliss. Ethan could overpower him at any moment, control him, use him, but he gave himself to Bash instead.

Ethan came soon after with a stutter of his hips milking Bash's cock. He bit down firmer with those last spurts of come staining his stomach and then lapped at the drawn blood, licking the marks away. That, this, all of it, was something Bash never thought he'd want. Certainly not a vampire in his bed, but not anyone stable either. Or monogamous. He'd never been on the lookout for a mate, yet Ethan kept making that word ring true. Bash might even say he….

No. He couldn't say *that*. They hadn't said it. Bash never said it to anyone, because that sort of emotion and devotion, those words, were a danger he didn't think he could brave.

Even riskier than bedding a vampire.

"Wow." Ethan dropped his head back onto the pillow with fangs still peeking between reddened lips. "How is it literally better every time?"

"I'm that good."

Ethan giggled, and oh, Bash adored that sound.

Adored was easier to think than the other word.

Already deflating from having fur nearly everywhere and his nose close to elongating, the last wolf bits to fade were Bash's claws and fangs and the glow of his eyes. He kept the fangs a while longer, just to nip once more at Ethan's neck, and took another deep inhale of the storm.

Their alarm went off like they'd planned things to the minute, and Bash rolled away to cease its chime. Ethan grunted from the disconnect and kicked down his briefs to snatch them up as a rag. The view of him rolling his hips back again, hole agape and oozing Bash's come, was a fine addition to their good morning.

Ethan caught Bash staring as he cleaned the mess and slowed, fingering where he'd been thoroughly fucked open. "You are that good. Did you actually get bigger inside me?"

"Maybe."

Ethan hummed, circling his tender hole with a fingertip. "Is it wrong if I want to try the full werewolf version some time?"

Bash had half a mind to stuff Ethan full again right now, and would have if he didn't have to go and be Alpha. "Maybe I'll spring it on you when you least expect it. Tie you up and take you standing, arms chained above your head, like a sacrificial virgin to the beast."

"*Urg.*" Ethan dropped his legs with a groan, knowing full well they couldn't make good on that promise for a while. "You're mean."

"You started it." Bash leaned over and kissed him, feeling the press of Ethan's fangs between their lips, and then a gentle graze when his tongue slid between them. "Come on, we both have responsibilities to get to."

The flushed beauty of afterglow faded from Ethan's face, because his first true task each day wasn't as much fun as their wake-up. Part of the reason for a routine fuck, besides it being the best way to start the day, was to help Ethan forget for a while that before he went to work, he had to tend to their prisoner in the basement.

Bash and Ethan showered together, and a few extra gropes and lingering kisses beneath the water helped clear some of the clouds from Ethan's eyes—green again, like he was simply human, though the smell of him said otherwise. The scent of a vampire was unmistakable to any shifter, but for Bash, it had the bonus of smelling right.

Ethan dressed a little smarter these days, an investigator once more, although the private kind instead of on the force. Bash had a feeling that Bari, his twin brother, may have had a hand in Ethan's wardrobe change, given its more fashionable leaning over Ethan's previous collection of T-shirts.

A sage-green button-down brought out the emerald in Ethan's eyes, and navy slacks should have clashed, yet they worked perfectly with the green-and-blue-striped tie he failed for the third time to knot correctly.

"Get over here." Bash tied it for him with a few quick twists and pulls.

"Thanks." The storm clouds were back in Ethan's eyes. Bash preferred for the storm to only ever be pleasant.

"You're making progress."

"I know."

"He's been alone, planning all this for decades."

"I *know*."

"Then stop moping. It's very unattractive."

Ethan cracked a smile just as Bash hoped.

If Halloween at the den had been like the holiday threw up everywhere, then the weeks leading into Christmas made it the place where Saint Nick recovered from his latest bender. Preston, rat shifter, Rat King who could control rodents with sheer will, and the pack's Magister in charge of magic, was also a menace when it came to holiday decorations. They were everywhere, including a set of child-sized porcelain Mr. and Mrs. Claus figures with auras so creepy Bash wouldn't have been surprised if they came to life at night.

"Mornin', boss. Leech," Deanna greeted them at the bottom of the stairs. What had started as a deriding nickname for Ethan had become a fond pet name.

Deanna was an Asian panther, with a short black bob, violet eyes, and the sort of sturdy muscled frame that would have made her an ideal— and deadly—MMA fighter. Everyone in Bash's inner circle lived under the same large manor roof. Made up of him, Deanna as Second, Preston as Magister, Luke as Counselor to the people, Siobhan as Warden to police them, and Nell as Shaman to heal and protect, the circle living together was one of the few traditions Bash hadn't done away with. If he'd followed other traditions when he took over the pack, everyone in his inner circle would have been a wolf like him, but instead, his core advisors represented each of the other shifter tribes: a rat, two cats, and a lizard. The only tribe missing from his circle was a raptor—meaning the avian kind, not a dinosaur.

"Got another call from Shorehaven." Deanna got straight to business as they reached the first floor, which made sense given she'd been waiting for them. "I think you might need to return this one, boss. Their Alpha's gettin' twitchy."

All the neighboring cities were twitchy, particularly Shorehaven and Metro City, both of which had been poised to attempt takeovers of Centrus weeks ago. Forming a strong bond with Brookdale—despite having called off his engagement to Brookdale's Alpha, Jeffrey "Jay" Russell, who instead was currently engaged to be engaged to Bash's brother, Bari—had helped ease some of the tensions. So had reforming old bonds with nearby Glenwood, but with vampires showing up and having influence over Brookdale—and possibly Glenwood now too— any headway Bash had made was crumbling. The other cities had always been skeptical of his rule, but now they thought a plague was spreading through the packs, and it all started with Ethan.

Another thing tradition stated was that vampires should be killed on sight.

"See you later?" Ethan asked, giving Bash leave to go be boss.

"Can't wait," Bash said. They kissed, just a quick peck, before Ethan headed for the cellar and Bash went with Deanna into the side lounge he used as an office. Even that kiss was domestic.

"Ain't you two so cute?" Deanna elbowed Bash along the way.

"Can it. As if you're any better. Where's your counterpart this morning?"

"Rio left early. Gotta get up with the sun to tend to flowers right, apparently."

Rio was one of the owners of a local flower shop. He was a human Focus, who they'd taken into the fold after his abilities were discovered and he got thrown into their world basically headfirst. He was instantly likable, the type of person who drew people in, because just like Ethan and Ethan's father, Gordon, his presence amplified the innate abilities of anyone around him. It could be directed so the wrong type of person wasn't given the same boost as someone else, but Rio was still learning. So was Ethan, really. And Bash.

Bash was a Focus too, since his father had been one, but the only power he'd been aware of before recent events was being a Seer like his mother. He hadn't had a prophecy in weeks, but it was only a matter of time, being the child of a Seer and Focus, with abilities from both, like Ethan had proven to be too. Now, with Bari manifesting the same, the three of them were the rarest and possibly most powerful people on earth.

If only that eased Bash's anxiety about their mystery villain, orchestrating events from the shadows across cities and that spanned decades, maybe centuries worth of planning. They only knew it was a she, some ancient vampire who wanted to seize power from shifters. She'd almost succeeded too. Twice.

And they didn't even know her name.

"Any idea what you're gonna say to Shorehaven?" Deanna asked.

"Nope. But I'm sure something will come to me. Eventually we're going to need to stop stalling or we'll be back to square one, waiting for war to break out on all sides and some traditionalist to try stealing my city."

"Not on my watch, boss."

Bash hoped not, but as much as Ethan hadn't been able to shake the storm clouds from his eyes, Bash couldn't shake that something was off. Very little was right lately, but there was something else in the air this morning, and it wasn't only because a twitchy Alpha was pestering him.

They were in for bad news, Bash could sense it, and it would likely come from Preston and Luke on assignment in Glenwood, right where they suspected their mystery vampire might strike next.

At least Bash was prepared for it. After all, his hunches were never wrong.

ETHAN WAVED to Siobhan and Nell in the kitchen as he went to the cellar door. The pair was a true set of opposites this morning. Nell, their human Shaman and resident long-haired flower child, was wide-eyed and enjoying what looked like tea and avocado toast. In contrast, Siobhan barely had her eyes open, more a night owl—or night lizard, Ethan supposed, since she was a shifter with scales. Her short platinum hair was stuck up in every direction as she held a giant mug of coffee and sipped from it like a child drinking soup.

The brief smile evoked from seeing them vanished as soon as Ethan started down the steps, even if he did have to duck beneath a strand of garland draped across the archway.

All this, at least for him, had started when he got out of prison and returned to Centrus City for the first time since he was a boy. He'd wanted a fresh start, just a way to make money until he got a PI license. Being an ex-con could have made that difficult, but Bash had connections, and it helped that what Ethan went to prison for was trying to right a wrong.

A guilty man had been about to escape jail time, and Ethan had foolishly tried falsifying evidence to change that. Even if his heart was in the right place, he shouldn't have done it, but he often wondered if he only felt guilty because he'd been caught.

Was that how his dad felt too?

The echo of Ethan's footfalls enhanced the claustrophobia of the space as he descended. He'd spent his first night as a vampire in this cellar. Or rather, *cell*.

It was livable. Bash had ensured that even back then, with a bed, desk, entertainment. It wasn't as though a vampire needed to eat or use the bathroom, but isolation was its own torture. Ethan felt like Clarice going to see Hannibal Lector, even though this was his father he was visiting.

There was a door at the top of the stairs and one into the enclosed cellar room at the bottom, tightly bolted. The room had been intended to be a wine cellar but might never become one now. Ethan didn't have to worry about his father trying to rush out when he unbolted and opened it, because Nell had reinforced the archway with runes, and only someone with a corresponding rune placed on them, like Ethan, could pass through it.

His eyes adjusted to the darkness the moment he creaked the door open, but in that brief second when everything was black, the outline of his father within was an ominous silhouette.

Ethan thought of the charcoal drawing he'd once made before he knew his father was his sire, just a tall, broad shadow down a long, dark alley, like a storybook monster lurking. He'd seen that figure in his dreams too, calling to him, manipulating him, enthralling him to in turn enthrall Bash to do terrible things.

He'd believed for years his father was dead. The last time he'd seen him before all this, Ethan was just a kid. Facing him now made Ethan feel like that same little boy.

Gordon sat on the bed like every morning, as if waiting for Ethan, or maybe never having slept. When Ethan stepped inside, Gordon didn't try to move closer. He hadn't since the first night. Contact, luxuries, freedom, all had to be earned. The only way Gordon was ever getting out of the cellar alive was if he proved he could be trusted. More than that, Ethan needed to believe his father knew what he'd done was wrong.

Nothing justified trying to enslave an entire city. Nothing justified the deaths Gordon had almost caused. Even if it had been for Ethan's sake, some twisted logic to make up for that long-ago night when Gordon, a frenzied newborn vampire, killed Ethan's mother.

He *was* the shadow from Ethan's dreams, a monster in the dark, detached from reality and unsettling, but someone Ethan never imagined he'd fear this much. Especially with how Gordon sat there. Waiting. Smiling.

"Good morning, Ethan."

"Hi, Dad."

Chapter 2

GORDON SHOULD have been in his fifties, but because he'd been turned into a vampire nearly twenty years ago, he didn't look much older than Ethan. He was the same height as Ethan too, but broader, giving him an overall larger presence. He had brown hair and eyes, but otherwise looked very much like Ethan, with a more masculine jawline, whereas Ethan had a delicate curve to his chin like his mother.

Ethan turned on the light.

"You look good," Gordon said, his smile seemingly serene but still unnerving. "Going to the office today? It continues to be strange, seeing you grown up like this, and a detective too."

"I'm just a PI, Dad." Ethan kept his distance but pulled over the chair from the desk to face his father as he sat. "I barely have any cases yet."

Ethan hadn't wanted to push too hard too soon, so these first few weeks had mostly been about chitchatting and catching up on twenty years missed. Ethan had been raised by someone who, at the time, he'd thought was a family friend. He called him Uncle Leo and loved him like a second father, but he hadn't learned until he became a vampire that Leo was more like his grandfather, because Leo was a vampire too.

One night, starved and frenzied, Leo attacked Gordon, nearly killing him, and turned him in an attempt to make up for the accident. A young Ethan and his mother had come home then, and Leo hid, just in time for Gordon to wake, frenzied himself as a newborn. Who wouldn't have gone a little mad waking later to their wife's blood on their hands, a monster who'd killed his child's mother in front of him? Ethan was glad he'd blocked most of it from his mind.

Gordon had begged Leo to take Ethan away that night, but over time, his mental state deteriorated more and more. He wanted Ethan back, and Leo, recognizing Gordon wasn't well, kept Ethan hidden and safe in Glenwood. Too safe in some ways, because the spell used to keep Ethan from standing out to others meant he'd never been close to anyone. People dismissed him, even disliked him because of it, and that same magic had kept his abilities from manifesting until the spell was no longer being reinforced when he went to prison.

Ironic that the first time Ethan had felt like himself, making connections with people, finding his inner voice in his drawings and eventual tattooing, was while he was locked up.

"You're doing something that's important to you," Gordon said, "trying to make a difference for the sake of others. Your mother would be very proud. *I'm* very proud."

Ethan's eyes prickled, and he looked away, not able to meet his father's stare when he said something so normal like that, so much what Ethan wanted to hear.

Sometimes he still waited for that strange pressure that signaled his father was trying to control him. Ethan liked to believe his combined strength as a Seer and Focus would prevent his father from ever controlling him again, but even if he might have succumbed, other runes Nell placed on him were able to disrupt the connection a sire would normally have over their fledgling.

"Thanks, Dad. I…." Ethan's eyes fell on the minifridge in the corner, with a glass door, showing the blood bags inside, donated from members of the household. Ethan could get by fine drinking here and there from Bash. Bash rejuvenated faster than a human, but Ethan could feed from the others if needed. They trusted him. No one trusted Gordon, so it had been agreed he'd be fed more clinically.

Only none of this week's bags were empty.

"Have you been eating?" Ethan hurried to the fridge and opened it to be sure his guess was right. He knew it hadn't been restocked. There were three bags, enough to sate Gordon even more than he needed, but none of them were missing a drop. "*Dad?*" Ethan turned to him with a wilder crack to his voice.

Gordon's eyes flashed in the dark, glowing such a brilliant shade of amber, they almost looked red.

"Don't you understand what could happen?" Ethan nearly rushed his father but held back, knowing the precarious tightrope being walked between sanity and animal rage. "You could kill someone! Kill me! Don't you get that?"

"Yes," Gordon said, infuriatingly calm. "But I won't be a danger to anyone if you kill me first."

"What?"

"You've been so patient." Gordon let his eyes dim to brown, but Ethan knew how close he must be to losing control. "All I've ever brought you is pain. I killed your mother—"

"That wasn't your fault—"

"Forced you to live with a stranger who secluded you—"

"Leo meant well—"

"And threatened the people you've come to care for. I should have died the night Leo fed from me. It would have been better. But you can remedy that now. You can end this cycle and keep living the good life you've built for yourself despite me."

"Dad, no." Ethan pushed good sense aside and went to his father, dropping to his knees in front of him. How much of this had escalated because someone wanted to right a wrong in the worst possible way? "I had them spare you. They let me spare you. I am not going to kill you just because this is hard. You know it was the wrong path. That's all I wanted. That's all anyone was hoping for. We can rebuild from that. We can make things right."

Gordon looked so serene, so much like the kind soul Ethan remembered from when he was a boy, as he took hold of Ethan's face in both hands. Ethan choked on more tears, grateful to have his father touching him, because he'd missed him so much and denied them both the chance to even embrace until now.

"I've made mistakes too," Ethan whispered, "but I'm working to right them. That's how you make this up to me, Dad. And not *Mom*. You can't make it up to me what happened to Mom because it wasn't your fault. Now here." Much as he wanted to press his face into Gordon's hands, time was short, and too many people counted on him to keep Gordon caged until it was safe.

Ethan sat beside his father, unbuttoning the cuff of his left sleeve, and rolled it up to the elbow. He held his wrist in front of his father's mouth, a safer alternative to baring his throat.

"You can take a little from me to tide you over. Then I need you to drink at least one of those bags today, okay?"

Gordon didn't take the offered wrist but faced Ethan. "You look like her. Like me, too, but I see so much of your mother in you."

"Dad...."

"If this is what you want, Ethan."

"It is, but I need you to want it too." Ethan thrust his wrist closer to his father's face, and at last, Gordon looked at it. He breathed in, no doubt smelling the tang of blood in Ethan's veins, even if not as tempting as a human's. To Ethan, Bash's blood tasted better than anyone's, but a hungry vampire could feed on almost anything.

Gordon's fangs latched on to Ethan's wrist so suddenly, he gasped, not even having seen them extend. Gordon's eyes went amber again, so close to red, Ethan tried not to think of what might have happened—or would have needed to happen—if his father had already been frenzied when he came down to see him this morning.

The bite didn't hurt. And maybe because Ethan was also a vampire, he didn't feel the way Bash or others described the sensation. He was grateful there was no stir of arousal, but it was sort of peaceful. Comforting. Like Ethan remembered when his dad would hold him tight as a kid after a nightmare.

It was Ethan who held on to Gordon now, wrapping his free arm around Gordon's shoulders as his father drank. He pressed his face to the side of Gordon's neck and closed his eyes, trying to be mindful of the amount being taken. It helped that he'd fed from Bash earlier, but he focused on each rapid beat of his own heart, faster than a human's but slowing as the blood drained.

Behind his eyes, he thought he saw an image in the dark, like five silhouettes standing in a lopsided circle around a sixth figure in the center—

Heaviness in body and mind nearly made Ethan sway. He opened his eyes. His father still had hold of him, grasping his wrist with both hands, fangs sunk in tight. Ethan wanted to let him out of the cellar, to lead him upstairs and out to freedom. He couldn't. He shouldn't even wish it yet. Then he realized why he had.

Ethan was a masterpiece of invisible runic wards, almost more than the visible marks on him in the form of tattoos. The unfortunate thing was the blue glow of a rune on his father's left arm, just like a matching red one glowed on Ethan's, blocking what Gordon had attempted to do.

Ethan pulled from his father's grasp, and the runes dimmed. "You were trying to enthrall me again," he said, hurt and feeling so foolish as he licked the bite marks clean and then pulled his sleeve down with angry tugs. "You starved yourself to trick me?"

"No." Gordon reached for him, but Ethan used his vampiric speed to be across the room before Gordon could so much as graze the cuff of his shirt. "Ethan!" He made to spring upward, vampire eyes safely yellow again.

"*Don't* come near me," Ethan warned, already stepping outside so that, even if his father tried, he couldn't reach him.

"I wouldn't harm anyone from the pack," Gordon said, remaining sitting but beckoning to Ethan with outstretched arms. "I swear. I know how much they mean to you."

"The push I felt wasn't you trying to convince me to kill you. You were telling me to set you free."

"Only for your own good! This has always been about you, Ethan, all for you. I don't want to hurt you anymore."

The tears made it difficult for Ethan to see clearly, even with vampire eyes, but he welcomed the blur. "You lied and manipulated me again. You don't want to die, and I'd be glad for that, Dad, but that still might be how this ends. Please don't make me be the one who has to do it."

"Ethan—"

Ethan slammed the door shut, sniffling back the sobs that threatened to overtake him. He sped upstairs, trying to not go too fast and risk Nell and Siobhan's worry if they were still in the kitchen. He'd never been so relieved to need sunglasses before meeting the sun, because donning them hid the stains on his cheeks.

If Nell and Siobhan were there, he didn't notice them, eyes still blurry, focused on reaching his office. He barely remembered to grab his winter coat. There hadn't been a first snowfall yet, and as a vampire, he was resistant enough to the cold, but it was still December. He didn't need any strange looks this morning.

Thankfully, his office was close, within walking distance from the den, across the street from Rio's flower shop and kitty-corner from the Rogue's Gallery tattoo parlor that the pack owned as a money laundering front. They still legitimately offered tattooing, but the state of their finances may have been questionable.

The lawful side of Ethan would have cared if he didn't understand that looking out for an entire species unknown to most of the human populace sometimes required money exchanging hands off the books.

There was something especially comforting about the sight of the glass door to his office when he reached it, frosted and etched with the name Lambert Investigations. Bash had rented the space for him, in a building filled with other small businesses. He said he'd only foot the bill until Ethan started bringing in clients and money of his own, but Ethan doubted Bash would kick him to the curb if business was slow.

There was a mail slot by the door, but packages were left in the hall, like today, where a larger one from a name Ethan knew well awaited him. Finding it almost buoyed his spirits.

The door was the fanciest part of his office, the rest merely a single room with a desk, chair, shelving, filing cabinets, and other usual trimmings. Though he did have a bamboo plant by the window, courtesy of Nell, for luck. All he needed was a fedora to perch atop his coat rack and he'd be a regular gumshoe.

There were only a few pieces of regular mail today, which he retrieved to toss on his desk. He focused first on the package. Mrs. Decker was too kind. She'd sent him care packages every week the six months he was in prison. Often little things, like a jar of peanut butter or a clever or interesting news clipping, but always with a drawing included from her daughter, Rosie.

She'd drawn a snowman for Ethan today. He wondered if Glenwood had already gotten their first snowfall. There was also a succulent in the box, so another plant to add beside his bamboo, and a note from Mrs. Decker wishing him luck in the new job. At least the gifts cleared the last of the tears from Ethan's eyes.

He wished he'd been able to give Mrs. Decker justice for her son's death. It was her husband who Ethan had tried falsifying evidence against, the case of her son, dead at the hands of *Carson* Decker, that had ended with Ethan in prison instead and a guilty man set free. Even so, all Mrs. Decker cared about was that Ethan had tried.

He set the succulent in the window, the box on the floor to recycle later, and the note and drawing in the corner of his desk beside Decker's case file. Bash had given him the file almost a month ago as a gift with the office. Decker was in Centrus City. He hadn't been a murderer before, just a thug, a thief, a low-rank criminal. He'd tried covering up his son's death, and poorly, but there hadn't been enough solid evidence to convict him.

Recently he'd been spotted in shady neighborhoods in Centrus, neighborhoods Siobhan's agents had eyes on. Nothing truly incriminating had been recorded, but it was proof enough to Ethan that Decker was up to his old tricks. He'd make a mistake eventually, and Ethan would be there to finally take him down.

Ethan was lucky he'd only gone to prison for six months. It should have been longer, but Leo had pulled strings—what strings, Ethan never really knew—and got him out early on good behavior.

Beneath Decker's file were a few smaller cases and tasks he'd completed since opening his door to clients, slowly building up word of mouth and a little income. Decker was priority, though. It wasn't a case that would pay, but Ethan couldn't let it go, that last chapter of his old life that needed to be closed.

Along with Gordon.

One of today's letters was another reminder from the recent past, from Ethan's old cellmate, Dave Golding. Ethan never could have survived prison without him—his teddy bear in a hitman's casing. Dave had looked out for Ethan in prison, a large and intimidating man who'd had some tough breaks but ultimately wanted to do better when he got out.

The letter was mostly Dave checking in on how Ethan was doing and assuring him that he was okay too and still on track to be released early next year. Ethan was happy for him and would have to write back to Dave soon so he wouldn't worry. They hadn't talked much since Ethan's release. It was signed, like all Dave's letters, with the nickname he'd given Ethan the first day they met.

Stay good, little Lamb.

Beneath where he'd set the mail was Ethan's sketchpad. He had one at home too, but this one was for those moments between cases when something struck him or stirred in his mind that he had to get down on paper. He mostly used pencil, sometimes with color, some detailed, some abstract. It depended on what he saw when he closed his eyes, but he'd learned to trust what he drew as more than mere doodles.

He flipped it open to a drawing of Decker, first done from memory and then updated after he'd seen the man from afar while scoping out his haunts. His hair was longer now, face clean-shaven, eyes less glazed than Ethan remembered, so he'd been laying off the booze, but what Ethan hated was Decker's smile. He could never draw it right. It always turned out too kind, and Decker was not kind.

The next page in the sketchpad made Ethan shiver. It reminded him of the one he'd done of his father's silhouette, but this was of their vampire villain, whoever she may be. Even Ethan's Seer abilities couldn't conjure a face, so she was just a feminine outline from the bust up, with long wavy hair, a thin frame but powerful presence, and blank features.

There weren't placeholders for eyes or a mouth, but what Ethan had drawn was what he'd thought was a constellation, since so much of the prophecies between him, Bash, and Bari included celestial bodies.

He looked closer at the points of light in the woman's shadowed visage. They matched what he'd seen when he closed his eyes that morning while his father fed from him—like five points in a lopsided circle around a sixth.

"Knock-knock! Any private *dicks* arou—yeah, that isn't gonna land, sorry. Couldn't think of a joke."

Ethan smiled as he looked up from the sketchpad at the entrance of his friend Rio. They hadn't known each other for long, but both had been thrown without warning into the world of shifters, vampires, and magical humans in only the past couple of months. It was nice to have someone to commiserate with over that.

Rio was slight of stature with long dark hair, dark eyes, and a friendly smile. Today's graphic T-shirt had a black cat holding a bone and read: I found this humerus. Rio also carried a leafy potted plant larger than any of the others Ethan had been gifted so far.

"At this rate, I'll run out of room." Ethan chuckled, indicating his window. "How about the desk? Assuming that's enough sun?"

"Like I'd give you a plant that needs sun." Rio strolled in to deposit the plant on Ethan's desk. He'd been a little wary initially upon discovering Ethan was a vampire, but had eased in quickly, especially after learning that Ethan was already a vampire when he gave Rio his Bulbasaur tattoo. It was hard to imagine a vampire being a danger to you when they'd literally smelled your blood for an hour straight.

"I love it, Rio. Thanks."

"One whole month in business, man! Figured that deserved a present. Plus, it's been slow at the shop today, and Caity is on one of her rampaging rearranging binges. Best to stay out of her way."

Caity was another owner of the flower shop, along with her husband. They and Rio owned it together, the others being normal humans who had no idea the number of nonhumans working in and around their neighborhood.

A tingle shot down Ethan's back, and what he once might have thought was the alluring smell of human blood so near him was better understood as the empowering zing that Rio projected as a Focus. Everyone said Ethan made them feel the same. Bash certainly made Ethan feel that way, but he didn't feel it around Gordon, even though he was also a Focus. Part of that was all the warding around the cellar, but also because even the strongest of empowering energy couldn't negate the dip in Ethan's stomach when he faced his father.

Like earlier.

Ethan absently touched his wrist, despite knowing the marks were gone, and glanced at his sketch of the unknown vampire.

The tingle raced down his spine again. Five points around a sixth....

"So anyway, it's only a couple weeks from my and Deanna's two-month anniversary, and I could really use some advice. We didn't do anything for the one-month, 'cause, ya know, I was still partially in shock and moving into a den of were-people. I gotta think of something special this time. *She's* special and deserves, like, all the special things."

They weren't stars. They were figures. People.

"Ethan? Dude, it's hard to tell where your mind is when you're wearing the shades. I mean, those round Ray-Bans are *sweet*, but I thought you told me you weren't the sunglasses indoors kinda guy?"

People... and they were needed.

Because she was coming.

"Ethan?"

The flash of a vision assaulted Ethan so suddenly, too suddenly, that he couldn't grasp it or fully understand what was being shown to him. All he saw was a daunting flicker of two outcomes side by side.

Five people around a sixth—succeeding.

Or many, many people laid out and unmoving on the ground like a scattering of ashes around the center person's feet.

"Ethan!"

THE LANDLINE dropped from Bash's hand.

"Boss?"

He shook the start of the vision from his mind. That was different from what he was used to. He wasn't really used to how his powers manifested these days because it was all so new. Before, he'd barely remember his visions, speaking riddles he had to hope others overheard or he might forget them.

Since meeting Ethan, having Bari come into his powers too, and with so many other Focuses and magical people around, the visions were stronger, clearer. But this was almost like something too big to compute, trickling in like a preview.

"Bash?" Deanna asked more seriously. When all he did was stare at her, she picked up the dropped landline and spoke to the confused voice still talking on the other end. "Somethin' came up." She slammed the receiver down, just as the cellphone in Bash's pocket began to ring.

"Ethan?" Bash answered without checking the caller ID.

"You saw it too?"

"Not enough to understand anything clearly. You?"

"Same. It was like a precursor to something bigger. I think I've been feeling it all morning."

"Me too."

"Rio's here. I think that might have been what pushed it for me."

"Love being of help!" Rio called half-hysterically from Ethan's end.

But it wasn't only Rio. There was more coming, more of the vision on its way. Bash felt it like a tide rolling in, like something, *someone*, was creeping ever closer.

"Ethan—"

"Bash—"

They overlapped in their warning cries, both cutting off as the next wave hit them.

Bash clutched his phone tighter to prevent his hand from dropping it like the landline and let the words flow from him, as they also flowed from Ethan over the phone. Both their eyes changed, he knew, the whites going black, irises bright blue, with a third eye appearing on their foreheads as they spoke in unison.

Blood Moon to Blue Moon, the harvest is ripe
For the old queen to conquer by Cold Moon's night
Four corners connect where a fifth is born
As a united star they can hold back the morn

A series of rapid knocks on the front door made Bash gasp as the vision and prophecy ended. He couldn't deny what he'd seen, but it still hadn't been clear enough, not nearly enough, a mere flash of hazy figures around a sixth, contrasted against a devastating landscape of fallen bodies should their mystery villain win.

He lurched up from the desk, still clutching his phone, and hurried toward the front door.

"Boss!" Deanna chased after him.

Bash was unsteady, knees quaking, and nearly crumpled as he reached the foyer, only for Deanna to be there, as she always was, to support him when he needed her.

The knocking was loud, continuous, desperate.

It couldn't be the enemy. Not yet.

Then the door burst open, the knocker not waiting any longer for admittance, and in came Preston and Luke helping Jay bring in Bari, who looked as unsteady and spooked as Bash.

"We told you to go in!" Preston growled, his long dark hair tied up in a messy bun, unshaven face more scruffy than usual and glasses askew from their harried entrance.

"It seemed rude!" Jay argued, a massive contrast to Preston and Luke's smaller statures, since the Alpha werewolf of Brookdale was basically a linebacker, tall and thick with muscle, his short sandy hair dusted with gray despite only being a few years older than Bash.

"You too?" Bash asked his brother without greeting.

Bari nodded. He was Bash's twin in everything but fashion sense and, normally, countenance, but his grave expression made him look far too serious and it was more like looking in a mirror than usual.

"Ethan," Bash spoke into his phone.

"I'm here."

"Get back to the den. Now."

Chapter 3

BASH HAD known something was coming even before the looming threat of it building in the back of his mind that morning, but he'd still hoped it wouldn't blindside them like it had.

"Guess we won't be needing that round-robin update call this week," Bari said with his usual jovial tone falling to weariness. They'd been checking in via magical "Zoom" calls ever since Bari went to Brookdale, but for the first time in a long time, they were all under the same roof.

With every member of the inner circle, including Preston and Luke, as well as Ethan, Rio, and newcomers Bari and Jay, it was a full house. At least it didn't appear that Jay's Second, Maximus, had accompanied them. He wasn't the most cordial of werewolves.

Bash stood in the center of the living room, no matter how much Ethan tried urging him to sit. Ethan wasn't sitting either but stood beside Bash as they faced the others. The somber atmosphere was only partially belied by the Christmas tree towering the full height of the two-storied space, with lighted snowflakes dangling from the ceiling, more tinsel and garland over every possible surface, and wreaths—so many wreaths.

If Preston could have re-wallpapered the den in literal candy canes, he would have.

Preston and Luke had claimed their usual corner of the sofa. Although usual hadn't been as true of late. Tension had been brewing since their adoption of young tiger shifter Jesse, who'd been left behind in Glenwood to keep her safe. Their trip had cured them of any conflict, apparently, for Preston was snug against the armrest, with Luke equally snug against him.

His rat companions, Basil and Dr. Dawson, had appeared at his arrival, since he'd left them here while traveling to Glenwood, but there was a third now. It was smaller, a mouse, which he'd pulled from his pocket and set on the end table to introduce to the others. Another rodent in the house might have been upsetting if Preston wasn't a Rat King.

"Speaking of our weekly calls," Bash addressed Preston and Luke, "why didn't you two call ahead that you were coming back, and how did you—" He returned to Bari. "—know to come here at all?"

Bari had claimed one of the larger plush chairs, with Jay sitting on the arm. Bari's outfit was somewhat subdued today, a color-blocked burgundy-and-black sweater split down the middle over slim-fit slacks. He still made the rest of them look like punks.

"We were maybe working out what to say." Luke shrugged. "We learned a lot in Glenwood."

Luke, classic ginger in coloring, with pale skin and blue eyes, was the youngest among them at twenty-eight but still could have passed for a teenager. He wore a graphic T-shirt he easily could have stolen from Rio's closet, or vice versa, with a Christmas tree on it made of Super Mario Bros. characters and, naturally, a Super Star on top.

"And I had a… hunch—" Bari wrinkled his nose. "—that you were going to need us. I'm becoming even more like you, brother. How wonderful."

"We jumped on the train as soon as we woke up this morning," Jay explained. "Maximus is watching over Brookdale with the new circle."

"And he trusted Bari to watch over you?" Ethan asked, no doubt meaning it as a compliment, since Maximus hadn't been the biggest fan of their coupling initially, especially after what happened between Bash and Jay. Bash breaking his engagement to Jay for a vampire, although it would have been a marriage of convenience, not love, hadn't exactly endeared Maximus to the Bain family.

"Bari is a member of my circle now too." Jay leaned down to drape his arm over Bari's shoulders, who smiled despite his obvious anxiety. One would never guess they'd only been dating a few weeks, but Bari would gush that they were destined to be mated. Funny how no one minded fate when it offered something good.

"Yes, yes, you're adorable," Preston droned. "We're adorable. Isn't everyone *so* adorable? Can we get back to this newest prophecy? Bari said the whole poem thing outside."

"Us too." Ethan nodded.

"Why, though?" Bari asked. "Before Ethan got shot in Brookdale, none of us said anything out loud. No weird riddles. I thought we were getting stronger."

"We are," Bash said, "but so is the breadth of what's coming. That warning in Brookdale was a mere blip of premonition." Not that it hadn't been harrowing.

A conspirator in Brookdale, a werewolf named Ursula, had been orchestrating her own takeover. Planning to overthrow Jay as Alpha to reinforce traditionalist views that wolves should always be on top over other tribes, she and her cronies had been murdering people who were part of mixed-tribe couples, especially if they were trying to get pregnant. She was secretly working under the vampire villain's direction, who also wanted such couples stopped, since it was mixed births in ancient times that first created Focuses, Seers, and Nulls, allowing such people to resist a vampire's thrall.

Ursula had Ethan shot to keep him and Bash out of the way. All the better, really, because Bash had been eager to escape after that. He'd said it was because Bari was clearly meant to save Brookdale without them, but he'd also had the selfish reason of not wanting to see Ethan hurt again.

He'd never thought he could be so terrified of losing someone. If it had been Bari or another circle member, his close friends and family, certainly, but Ethan had only been part of his life for a short time. Yet seeing Ethan shot and at threat of bleeding out in his arms had been one of his worst experiences to weather.

"This is bigger," Bash went on, shaking the memories of that day from his mind. "My guess is the potential for good or bad outcomes is too split. Nothing is certain, so we need to learn all we can."

"What were the words?" Nell asked, since she and Siobhan hadn't overheard with the others. She had the other end of the sofa, with Siobhan sitting beneath her on the floor.

Ethan spoke it:

Blood Moon to Blue Moon, the harvest is ripe
For the old queen to conquer by Cold Moon's night
Four corners connect where a fifth is born
As a united star they can hold back the morn

Bari nodded, confirming he'd said the same.

"First line's easy, right?" Siobhan surfaced from her coffee mug. Many of those gathered had tattoos, but she was the true canvas, even with some stretching up the length of her neck. She nursed what must have been her second mug of coffee, given she was more awake than usual this early. "All this started on Halloween, with that red moon, continued in Brookdale a month later, and now we're headed toward something else."

"Old queen must mean the ancient vampire chick," said Deanna. She and Rio had the other armchair, with the more petite Rio sitting in her lap.

"*Alexa*," Preston spat, drawing a snap of all heads in his direction. A name. They finally had a name. "That's what we found out from Leo in Glenwood. She was his sire. He sent the creation tablets to Brookdale to keep them away from her. She'd usually kept him from remembering and set a whole bunch of other things in motion, including the incident with the totem our first week in power."

The totem. Bash could never forget it. It was just after he'd taken over the pack from his father, formed his young and mixed-tribe circle, and already he'd had a prophecy spelling their doom. At the time, they'd never learned the totem's source, but it had been stolen from a museum in Glenwood and smuggled to their city by a pair of fox siblings. The brother, Jude, was Second to the Alpha in Glenwood now, Kate Romero, and his sister, Jordana, was Kate's mate.

The totem had corrupted Jordana into using it on others, which turned them into their animal forms, completely under her power, like an even more twisted Pied Piper. Bash and his circle had stopped her and destroyed the totem before shifter culture could be exposed to humans, but they'd never known how it all started.

The creation tablets could have been an equally devastating incident. They told the true story of where shifters came from. Shifter history usually said they were the first species on earth and vampires and humans were a corruption that came after. The truth was that humans were the originators, and those seeking immortality made themselves vampires. The experiments that led to vampirism created shifters as a byproduct. Once, vampires ruled everyone, with shifters beneath them and humans at the bottom.

The story alone wasn't something shifters would believe readily, but the real threat had been how the tablets could have been used to enslave shifters under Alexa's singular thrall—if Bari hadn't destroyed one.

"She took Leo over and spoke to us through him," Preston finished.

"She made Leo?" Ethan questioned in awe—or more likely horror. Leo had raised him, turned his father into a vampire, and now that line of succession started with the enemy.

"And forced him to frenzy the night he made your father," Preston continued.

At that, Ethan looked like he might throw up.

"Kinda why we weren't sure what to say," Luke said. "Kate's circle has him locked up for now, for his and everyone else's protection. He told us to tell you not to worry, but we get if that might be impossible."

"She also made Reggie," said Jay. "Preston called to let me know while we were on our way here."

"*Him* you call," Deanna shot at Preston.

"It seemed more pressing, considering Reggie was still on the loose," Preston argued.

"I informed my circle, and Reggie voluntarily allowed himself to be locked up as well," Jay went on, easing Bash's growing concerns at least a little. "He had no idea and says he has no memories of Alexa or Leo, but that's likely her doing. If she doesn't want her children to remember her, they won't. When you're not a Focus"—he nodded at Ethan—"it's practically impossible to resist your sire's call."

"She could take control of them from a city away?" Rio asked.

"Not that far," explained Nell. "She'd still have to be somewhat near to trigger anything. Even Ethan's father couldn't be across the whole city while enthralling him. He was always close. Then again, a vampire can move so fast, it probably doesn't take Alexa much time to move between cities."

"What matters most," Bash broke in, "is she's likely here now, and we only have two weeks to prevent her takeover."

"Two weeks?" Ethan sputtered.

"*By Cold Moon's night*. The Cold Moon is the last full moon of the year. Two weeks from today." A somber silence settled, until Luke broke it with an attempt at levity.

"We've fought off prophecies in one week before. Two should be easy!"

"Did Alexa give any indication of what she's planning?" Bash asked Preston.

"Only her certainty that she has more in the works than we can counteract."

"Oh!" Luke jumped in again. "And we should have Kate and Jude's help soon. They were securing things back in Glenwood and keeping Jesse safe too, but they'll be coming."

Another Alpha and Second certainly wouldn't hurt.

"Jay." Bash turned to the other Alpha in the room. "I hope you don't mind me taking point, but this is my city."

"Your pack, your call," Jay affirmed. "I told you I'd help Centrus whenever you needed me. Nothing is going to sever the ties we've made now." He squeezed Bari's shoulder.

They were basically engaged now, and they really were… cute, domestic, doting, all the things Jay had wanted of his and Bash's engagement, but that Bash hadn't been able to give him. He didn't do commitment or forever to one person. He'd wanted leave to sleep with others and not be tied down to romantic notions getting in the way of a business deal.

Ethan's hand slid into his, drawing Bash's gaze. "What should we do?"

How quickly things could change.

Bash tightened his grip and then slipped free to command the room. "Everyone stays in pairs. Deanna, Rio, keep watch over the businesses. Try to appear normal and not attract attention. If one of you has a shift at the flower shop or tattoo parlor, the other goes with them. Otherwise, keep watch over the den.

"Nell, Siobhan, it's business as usual for you too, guarding the streets and helping anyone who needs it, but put extra wards around all places of importance, especially here.

"Luke, Preston, help Nell with wards as best you can, but I primarily want you watching the Shelter.

"Jay, Bari, you two coordinate with Brookdale and Glenwood, relay any incidents or messages as soon as you learn them."

"I can detect spells too!" Bari blurted before Bash could continue. "Cast wards, protect… people." He shrugged with a bit less confidence than Bash would have liked, but he wasn't going to argue. "I'm a Magister now too, albeit a bit new to it."

"Be my guest," Bash said. "The important thing is for no one to be alone. Pairs or groups, always. Never solo acts."

"What are you two going to do?" Deanna asked.

"Dad!" Ethan cried in apparent epiphany and sprinted from the living room.

Bash thrust out a hand to tell everyone to stay put before hurrying after him, catching him just as Ethan threw open the cellar door. "What did I *just* say about no one going anywhere alone?"

"I have to check on him!" Ethan yanked free and flew down the stairs.

"You saw him this morning." Bash followed.

"I...." Ethan didn't finish whatever explanation he might have given, but clamped his mouth shut with a click of his teeth. When he reached the bottom, he opened the cellar door, but Bash held fast to his arm to prevent him from going inside. He couldn't risk Ethan's panic causing him to do something stupid. He gave the young vampire enough leeway as it was.

"Ethan?" Gordon sat at the desk, reading. "Did something happen?"

Ethan sagged, like he'd almost expected Gordon to be gone.

"Nothing that concerns you," Bash said. "Just giving Ethan some added peace of mind."

"But—"

He shut the door in Ethan's stead, knowing damn well this was about more than simple comfort. He led a quiet Ethan back upstairs but didn't let him head off to rejoin the others right away. He hadn't let go of Ethan's arm since he caught it at the bottom of the steps and tugged on it now to draw Ethan's eyes upward.

"Was it for peace of mind?"

A worse war of emotions was on Ethan's face than when he'd arrived back at the den. "I first saw hints of the prophecy when Dad was feeding from me this morning."

"*Feeding* from you?"

"He'd been starving himself all week. Nothing from the fridge was gone. I had to."

Tightness seized Bash's insides like a succession of sharp kicks. "And?"

"And he tried to enthrall me."

Bash felt such a bristle at that, he nearly sprouted fur.

"It didn't work, obviously!" Ethan said like a defense.

But there was no defense, not when the entire household had been in danger, and now they knew Alexa was the start of that entire vampire line. "You cannot take risks like that, especially not now, and not after we learned Alexa orchestrated his turning."

"I know, but he's my dad, and he was telling me to kill him, and…
I never thought he'd stoop to pretending something like that just to…."
Ethan shook his head, eyes damp and face contorted with his efforts to
keep tears from springing free.

Bash lessened the tightness of his hold on Ethan's arm. "I'm glad
you have a father who you have good memories of as a boy, but you
don't know the man he is now."

"I know." Ethan smiled bitterly. "So much for progress."

These were the moments when Bash most wished he could be
effortlessly affectionate, and in his best attempt, he gathered Ethan
against him.

Ethan's returned crushing grip was grounding. They hadn't had the
chance to breathe much since Halloween. Bash felt forever on edge and
knew everyone else did too, especially Ethan, who'd been the catalyst.

"Thanks." Ethan squeezed him tighter. "I don't think I could handle
this without you."

Bash's phone rang.

Ethan laughed, drawing away with slowly uncoiling limbs. "Isn't
everyone we know in the other room?"

"With a few exceptions." Bash sighed upon seeing the name
blinking back at him—Robert Hedin. "Mr. Mayor," he answered, "I'm
afraid right now is a bad time—"

"No *shit*, it's a bad time," Robert barked. "For me! Because if you
don't do something to help me right now, in a few days, I might not be
the mayor anymore."

Chapter 4

WHAT HAD started as annoyance had quickly turned into that damn hunch feeling Ethan had been picking up from Bash. The timing and extent of the potential damage made Ethan certain that a scandal hitting the mayor right now—who was secretly a Null, capable of depowering anyone near him, the opposite of how a Focus enhanced someone—couldn't be a coincidence.

As much as Ethan might have enjoyed a visit to the mayor's office, meeting Robert there wasn't an option right now, or it risked someone connecting him to Bash. Having an in with the mayor made keeping pack business out of the public eye easier. And maybe allowed for some personal favors, like the ease with which Ethan had gotten his PI license.

Instead of anywhere high-profile, then, they were meeting where Bash always had his rendezvouses with Robert: the bar at the same hotel where Ethan once stayed when he first returned to Centrus City.

Different from the last time they'd been here, Robert was waiting for them. He was a tall man, late thirties, lanky, with angular features and a long chin. His suit looked rumpled as they got closer, and he had two empty whiskey glasses in front of him, though at least this time he hadn't bothered with the '50s-style spy movie sunglasses, trench coat, and hat.

"Bain. Rookie. 'Bout time," Robert greeted when they claimed the stools on either side of him.

"You know I'm not really a rookie anymore, right?" Ethan said. "I live at the den, feed regularly without issue, understand all the weird shifter politics and history."

"And it's been, what? Six weeks for you? I've lived with this shit for years. You're a rookie." Robert waved the bartender over, who scowled but refilled both glasses with double shots, and then looked to Bash and Ethan.

"One of the same," Bash said.

"Nothing for me, thanks." Though sometimes Ethan wished he could slam back a few fingers of booze when times got tough.

Robert waited for the bartender to finish pouring Bash's drink before he said more, which proved he wasn't drunk enough to be careless. He was the only human with any power in Centrus City who knew about the supernatural, but then, he was supernatural too.

As a Null, Robert was a blank space. Magic didn't work on him and was mostly nullified anywhere near him. If being around a Focus made someone instantly want to like that person, then being around a Null was, well, it wasn't as if Ethan wanted to hate Robert, but his feelings toward the man seemed to balance between like and dislike the way only the best of politicians could manage.

"Hooboy, I forget what a thrill being in you boys' presence feels like," Robert said in contrast, side-eyeing them both. "Was it always this potent?"

"Now would be the time I hope you're sober enough to explain yourself," Bash said.

"I'll get to it." Robert downed one of his doubles and sat back with a smack of his lips. This time of day, the place was empty of patrons other than them, and the bartender busied himself with restocking unless summoned. "Sad thing is, me being me, that thrilling feeling goes away too soon."

Reaching awkwardly between his legs for something leaned against the bar, Robert produced a briefcase. He set it on the countertop mostly in front of Ethan, since he didn't have a drink to disturb, popping the latches to reveal a stack of manilla envelopes.

Feeling prompted, Ethan opened the topmost folder.

"*Wow.*" He quickly closed it again. "Was that you?"

"Expected me to be more or less endowed?" Robert winked, much as his weariness and the bags under his eyes diminished the intended charm. "It's me. I have a… specific appetite."

Bash reached across Robert to pluck the folder from the briefcase and opened it to see for himself. The photograph was of a man, who Ethan had correctly guessed was Robert, wearing a full-cowl bondage mask with a zippered mouth, a harness that helped suspend him midair, arms spread, and wearing nothing else. While one heavily bondage-geared woman stood with a whip in hand behind him, two similarly dressed men knelt beneath, one tonguing Robert's full-mast cock and the other, mostly hidden behind Robert, very likely tonguing elsewhere.

Ethan shifted in his stool upon glancing at it again.

"Mr. Hedin," Bash said with an audible sigh as he closed the folder, "I believe our continued relationship was contingent on you maintaining discretion of such activities."

"I do!" Robert contested, snatching the folder back from him. "I have been. The only people who'd even know about this are ones I trust. Who now, all of a sudden, are apparently turning on me without cause. The other folders are mostly filled with the same." He chucked it back into the briefcase.

"You have yet to explain how this is my problem," Bash spat. He had an edge to him that Ethan couldn't deny, much as he'd seen Bash's softer side.

"You're not married, right?" Ethan tried. "How bad can this be?"

"Just because I'm not a cheater doesn't mean my more conservative constituents want to read the words 'sex' and 'dungeon' in the same headline."

Ethan choked.

"This won't get you impeached," Bash held firm, "just a few negative headlines for a month or two until something else draws the public's attention. You can clean up your own scandal."

Robert slapped a hand on Bash's wrist when he made to leave the stool. "Do you think I'd bother you with this if that's all it was?" Unperturbed by Bash's flash of angry wolf eyes, Robert pulled one of the bottom folders onto the top and flipped it open himself. No scandalous image stared back at them, but a collection of statements. "There are also reports saying I used city funds to feed my habit. Which isn't true! But it's sure as hell looking like it."

Ethan reached for those pages to scan through them, seeing dates, times, amounts. It was thorough, including an official-looking spreadsheet highlighting areas that seemed to be about discrepancies in the city's bookkeeping.

"Doesn't look good, does it?" Robert said. "But I swear it's not true."

"Who gathered all this?" Ethan asked.

"I did. I still got contacts. I was a PI too, remember? But I can't be the one who keeps digging. I got you your license, Rookie. Use it to help me."

"I...." Ethan hadn't expected to be the point person on this. He'd only come along because Bash didn't want him to be alone. "Normally, absolutely, I would, but right now—"

"You *owe* me. Not only for the license and letting you sink those pearly whites into my veins the other week." Robert let his voice drop lower, but more like a mock-whisper that warned he could be very loud if he wanted to be. "Maybe for, oh, I don't know, stopping a psycho vampire from taking over the city!"

Bash slammed his whiskey glass on the counter in time to the plummeting of Ethan's stomach. The bartender returned, filled Bash's glass, then sped away before Robert could down his other double and demand another. "You may recall, Mr. Hedin, that the psycho in question is Ethan's father."

"Shit. Sorry, Rookie." Robert grimaced.

If it hadn't been for Robert's well-timed arrival that night, they might not have stopped Gordon at all. He was a powerful Focus, bolstered more at the time by having kidnapped and enthralled Rio. Robert nullifying Gordon's influence had been the leverage they needed to win.

"It's not a wrong observation," Ethan admitted. "And I do want to help, but...." He looked to Bash because none of this was his decision to make alone.

"You'll help," Bash said. "So will I. It seems this is worth our attention, and it can't be chance. If we lose Robert from office, not only does that take away some very important ins around the city, but if he's sentenced to jail time, we lose our trump card."

"You think Alexa is behind this?"

"Even if she's not, we can't afford to let this get worse."

"So glad for the altruism on my behalf," Robert said loudly, leaning forward to get between Ethan and Bash, talking over him, "but who the hell's Alexa?"

"Another time," Bash said. "But maybe don't get caught in any dark alleys in the near future. In fact, you shouldn't be alone at all, and I don't trust anyone other than my own people to keep an eye on you. Stay right here when we leave. I'll send some of my circle to you."

"Plenty to keep me occupied." Robert downed the last of his booze and then made quite the show of waving his arms to get the bartender's attention. Thankfully, of his own volition, he only asked for one more double and sipped it instead of knocking it back.

"Do what you need to. We'll do our part." Bash slid from the stool like he'd tried to do before. "When you're not at your office, you'll be at the den, staying with us."

"What, not footing the bill?" Robert scoffed. "And how am I supposed to explain that kind of move to my constituents?"

"You don't. We'll teleport you back and forth so no one's the wiser." Bash downed the remains of his own drink and got out his wallet.

"Tele… isn't that magic? It won't work on me."

"It will if you don't dally. But take too long and you might cut yourself in half. Besides, it's the only way to prevent you from nullifying the wards around the den every time you enter and exit. By using portals, we can avoid that."

Ethan slipped from his stool too.

"Um…." Robert's arm shot out, this time catching Ethan. "Don't suppose you need your own drink like last time? Might help me relax." His glassy eyes looked pleading. Despite his earlier accusation, and given his penchant for being dominated, he probably enjoyed the prick of fangs. He'd been Ethan's first test drink from a human, and he'd certainly seemed to enjoy it then.

"I did lose a little blood this morning." Ethan eyed Bash over Robert's head.

"Go ahead."

Robert might be immune to being enthralled, but Ethan remembered he tasted incredible. The hunger left in Ethan from his father's feeding earlier meant the smell of human blood was already tempting, enhanced by knowing how deliciously Robert's blood would tingle on his tongue.

First checking that no new patrons had entered and the bartender was turned away, Ethan shouldered closer. Reversing the positions of their hands in one swift sweep, he quickly had hold of Robert's wrist. Bash was his preferred meal, always, but there was something unique in human blood, especially Robert's, like him being a Null made his blood purer and more simply human than anyone else who might be touched by magic.

Ethan's eyes sharpened to the point where he knew they glowed yellow. Not amber. He wasn't that hungry, but he saw the way Robert fixated on the changed color as he lifted Robert's wrist to his mouth and bit down with a tender but sure puncture of fangs.

The flow of blood was always a rush, not tangy or metallic the way Ethan remembered from a lick at a wound as a human, but like wine and sex and the best meal he'd ever tasted combined into one experience. He might have moaned as he sucked and nourished himself on the heady flow, but he was careful to not draw attention, wondering if, instead, Robert might be the one to moan. His eyes certainly did enough fluttering.

Once Ethan was sated, he licked languidly along the bite marks to close them, erasing any evidence of what he'd done. It was no wonder few humans knew what went bump in the night when the truth could be covered up so easily. Ethan's solace, besides the pleasing taste, was that he trusted himself to never take too much, never hurt another, no matter how good they smelled or hungry he might be.

"Oh yeah, that helps," Robert hummed. "One more for the road." He called the bartender over once more and then tapped the briefcase closed and nudged it over for Ethan to take.

As Bash jerked his head to the exit and turned to leave, Ethan grabbed the briefcase and hastily followed. Though maybe *unsteadily* followed was the better term, because he'd swear he felt some of the effects from the alcohol in Robert's bloodstream.

"If we're right, then Alexa is already making moves against us," Bash said once they met the crisp winter air, "setting the stage to make this fight very difficult. So maybe don't set yourself up to need extra meals again anytime soon."

Ethan huffed, not actually believing Bash was jealous—though he was probably still halfway serious. "I'll try."

Bash paused outside the hotel entrance to pull out his phone. He called Siobhan and began filling her in on what they'd learned from Robert, and that she and Nell were to finish up whatever else they were working on and get to the hotel immediately to pick him up. Siobhan's agents could do some digging as well and had also been instructed to never go anywhere in less than pairs. They needed to prove the worst of this scandal was fake, even if they couldn't sweep it all under the rug, and they didn't have much time.

"Then tell Preston to be on call. We'll need him to use teleportation to avoid creating any new scandals of where Mr. Hedin might be laying his head tonight, but we're going to be adding one more to our full house."

"You got it, boss," Siobhan was heard on the other end.

A couple more details were exchanged as Ethan drifted his gaze around the nearby streets. This was a midrange area as far as fancy versus rough. He hadn't been able to afford much when he first got out of prison and stayed in one of the hotel's extended-stay rooms, but he hadn't ended up somewhere run-down or truly dangerous. It was the type of area mostly populated by those with working class and civil service jobs.

Still more upscale than anywhere he would have expected to see Carson Decker.

Ethan straightened, recognizing with a hawk's precision the figure across the street. Longish dark hair was tied back, face clean-shaven like usual lately, and he wore a nice enough pair of jeans, button-down, and winter coat. It was Decker, walking with purpose in the same streets where Ethan had once stayed, where they'd just met with the mayor, and on a day when said mayor was fighting the release of scandals that could ruin him.

This couldn't be a coincidence either. It couldn't be. Decker was too important to Ethan to not be something their enemy might use against him.

"*Ethan.*" Bash's hand clamped around Ethan's arm when he made to pursue. "Get it done, Siobhan. We'll be in touch." He ended the call before snarling, "Are we going to have the 'don't run off alone' conversation a third time today?"

"It's Decker," Ethan hissed back and thrust his chin in the direction where—shit, Decker was already disappearing around a corner. "Bash, please. I've never tracked him to these streets before. It might mean something."

Bash sighed but released Ethan. "Don't get ahead of me."

They hurried across the street and down the block where they'd seen Decker turn. Ethan could have caught up to him in a blink, but he kept pace with Bash. They had scent on their side, both of them, and after following Decker for weeks already, Ethan knew what the man smelled like. What his *blood* smelled like, stewing in his rotten veins.

Wherever Decker was headed, his pace was swift, in a hurry like he was running late. For what? A job? A meeting with some new lowlife contact? Alexa herself? Decker didn't smell like anything but human, but his presence here had to mean—

"Wait." Bash held Ethan back as Decker's destination took him inside a large official-looking building.

"What? What is that place?"

"I know that building." Bash took hold of Ethan again and, instead of heading up the steps after Decker, turned them down the alley.

It led around the building, where a branching of alleyways met, and a back door into where Decker had gone sported a security camera.

"Don't worry, it's a decoy," Bash said. "I should know, since I had Mayor Hedin ensure it stayed that way. This is where Siobhan and her agents are passed appropriate building permits when we need to work on the Shelter or secure other housing for pack members. It's a DLI office."

"Department of Labor and Industry?" Ethan questioned. "Why would Decker go in there?"

"A good question, and given the current situation, I don't like any of the answers. If Alexa is connected to this too…."

"Then taking away the buildings where shifters live would be a really good way to destabilize us further."

"Let's not jump to conclusions. First—"

Ethan felt the now familiar sinking feeling before he saw the change in expression on Bash, though he knew his own features changed in tandem.

The whites of their eyes went black, irises glowing blue, with a third eye appearing on their foreheads, as a brief, simpler premonition surged through them that didn't require any riddles to pour forth.

Blood. *Theirs*. Sprayed all over the pavement and the back door to the building. It was just like when Ethan had been shot, giving them precious seconds to act before the worst happened.

They jumped away from each other the moment the vision ended, as something like a spear on a length of chain launched through where they'd been huddled and embedded into the building's brick.

Chapter 5

ESPECIALLY BEING a Seer, Bash really hated surprises.

The spear end to the weapon that had flown between him and Ethan was yanked from the brick. After soaring back into a skilled hand, it began to immediately swing on its chain for another attack.

"Who the—?"

"Ethan!" Bash snarled as the chain deployed once more, wrapping around Ethan's ankle. One great heave knocked him off his feet, and a pained cry left him from the bladed end digging into his calf as the briefcase he'd taken from Robert went flying.

Their attacker launched upward, achieving such height and speed, Bash wouldn't have needed to see the sprout of wings from her back to know they were dealing with a raptor. She became such a blur that he barely saw her draw the knife from her belt as she descended on the downed Ethan.

Every ounce of Bash's animal instincts leaped with him to intercept, shoes splitting open and clothes tearing apart as he made the pained completion to Stage Three in a blink to overtake her in time. *Not again.* He wouldn't watch Ethan get so close to death ever again.

He made it, inches from the tip of her blade sinking into the dip of Ethan's throat, and they tumbled across the alley. The moment their roll ended with Bash on top, he roared in her face, slamming her wrist into the pavement to loosen the knife from her grip.

A cry like a prey bird's screech made his sharpened ears ring, and he resisted the urge to let her go to cover them. She slammed what felt like a hard beak into his forehead, dazing him further, and flung him away with seemingly twice his strength.

He'd seen her clearly now. A formidably built woman, as tough and well-muscled as Deanna, but someone this strong, with hair like an ombre of black to periwinkle-gray....

She was a damn harpy eagle, one of the best shifter tribes for assassins.

Her knife was gone, but her other hand had never lost hold of the chain. She tugged as she looked to where Ethan had last been—only for the spear end to strike her in the chest. *Blunt* end first, but it had the desired effect of knocking her backward into the nearby wall.

The damage to Ethan's ankle didn't stop him from moving like a far faster blur than she'd been. Bash's head and ears ached as he gasped into the pavement, watching Ethan's jumble of green and blue, with only brief flashes of red, as he pummeled their attacker's midsection. The chain whip fell between them, the eagle too shocked from the barrage to defend—

Until she caught Ethan's next incoming blow with claws and headbutted him with the same sharp point of her beak, knocking the sunglasses from his face.

Ethan nearly tripped over the collection of metal beneath his feet as he stumbled back. She completed her shift to Stage Three while he was stunned, massive, already six feet tall, and towering now on her quickly formed talons. She was a mix of white and dark blueish gray, her similarly colored hair becoming a feathered mane. Even with her wings connected to her arms now, face formed into a black beak and eyes equally black and piercing, there was a humanness in the depths of her features.

Humanity did nothing to quell the look of predator.

She darted toward Ethan with a screech and lash of deadly talons.

Bash sprang to his feet and roared, concussion be damned, and the primal *Alpha* challenge halted the eagle's attack with a flutter of wings. She looked shocked, furious that he'd made her hesitate, but Bash was no normal werewolf, and more than any normal Alpha.

"*Stop*," Ethan's voice rang through the alley with a tremor.

The last of the eagle's fortitude dwindled, and she dropped to her taloned feet on the pavement. Ethan was no normal vampire either, and enthralling a trained assassin was as easy as he could have overpowered an Alpha—other than Bash.

"*Tell us what you're doing here.*"

She immediately began to shrink and lose her feathers. Large as she'd become, her clothing hadn't torn the way Bash's had, designed to withstand her Stage Three shift. She'd probably even come barefoot. Her outfit was all black leather, like armor, cut off at the knees and backless to accommodate her raptor feet and wings.

Her ombre hair was chin-length and wavy when free of feathers, her skin and eyes still dark. Tall, lithe, and beautiful, she looked like the proverbial Amazon in a modern uniform. When she spoke, her faint accent made Bash guess she was originally from South America, Brazilian maybe, where this type of shifter was most common.

"I was sent to kill the vampire, Ethan Lambert, and anyone who stands in my way."

"*By Alexa?*" Ethan demanded.

"I do not know any Alexa."

Just a friendly neighborhood assassin, then, sent by someone else. "Use her chain to tie her up before you release her," Bash ordered, losing his own shift and briefly mourning the loss of his newest pair of shoes. If he ruined any more outfits, he'd have to start borrowing from Bari. "I have questions too."

The beak punctures in his and Ethan's forehead were healed by the time they had the eagle secure, with Bash situated enough in his torn clothing to not feel too unkempt, though his head still throbbed from the combined blow and eagle cries.

They sat her against the wall of the alley before Ethan snapped her from her stupor.

"Raptor, huh?" Ethan retrieved his sunglasses and the briefcase.

"Raptor," Bash affirmed. "Why don't you tell us in your own words who you are and what you hoped to accomplish here?"

The fog cleared from the eagle's eyes—and she immediately spat at Ethan, snarling, "I do not answer to fangers!"

She'd missed, but Ethan still scooted back from where he knelt to avoid where the spittle landed. "I was almost starting to forget that slur."

"You do answer to him," Bash said, "and can again with a simple order from me. Allowing you any autonomy is a courtesy. You just attempted to kill the Alpha of Centrus City, which gives me full leave to kill you without repercussion."

"You think I care, *Alpha?*" The eagle remained unmoved, even wrapped in her own chains. "You are a disgrace, and death is always a risk in my job."

"But I know there are two kinds of assassins—those only in it for the money or enjoyment, maybe both, and those who believe in the cause." Bash slammed a hand into the brick above her head, allowing it to impact with more force from sprouted claws. She didn't flinch. "I think you're the latter."

Her black eyes slid to Ethan. "Vampires are a blight upon this world, and you let one into your bed, your pack, spreading that corruption to other cities like a virus."

"And news of how Ethan helped prevent a takeover, both here and in Brookdale—"

"Convenient lies."

Naturally. Bash had expected the good rumors to be ignored. Funny how the bad ones were always believed. "Which Alpha sent you? Shorehaven's?"

She said nothing, so Bash nodded at Ethan.

"*Which Alpha?*"

"Metro City," she intoned and then blinked away the renewed thrall with a sneer.

"See, I can get everything I need without permission." Bash hovered, careful to not get too close. "But I'd prefer to play nice. I don't want war. I don't want to spread across the country with a vampire army and my nontraditional views. Well, a break in tradition I wouldn't mind spreading, because I have proven for a decade that my way is as right and workable as any other, but it just won't sink in for the rest of you, will it?"

"Not when your rule is but a false bend of the knee to him," she hissed at Ethan, a bit of her eagle chirp bleeding into her words, "the source of so many deaths and all the chaos these past months."

"It's not my fault!" Ethan lunged closer than he should have. "I didn't ask to be turned."

"Then you should bare your throat to your Alpha and let him end your sorry existence." She made to ram a knee up into Ethan's rib cage, but Bash saw it coming and lashed out with his own arm to hold her down.

"There will be none of that," Bash cautioned. "Besides a vampire being here, you've obviously heard there is one in Brookdale's circle, and one protected in Glenwood, but the chaos and bloodshed were caused by one rogue vampire's actions, and it was none of them."

"More than one if you count that creature's maker," she sneered.

Ethan hunched inward, on his knees like Bash but slumped onto his ankles.

"A disturbed and mourning father aside," Bash said, "who is imprisoned by my circle, as you should also know, Ethan and the others in these cities are not to blame. No less than three vampires have proven themselves allies to those in power."

"Allies? Or masters? Even if you are right, so what if your pet is tamed, and maybe a few others too. Letting them run free is why we are dealing with a worse enemy now. You just said so. Another vampire is behind this, your Alexa, was it? Using younger vampires and shifters to achieve her goals. The enemy is still a *fanger*, and we would be better off with their vermin eradicated."

"So that's it?" Ethan said softly, staring at his hands and then at the eagle with a flash of yellow eyes. "It doesn't matter who I am, what I want, the good I try to do, I'm just supposed to bare my throat because of what someone else is causing?"

The eagle met his stare with no more flinch than she had at the slam of Bash's claws. "I can only speak to what I would be willing to do for my pack, but if our positions were reversed, I would gladly welcome death." She stretched her neck aside to bare her throat to Ethan, as if daring him to sink his fangs.

His eyes flickered back to green.

"Unfortunately for you, we don't kill our prisoners… right away," Bash warned.

He stood, and Ethan jumped to his feet after him.

"What about Decker?" Ethan looked to the eagle once more. "Why were you following Carson Decker? What's he doing in that building?"

"I do not know any Decker, no more than I know Alexa. I followed you from the hotel and acted once you were out of sight from others."

"*Are you telling the truth*?" Ethan asked through his thrall.

"Yes."

His expression fell further. Rather than answers, they simply had another obstacle.

The other cities weren't sitting on their laurels anymore.

"We'll get some of Siobhan's agents to keep an eye on Decker," Bash said and pulled out his phone, which was thankfully still in his pocket despite the tears in his slacks.

"But—"

"We have more pressing matters, Ethan. Decker is a lower priority."

Ethan clenched his fists but didn't object. Bash wished there was time to ease his concerns, to wipe away the anguish the assassin's words had caused in him, but that would have to come later.

As Bash dialed Preston, Ethan picked up the briefcase once more and grabbed the chains holding the eagle to yank her to her feet. She didn't fight him, and Ethan was careful to not give her any more openings.

Preston answered with an annoyed, "What now?"

"Did Siobhan have the chance to prep you?" She had, and Preston assumed it was time to port Robert. "Actually, you'll be picking us up first. We have another guest."

ETHAN FELT like he'd been in a daze since morning—or maybe that was the alcoholic blood burning through him. The hits just kept on coming, when all he wanted was to act, take back control of his life, and do his job. He needed to know how Decker might be involved, but a pair of Siobhan's agents were following him now, and Ethan was relegated to staying at the den, close within Bash's purview.

He might have allowed himself to enjoy the overprotectiveness if it wasn't so maddening being on the sidelines. Even starting to work on Robert's scandal would have been preferable to twiddling his thumbs, but what was in the briefcase merely pointed at people and places to investigate, and after the assassin, Bash didn't want Ethan going anywhere until morning. Hopefully, Siobhan's agents would have extra leads by then.

She and Nell were gone, playing bodyguard for Robert until he was ready to call it a day. Preston and Luke left to check on the Shelter, still on call for whenever Robert was ready, while Bash continued questioning the eagle.

Once Preston and Luke returned, Deanna took over watching the assassin with a nervous Rio, while Preston prepared wards around one of the guest rooms to prevent her from getting out, unlike the ones Bari was helping create around the den and everyone else's rooms to keep unwanted guests from getting in. Jay was just as busy, almost constantly on the phone to Brookdale, coordinating and checking with his own pack.

All Ethan could do was watch, eventually leaning in the doorway to Bash's office while Bash gave an earful to the Alpha of Metro City, who was trying very unsuccessfully to deny she had sent an assassin at all.

"Wanna swap partners?"

"Huh?" Ethan startled at the appearance of Luke in front of him, just as Preston breezed by into the office.

"He means for an art question, Ethan, not sleeping arrangements." Preston smirked, barely glancing at Ethan as he began drawing a protection rune over the glass of one of the windows as if painting with neon light from his fingertip.

Art question had been their code for any time someone had a new addition to the Christmas present Ethan was planning for Bash. It was a group effort and something he'd been working on for weeks, carefully tucked away into his closet. Thankfully, the bedroom he and Bash shared had two, and Ethan had been careful to not let Bash see inside his.

With everything going on, he'd honestly forgotten the present wasn't finished.

"Please." Ethan jumped at the distraction. He motioned to Bash that he was going with Luke and leaving Preston to keep Bash company.

Bash glanced up just long enough from his passive-aggressive Alpha-off to nod.

Ethan and Luke slipped upstairs, and as soon as they were safely tucked into Ethan and Bash's bedroom, Luke pulled a figure from his pocket.

"Pres finally finished it but hadn't had the chance to show you since he's, ya know, a bit busier than me when magic calls." Luke handed the figure over, arguably one of the most important pieces for the gift.

It was an Ork *Warhammer* mini augmented to look like Santa Claus and had turned out perfectly, complete with beard and hat and still left unpainted, since Bash being able to paint it himself was part of the present.

"If we're not at the Shelter, I sort of feel like my own third wheel sometimes," Luke added with a snort.

"I know what you mean. But this is incredible, Luke. Thank you. Be sure to tell Preston how much I appreciate it." Ethan headed for the closet.

"Can I see how it's turning out?"

"Of course." Ethan kept the closet door wide as he deposited the Ork warlord into the spot in the display he'd been saving for it.

The large diorama was the most impressively crafted battle display Ethan had been able to produce, as if the Space Marines—naturally the Space Wolves chapter—were literally destroying Santa's village to defeat a horde of Orks, complete with fake snow, gingerbread houses, candy canes lining the roads, and lights and tinsel and other Christmas decorations all around. Even better was that the Orks were dressed as elves, and with this newest addition of "Santa," the grimdark Christmas village was complete.

"Holy crap! Bash is going to flip when he sees this!" Luke praised over Ethan's shoulder. "I can't remember the last time he took a 'treat yoself' day and got his geek on."

"Me either." Ethan shut the door again to hide the display from prying eyes. "Probably before he met me."

"Yeah, but I don't think he'd trade you for Ork Santa."

Ethan laughed. "Thanks. And hey, you and Preston seem like you're doing better."

"We are!" Luke scratched the back of his neck, nose wriggling very much like a cat. Whenever Ethan forgot his friends could all become animals, they usually reminded him with tics like that. "We were just letting old stupidity bleed back in from our early years. We come from totally different backgrounds, ya know, me the Shelter and city streets, Pres his rich, traditional family of assholes. Ten years together and even we forget sometimes to remember common ground. But just because a couple is from different walks of life doesn't mean they can't be mates, no matter what the naysayers say." He winked and gave Ethan's arm a firm pat.

"Oh, Bash and I aren't… I mean, it's only been a couple of months for us."

"Dude, I knew Pres was my mate the first time I saw his room."

"His room?"

"It's basically a geek museum. How could I not fall in love with him?"

Ethan laughed again, though the eruption dwindled faster this time. "Different tribes isn't the same as different species, though, especially with people like that assassin blaming me for everything wrong with shifter life lately, all because Bash let me live."

"Hey, pretty sure if you asked Maximus's wife, Theresa, you know, the *human*, she'd say fuck those people who think like that. I never thought I could be friends with a fanger, and look at us! You're my bro, bro." He punched Ethan's arm this time with a gentle fist bump. "All of us think so. Screw what outsiders say. You're part of the pack. Part of the family. Even if your dad still kinda scares the hell out of me. Sorry. But hey, maybe he just needs to make a connection too, like how we all got to know you. Not that I'm volunteering."

"It's okay. But maybe you're right. Just me talking to Dad might not be enough."

"Time to pick up mayor and company!" Preston yelled from downstairs.

Ethan and Luke hurried back down to return to their original partners. In a few minutes, the den was close to bursting, with Siobhan and Nell back and now Robert added too. It was a good thing they had plenty of rooms, even with an assassin locked up in one of them.

Here was a crowded den, and Ethan had no idea who might be a good fit to talk to his father in his stead. While everyone had come to accept Ethan into the pack, the den, this family, it was different with Gordon. He was the enemy. He couldn't be trusted. No one was lining up to be his friend when he represented everything they feared about vampires.

"There ya are." Robert pulled Ethan from his ruminating this time, as Siobhan and Nell moved past him into the office to give Bash their reports. "Thanks again for the nibble before. You ever need another, Rookie, just call me a blood bag." He waggled an eyebrow.

Then again, there was one person who didn't have any fear of vampires.

"Robert, can I borrow you for a minute?"

LATER, WHEN Ethan was leaving the cellar while Robert and Gordon got to know each other, Bash waited for him at the top of the stairs.

"Technically, neither of them is alone," Ethan defended. "And I checked with Nell weeks ago about Null effects on those wards. Just like with the ones around the den, as long as Robert stays outside the cellar and docsn't cross them, they should be fine."

"I know," Bash said. "And really, all of us should be safe inside the den, even Robert with your father, since he can't be enthralled."

"Just worried about me, then?"

"And the liability you might be to my pack."

Ethan tried to smirk, but he couldn't shake the grimace that formed instead. He *was* a liability and had been since day one. If Bash had been anyone else, Ethan would have died that night when he woke as a frenzied vampire in the back alley of a tattoo parlor, and the assassin telling him that everyone would be better off if he had, wasn't the first time he'd thought it.

He didn't believe it, he didn't want to believe it, but hearing it didn't make him feel much better.

"That was me being cheeky, in case you missed the joke," Bash said.

"I know."

"Come on. Most of the others are turning in, and I think we could both use a break from the thrum."

It was only as they moved into the living room that Ethan realized how dark it was outside. What had started off as a strange morning had turned into a long day that was already ending, and the others were getting settled into various rooms or filtered into other areas of the den. Ethan could sleep if he wanted to, but he doubted he'd get much tonight.

Upstairs, Deanna was finishing a final interrogation and locking the eagle into a heavily warded room. She shot Ethan one final withering glare before the door closed.

"It's not fair," he said once he and Bash were alone. "I didn't do anything. Not this time. And I keep trying to make up for the bad I did do, but it doesn't seem to matter." He threw himself onto the bed.

"Catching Decker in some nefarious act isn't going to change the larger issues we're facing, or anything with your father."

"Yeah. And proving your way of running a pack is valid doesn't change that you killed yours. *Shit*." Ethan lurched into a sitting position. "I didn't mean it like that. I'm just—"

"You're right." Bash climbed onto the bed beside him. "We all compensate for the things we regret. But I don't regret killing my father. I regret not doing it earlier. Might have kept Bari around. Might have saved a few lives and helped non-wolves live better lives sooner. But if that had happened, what might I have given up in exchange?"

There were a million what-ifs between them, but what Ethan knew Bash was saying was that one choice made differently meant all the good could get erased too. "Bari wouldn't be with Jay right now. Maybe Preston and Luke wouldn't be together, because they'd have been too young to be part of your circle if you formed it earlier. And you'd maybe be missing a certain fanger?"

Bash smiled. He often smirked, leered, or managed to curl his lips like a threat, but for Ethan, his smile, however subtle, was soft. "Maybe. I also don't mean to say it would be better if you killed Gordon—"

"I know." Ethan lunged swiftly forward to capture a kiss, allowing the soft, simple press to ground him. "And maybe Robert is an odd choice for a Band-Aid. I just hate waiting, not knowing what comes next or what we can do."

"We're doing all we can do. You need to be patient. But then, you do tend to demand things earlier than you've earned them." There came Bash's leer, an upward twist at the corner of his mouth.

"Yeah?"

"Yeah. Some outcomes are worth waiting for."

"But sometimes I want to get to the point." Ethan snapped at Bash's jugular, allowing his fangs to form so he could graze their tips along the skin. He didn't need another drink, but the smell of Bash always tempted him to take one.

"Seems I'll have to keep teaching you restraint," Bash purred.

He knocked Ethan flat, seized his wrists, and pinned them above his head, claiming a harsher kiss. Ethan needed the distraction, and even knowing that Bash did too, he also knew Bash was playing it coy and seductive to put his mind at ease first. Bash ground into him, coaxing heat to flood Ethan's belly that fattened his cock from the sudden rush of blood.

Easily freeing his wrists from Bash's hold, Ethan rolled them to pin Bash next. Shirts and slacks were deftly discarded, but their eager pawing wasn't patient enough for either to kick down their underwear. They reached beneath waistbands instead to get at each other's cocks and stroked, both panting, breaths hitching as they gasped into each other's mouths.

The grinding and sloppy laps of tongues reminded Ethan of their dreamlike first time on the cellar floor, which, while not as consensual as he would have liked, given he'd enthralled Bash for part of it, had been really, really hot.

Bash tried to flip them the other way again, but Ethan resisted, teetering them onto their sides. Even-footed as they writhed and fondled each other, they sought out a faster, more inelegant end than that morning. The urgency of their pumping fists managed to shove down their underwear, asses out and cocks sprung free. But soon, even their hands moving and arms colliding between them was more hindrance than help.

Bash grabbed hold of Ethan's shoulders as Ethan clutched possessively around Bash's waist, and they thrust, wet cocks battling and chasing each other toward their ends. As their fast and furious lovemaking crescendoed, Bash kissed Ethan harder, passionate, with fangs clacking but still sweet, even as they rutted like the beasts inside them. It felt more like home than the safety of the den's walls.

Heat splashed over Ethan's cock as Bash finished, and his come mixing with the prerelease still building from Ethan pushed him to blissfully follow. As his climax hit, bursting a puff of air and verbal shudder from his lips, something else slipped past his tongue that neither had yet said.

"I love you, Bash."

Bash tensed.

"Just… so you know." Ethan laughed lamely.

Slowly, Bash tilted his head up, glowing bronze meeting shimmering yellow, but his face was a cryptic mask. "Now I know."

It stung, worse than any fight or wound or even being shot, and the sting didn't lessen in the aftermath. They cleaned up too quietly. Both remained naked when they climbed under the covers, in the bed they'd shared since day one, but it felt obligatory. Maybe it hadn't been this bed, but they'd still shared one, first as a precaution and then….

Then what? Ethan thought because Bash wanted him there. That he was part of this family not only because the others wanted him, but because he and Bash were fated. Destined.

Mates.

"Good night, Bash."

"Good night, Ethan."

Fuck.

Ethan didn't sleep, and he knew it took a long while before Bash did either.

Chapter 6

STATIC HUNG in the air the next morning, and it was all Bash's fault.

For the first time in weeks, they didn't start the day with sex.

"I know there are more important things than Decker right now, but he could still be involved," Ethan said as he dressed, eyes constantly finding places to land on other than Bash's face. "I'll wait for you if there are things you need to finish up here, but can we go to my office today? Get some legwork in from my angles too?"

"Of course. But don't forget Robert also needs your help."

"I can do both. Thanks."

Bash tried to say more, to think of anything that could cut through the tension, but he knew the words Ethan wanted to hear wouldn't spill easily from his lips. He couldn't remember if he'd ever said them to Bari. Certainly, never to their father. To their mother, maybe, before she died. Never to a lover, though, not even as a convenient lie.

He'd thought once about Jay that he couldn't feel love toward someone who didn't make his heart race. Ethan did that. Bash wanted a challenge. Ethan gave him that too. Jay had even said it that first week seeing Bash and Ethan together, that clearly Bash thought he was falling in love with Ethan.

Bash had laughed and said, *"I don't do love."*

"You would for him."

Then why the fuck couldn't he say it?

"Ready?" Ethan fidgeted on a good day. His heart beat faster than a human's, pulse always racing, and Bash thought he could hear it this morning, thudding out of control as Ethan shifted and twitched before his green eyes finally flicked upward to catch Bash's.

Bash couldn't say it now. It would sound forced, fake, and only wound Ethan deeper. When he said it, if he said it, he needed to mean it without risk of ever walking it back. "Ready."

The rest of the household was awake when they joined them downstairs. Before, with only one mated pair at the den, both of whom were circle members, the manor had almost felt too big for six. Now it was a literal zoo.

"Find some open seats, darlings! We'll serve you," Bari called from the stove.

It seemed he had appointed himself and Jay to cook breakfast for everyone, and the pleasant smell of classic American fare in the form of bacon, eggs, and pancakes was a rare wave of old family values that they'd never grown up with. The novelty made Bash smile.

Until Ethan wrinkled his nose as if those smells were an inconvenient reminder of all he no longer craved.

The small kitchen table was already packed, only fitting four. They were almost at a dozen now, and with the larger dining table the only available space, Bash claimed his usual seat at the head with Ethan beside him. The open archway from dining room to kitchen left a clear path to see everyone, and the only occupants missing were their upstairs and downstairs prisoners.

Robert had claimed the other head, with Siobhan and Nell on either side of him, discussing border patrols and added warding. The shop talk had Robert very conspicuously pulling out a flask to pour into his coffee. Siobhan snatched it from him to do the same without missing a beat in the conversation.

At the smaller table, Preston, Luke, Deanna, and Rio were sharing ideas for better protection at the Shelter. Well, the circle members were. The serious topic didn't prevent Deanna from pressing a kiss to Rio's temple when she realized how lost he looked, or Luke from feeding Preston a bite of his eggs.

Bari and Jay were being just as homey at the stove, cooking and filling more plates while stealing small kisses and a far too noticeable grope of Bari's hand on Jay's ass.

Ethan giggled at the displays, clearly having witnessed them too. "Disaster is all around us, but it feels sort of far away when you see the good we have. If it wasn't for the potential vampire takeover, this would be just the kind of Christmas I wanted." He glanced wistfully at Bash, only for the sentimental expression to end in a cringe that Bash knew was his fault.

"I would have bullied Jay into making crumpets," Bari announced, appearing to take the other seat beside Bash and setting down plates both for Bash and for himself, "if they didn't take so long. You will have to try them sometime, though, but no changing your mind then, brother. Jay's all mine."

The sinking feeling in Bash's stomach—and expression on Ethan's face—fell further.

Siobhan got a call that made her rise from the table to cross to a quieter corner, taking her spiked coffee with her. When Ethan saw, he pushed back his chair so fast, it nearly hit the wall.

"I'm gonna check with Robert how things went with Dad last night." He moved for the other end of the table at an almost vampire blur.

"What did you do?"

"Huh?" Bash startled toward Bari. "What? Nothing."

"Bash."

"*Nothing.*"

Bash couldn't have mimicked the look his twin gave him then if he'd tried, equally skeptical and pouty with one eyebrow raised. Bari was still in pajamas, much as his hair looked flawless and skin perfectly moisturized. His buttoned top, which seemed plain from afar, was actually a mock-brocade pattern in emerald green, displaying thistles, Venus flytraps, and little flying bats among them.

Urg.

"Brother...."

"Why do you assume I did something?"

"Because that particular expression of unhappiness is reserved for internal contempt. Just because we've lived apart for years doesn't mean I don't know you best. Now, what did you do?"

The distracted attention of everyone at the table and the now empty chair beside Bash made it less daunting to lean toward Bari and confess, "More like something I didn't do." He still hesitated to say it and lowered his voice to almost inaudible to avoid perked ears. "Ethan said 'I love you' last night."

Bari's face lit up.

Then he slugged Bash in the arm.

"Ow!"

"Radio silence? After he said the words?" Bari hit him again. Then *again*, until Bash had to scoot his chair away. At least he was keeping his voice just as hushed. "What is wrong with you? I knew you loved that baby vampire from the first day I met him."

"You mean when you let him kiss you?"

"Let is a strong word."

Bash huffed. It helped that Ethan looked pleased by whatever Robert was telling him. Apparently the mayor and elder vampire had hit it off.

Bash pushed his chair back in but still leaned safely out of the line of fire when he asked, "How did you first say it?"

Bari glanced at the Alpha in an apron, still finishing up at the stove, piling the last of the food onto extra plates. "We haven't yet."

Bash kicked him under the table.

"But *if* Jay said it…." Bari kicked him back, and then hunkered closer over their plates. "You better believe I'd return the words. Forgive me for wanting a perfect movie moment before I first say *I love you*." He brightened again, patting the table like a drumroll. "How did Ethan do it? In the afterglow throes of lovemaking?"

Bash glowered.

"He *did*?" Bari slugged him again.

"Would you stop that!"

"What on earth possessed you to not say it back?"

It hit especially hard to hear something so close to his own voice say the exact words he'd been berating himself with all morning. Bash looked down the table at Ethan, who was smiling so beautifully, laughing with Robert over something before politely declining the booze-fueled coffee or a nip at Robert's wrist. "Because then it's real. Then it's… it."

"What? Fate? A mate? Time for a wedding da—"

Bash slugged Bari this time.

"*Ow*," Bari said pointedly but didn't back down. He did the insufferable thing and looked sympathetic. "I know now is the absolute worst time for sweet nothings, but isn't it also the best? We have no idea how this is going to play out. Missing the few truly good opportunities presented to us, well, I guess it's a family trait, because I almost did too. But *someone* convinced me to step up." He poked Bash this time, a little less harshly than a punch.

"To help save Brookdale, not to snag yourself an Alpha."

"It was both, and you know it. Just like I know you love Ethan."

"Then why is saying it so hard?"

"Because it *is* real. Because he is *it*. And admitting that makes it more terrifying to imagine losing him."

"While it pains me to admit when you're right…."

Bari snorted.

"None of that makes this easier."

"Since when has that stopped you before?"

Jay came over with his own piled-high plate, interrupting anything Bash might have said, and took the seat Ethan had vacated. "Don't let it get cold, now," he said, realizing that neither had dug into their breakfasts yet. He went right in for his own bite, which was not only covered in syrup but a mountain of whipped cream that immediately smeared on the end of his nose.

Bari giggled, rising to lean over the table and coaxing Jay up too with a come-hither curl of his fingers. "Come here, darling. You're a mess."

Jay leaned in as urged, only for Bari to forgo any swipe of his thumb or use of a napkin and lap up the cream with his tongue, ending with a quick kiss to the tip and a coy grin.

"I love you." Jay chuckled.

Fuck.

Bari melted into that perfect moment he'd been waiting for without hesitation. "I love you too," he said and kissed Jay firmly, right in Bash's face.

I hate you, Bash mouthed when only Bari's eyes were on him.

Jay had the tact to look bashful, but Bari mimed a kiss at the air, as if to say it could be as easy as Bash wanted it to be.

Nothing had been easy since Halloween, for Bash's entire life, but he wondered if it could be.

"Better bring our assassin something to eat," Deanna announced, getting up from the smaller table.

"Hang on!" Siobhan waved at everyone to quiet down, still on her phone but rushing to the corner of the kitchen counter to turn on the small TV set resting there. She flipped to the local news station and turned up the volume.

"While the mayor's office has yet to respond to these accusations," the newswoman was saying, "it seems the evidence is fairly substantial. Unfortunately, the photographs are not suitable for our audience to view in full, but as you can see from these censored images—"

"Ah, fuck," Robert groaned with his head dropped back. "So much for getting ahead on things."

"We tried, boss." Siobhan came over, phone pressed to her chest. "The source was the deputy mayor, and she went live with the findings earlier this morning. When my agents caught up to her, they found evidence she'd been enthralled."

"She didn't turn on me?" Robert perked up.

"Not of her own free will."

"Then I just need to talk to her—"

"It's too late," Bash said. "It won't look good if a visit from you changes her mind now."

"Then I gotta head this off another way." Robert got up from the table, thinking a moment before downing the last of his booze-filled coffee. "You need me, I'm there, but I can't sit around in the wolf's den. Animal den? Pet shop? Have Tom and Jerry port me away, and Butch and Sundance can keep me company, but I gotta go."

Luke and Preston, as well as Siobhan and Nell, eyed each other at the admittedly apt pet names but quickly jumped into gear.

"Any of you know a good defense attorney?" Robert joked.

They did, actually, and Jay nodded, picking his breakfast back up from the table. "I'll do what I can."

"And I will take another look at those spreadsheets that Mr. Mayor-Who-Can't-Keep-It-In-His-Pants gathered," Preston said. Besides being their Magister, he was also the pack's accountant, and a brilliant one. "If something can prove those books were doctored, I'll find it."

Robert promised to return at night, but now it was a race against jail time. Knowing the source of the scandal had been glamoured basically proved Alexa's involvement, and she knew right where to hurt them. A Null was a powerful ally and had already saved them from a takeover once.

The ensuing chaos, despite a swifter downing of Bash's breakfast than he would have liked, while Ethan did his usual morning check-in with Gordon, at least meant they had plenty to talk about—other than a botched I love you—once they were headed to Ethan's office. He just hoped the others had more success than he had a feeling they were going to.

Chapter 7

JAY RARELY got the opportunity to stretch his attorney muscles for non-pack-related issues. Although he supposed Robert was part of Bashir's pack and certainly not any normal human, considering he was a Null.

Jay and Bari had gone to City Hall with Robert, deposited by Preston via portal, along with Siobhan and Nell, who continued to act as Robert's bodyguards. Robert had told them to make themselves comfortable in his office, he'd handle explaining who they were to anyone who asked, and then he was off, trying to mitigate the chaos, while Siobhan and Nell kept a watchful eye on him.

This meant the office was otherwise empty, leaving Jay to his work, which mostly revolved around familiarizing himself with Robert, his track record as mayor, and what evidence there was, if any, besides the doctored books. If Preston couldn't prove they were doctored, was there any precedence to keep Robert from seeing jail time? Misuse of public funds was a serious offense, and if charged as a felony—

A sigh from across the desk interrupted Jay. He couldn't say he minded the forced proximity Bashir had ordered of everyone, always needing to have someone with him, especially when that someone was as pleasant company as Bari Bain.

"I believe I can feel your adoring stare with all five of my senses right now." Jay flicked his eyes up from the paperwork he was perusing.

Bari sat across from him, elbows propped on the desk and chin on laced fingers. He and Bashir might be twins, but they looked completely different to Jay the more he got to know Bari. Bari exuded such flamboyant and effortless charm that it changed his face, truly, from what Bashir kept as a stiff, beguiling mask to one of untainted joy for simply being alive. How could Jay not love him? And he'd said it for the first time less than an hour ago.

He honestly hadn't realized it until after Bari said it back and kissed him, because he'd felt love for Bari so early in their courting. He also planned to ask Bari to be his mate officially very soon. He knew what

Bari's answer would be. They were already engaged to be engaged, after all. It was a foregone conclusion.

Then again, so had been the engagement to Bashir.

This was nothing like that. It wasn't political, even if it had political benefits, bringing together two different packs. Bari was all the things Jay had found enticing about Bashir but with the important parts that had been missing, the many things they had in common, and how much Jay simply enjoyed being with Bari, that made them a much better match. Even if Bari was being adorably disruptive right now.

Especially then.

"Bari, you can be very distracting."

"Can I?" He batted his long lashes.

"Yes. In all the best ways. But still distracting."

"Sorry." Bari chuckled and dropped his hands to sit upright. "I can't help it. All this insanity and you still manage to make me swoon. Which, by the way… oh, I probably shouldn't tell you." He was a terrible gossip, and Jay could see the way he bounced in his seat, biting his lip in eagerness to be prodded to divulge whatever he knew.

Jay resolved to be distracted for at least a few more minutes. "As both your romantic partner and a lawyer, there is similar attorney-client privilege, you know."

"Ethan told Bash he loves him!" Bari blurted at the invitation. "But my dolt of a brother didn't say it back. Can you believe it? They're all in a kerfuffle over it."

Kerfuffle, Jay mused—and then registered what Bari had said. "He didn't say it back?"

"He does love Ethan. Of course he does! But it's… it's Bash! He never expected to find love. Cramps his style," Bari mocked, which was especially adorable again, but for a moment, all Jay could think about was how well he knew Bashir hadn't been the type for love.

Because he hadn't been able to love Jay.

Ever the empathetic one, Bari reached across the table to place his hand over Jay's. "It would take quite the patient and masochistic partner to put up with my brother. Not a burden I'd wish on many."

Jay smiled. He knew he needn't ever mourn the might-have-been with Bashir, because everything had worked out for the better. "And that's exactly who he found. He'll tell Ethan when he's ready."

"I think so too." Bari patted Jay's hand. "Which is why we need to be diligent to resolve all this. And I need to let you get back to work. I'll go get us some coffee." He rose from the desk to leave, which gave Jay a small, possibly silly jolt of panic.

"Bashir probably wouldn't like you going anywhere alone," he said, not trying to hide that he didn't like that either.

"Two minutes in a breakroom only a few doors down in City Hall is plenty safe. I'll be right back." Bari winked and slipped from the office with a grace that never failed to captivate Jay.

That was why he'd brought along a small wrapped box from Brookdale, stored in their guest room at Bashir's den, in case they were still here for Christmas.

I'LL BE right back? Bari thought. Possibly the worst four words to exit a room with if one didn't want to jinx themselves into not being able to fulfill that promise. He didn't like being the superstitious type, though. They *were* in City Hall, and the breakroom *was* only a few doors down, with people all about, none of whom smelled like shifters, let alone vampires.

Who cared about four words anyway when Bari was still twitterpated over the three words he'd heard from Jay over breakfast? Jay loved him, and he loved Jay, and no current crisis was going to spoil that.

Most people paid Bari little mind as he passed them, all thinking him Jay's assistant, attorney for the mayor. That thought brought Bari's mind straight to the gutter. Maybe if they solved this quickly, they could make use of Robert's office for a little roleplay—although that probably wouldn't look good if they got caught, considering what Robert's scandal was about.

Those photographs had been very inspiring, though.

Bari chuckled as he turned into the breakroom for the coffee maker, which, thankfully, looked to have been freshly replenished. He didn't mind being Jay's gopher for today. He was much more than that, personally and professionally, though he hadn't been much help with his actual expertise since the tablets in Brookdale. He doubted it would be a good thing if they needed his ancient artifact knowledge for this newest disaster, but at least he could have been more helpful than getting coffee and assisting with breakfast that morning.

And hopefully he'd given the necessary kick in the pants to his brother to confess his feelings for poor Ethan. They all had to keep thinking ahead to when these crises were finally behind them.

The coffee smelled about as burnt and unappealing as Bari expected of a government building, while he poured two mugs full. Normally, Jay took his black, but perhaps a little sugar—

A chill shot through Bari that made the hairs on his arms prickle, and he nearly sprouted fur. That never happened. The first thing a young shifter learned was how to keep instinct from causing a shift in public. The only time Bari had ever nearly unleashed his wolf with humans around was when facing his ex, Joseph, who'd accosted him in the Brookdale Museum. Bari had a catalyst then, but whatever had just alerted him that something was wrong had felt so… primal. He honestly felt a little scared and turned his head slowly to see what predator could possibly be making him feel this way.

No one was there, but he was certain someone had been a moment ago or passed by the breakroom with sinister intent.

He'd never been a fighter, and while he was Brookdale's Magister now, given his abilities to see things coming and sense and discern magic, he wasn't the expert wielder of it that Preston was, or like Nell and Reggie as Shamans. What could he possibly do if alone and faced with the enemy?

He really wished he hadn't said *I'll be right back*.

Hurrying out of the breakroom, Bari took one quick glance in each direction, still not noticing anyone who could explain why he felt so threatened and on edge, and made a panicked near-sprint back to Robert's office and the safety of Jay's presence. Sometimes he really hated having a Seer's intuition.

"Everything okay?" Jay asked when Bari slumped against the closed door with a huff.

"I'm not sure, but let's just say I have a… *hunch* that we're right to think Alexa has something to do with Robert's scandal."

Jay's eyes widened, and then he immediately dove back into work, while Bari brought him his coffee. They had a mayor to save and an ancient vampire to stop, after all.

Then they could get back to the twitterpated part.

"BELIEVE ME, I'd rather be there in person too," Luke said to one of his lieutenants at the Shelter. He didn't have the same network of agents that

Siobhan did, just a handful of former Shelter kids like him who wanted to help with the next generation when he couldn't be there to attend to the day-to-day.

Like now, when he couldn't even leave the den because he wasn't supposed to go anywhere alone and Preston needed to pore over spreadsheets.

Luke was actually with Rio at the moment, in the upstairs hallway guarding the room for the assassin Bash and Ethan had fought. They'd been trading off partners to avoid going too stir-crazy.

"Maybe when Pres isn't swamped, he can help me do a magical Zoom thingy to still do story time for the kiddos. Just keep me up-to-date, huh? Even if it's someone sneezing funny. Thanks." He hung up with a sigh. The pack members at the Shelter were taking things surprisingly well, given their circle members were split in every which direction.

Turning from how he'd been pacing down the hall, Luke discovered Rio laid out on the carpet, staring at the ceiling.

"Uh, you okay, dude?"

Rio didn't move but spoke to the ceiling too. "How do you do it? I mean, I know you're a cat, and, like, all this weirdness is somehow normal for you, but, like… how do you do it?"

"Avert disaster twenty-four seven? Comes with the job. Plus, you being around helps."

"It does?" He finally lifted his head.

"Totally! It's the same as being around Ethan. And Bash and Bari now. That little Focus jolt helps stave off the panic."

"You never seem panicked."

"Oh, I've been known to panic. Even recently." Luke glanced behind him back down the hall, thinking of Preston in Bash's office— and saw Deanna coming up the stairs to relieve him. "And hey…." He turned back to Rio. "Would you trade away all this insanity and your newfound abilities you didn't even know you had if it meant no more Deanna?"

Rio sat up fully and spotted her coming as well. "Not even for a second."

"Right there with ya, pal. All yours, D!" Luke spun around again. "How's my boy?"

"Gettin' there." She looked and sounded as equally exhausted as he was starting to feel. They both preferred to be out doing something rather than babysitting. "He's made a few pleased murmurs, if that says anything, but it's math, so I don't really know."

"You and me both." He laughed, patting her shoulder like a partner hand-off, and headed for the stairs, while he heard Rio scramble up from the floor.

"What were you doing down there?"

"Nothing."

Luke chuckled again. He couldn't imagine what it must be like for Rio, thrown into this world, never having known anything about shifters or vampires or magic. For him, it was all just life. So was facing disaster, really, but what had recently made him panic didn't have anything to do with vampires or ancient artifacts.

It had been the fear that he might lose Preston, that they were somehow growing apart and unable to connect the way they used to because adopting their daughter, Jesse, had brought up so many old wounds. Working their way through that, remembering back to when they first met and why they were mates, made even the craziest of Bash's prophecies seem possible to avert. Not only because Preston had smelled incredible to Luke from the moment they met, but because they did connect, even having come from different worlds—an orphan and a rich kid both longing for family.

Luke reached the bottom of the steps and peered into the office to see Preston furiously going through printouts and computer reports like the gorgeous little nerd he was. Then the small table beside the front door caught his attention. Someone must have brought in the mail, because a stack was piled there and included a box.

Luke knew what that must be and was proven right when he saw it was addressed to him. That should help turn Preston's serious work face into a smile, even if they did need to save the city with a ticking clock counting down to their doom.

Once again.

PRESTON HEARD Luke enter but couldn't tear his eyes from his current corroboration of the digital records showing payment to the BDSM club that Robert frequented and the printouts of city funds sitting on Bash's desk. He held up a hand as he continued through his train of thought, the familiar sign to his mate that he was not to be interrupted until he looked Luke in the eyes or there would be hell to pay.

He knew the books were doctored, and not only because Robert said so, but because he could see it, and he could almost trace exactly where and how and why, but he was still just out of reach of actually being able to prove it. He needed time, and that was something they were running out of far too quickly.

With a sigh, as he hit another dead end in verifying notable discrepancies, Preston allowed his eyes to drift from the screen to where Luke was strolling closer, carrying an armful of mail. He dropped the letters onto an unoccupied space on the desk but kept hold of a small package.

"Need a break?"

Preston glanced at his watch and saw that it was already past noon. "Fuck, I do. How's your end?"

"Quite nice, I've been told." Luke shifted his hips and smacked a hand on his ass.

"I would scowl at you, but that is a better view than spreadsheets."

Luke snorted. "I could cover them in tinsel for you."

"I suppose you could cover the BDSM photos with it. Make them more festive."

"How about this instead?" Luke set the package down and slid it across the desk.

Preston's mind was too fried to even guess at what it might be, but once he'd sliced through the packing tape and opened the flaps, he wasn't surprised by its contents.

It was their Christmas cards, a hastily made decision and rushed to the printers, with photos taken with Jesse right before they left Glenwood, but still with time enough to send them out before the holiday. They'd chosen a collage template so they could include multiple shots. Jesse had been a little reluctant, thinking the whole thing too lame, but Preston had been insistent, and Luke jumped on the idea only too readily.

They'd never sent out a Christmas card before. Most of the people they'd actually send one to they saw every day. But it was more about getting the pictures taken, something to remember and hold on to, than who else might see them.

Other than the sneer Preston hoped to conjure on his parents' faces when he sent one to them so he could rub their noses in a few snapshots of the family he'd made in their place.

Like the shot of the three of them huddled together smiling. The one of Preston and Luke kissing while Jesse rolled her eyes. And one of them all making silly faces that had little cartoon tails and ears drawn in—for two cats and a rat, respectively. Seeing the photos helped untie some of the knots forming in Preston's stomach.

"How about I start addressing them?" Luke pulled over a chair to sit beside Preston.

"You hate that sort of work."

"At least I'll have a nice view while I do it." He grinned, clearly meaning both the cards and being able to be beside Preston while he worked on them. "But first I gotta take a pic to send to Jess so she can see how awesome they turned out." He pulled out his phone to line up over one of the cards and sent off a text.

It was Luke's energy and excitement for the simple things that had been part of what first endeared him to Preston, and after ten years together, Luke hadn't lost that. Preston was so relieved they hadn't lost each other either. They'd come close to losing sight of what mattered and had to be reminded of just how much they wanted to build this family—a rat, a cat, and a tiger, beating the odds despite what so many in their world might consider wrong.

Luke laughed when Jesse almost immediately texted back and showed Preston the message.

Urg, we look like dorks. You guys are ridiculous. Miss you.

The final sentiment included an emoji with its tongue sticking out. Their little girl.

And both she and Luke, their family, the small and extended versions, were more than worth figuring this mess out before Christmas.

Preston kissed Luke, who smiled dopily back at him, and returned to the computer. "Back to work."

Chapter 8

BASH WOULD have preferred to stay at the den, but he could make do with a phone and a laptop just about anywhere. Sharing a desk all morning and into the afternoon, however, hadn't staved off all the awkwardness between him and Ethan. Anytime Ethan passed Bash a furtive glance, it was filled with the same pinch to his brow. After the dozenth time it happened, Bash had to say something.

"Good to hear, Luke." Bash was finishing an update call from the den. "Yes, I realize it would be easier to have something to react to other than headlines, but I'm sure Alexa won't keep us waiting long. She orchestrated anarchy with that damn totem and the creation tablets. Some other artifact or unexpected magic is bound to be her next play. Be wary of anything you hear from the Shelter that's out of the ordinary. Yes, I'm sure you already have been. I'll check in again soon."

Ethan was finishing a call too, an update from the agents tailing Decker, but it didn't sound like he'd deviated from his usual routine today. Much as Ethan wanted the man to slip up, they had nothing criminal against him—or any signs of secret meetings with vampires.

"If you learn anything about that DLI stop yesterday, call me back. Thanks again." Ethan hung up, and "awkward side-eye number thirteen" made its appearance.

"Ethan—"

A quick rap of knocks sounded at the door.

"It's open!" Ethan called back.

One of the largest men Bash had ever seen walked in—in height and widthwise, given the size of his muscles. He was at least six four and built like a professional wrestler, with a shaved head and graying beard. Despite his peak physical condition, he looked midfifties, with a few tattoos peeking up the sides of his neck from the collar of his winter coat. Everything about him screamed professional, and not in the suit-and-tie kind of way.

"Hey there, Lamb. Been a tick."

"Dave!"

ETHAN WAS so stunned to see his friend that he almost leaped up from the desk at superhuman speed. He raced at a more believable pace to the door and right into Dave's arms, for the first time ever experiencing the man's burly bear hug without his ribs feeling like they were bowing inward. Being a vampire had its perks.

"You look good!" Dave pounded the middle of Ethan's back.

"You too!" Ethan still choked a little from the impacts. "But am I a complete asshole? Did I miss your release? I thought you still had until January."

"I did, I did. Got out early. Call it a Christmas miracle." Dave noticed their silent onlooker with a flick of sharp eyes, immediately standing taller, like he was falling into old habits, always making himself look bigger when someone got too close to Ethan in prison. "Didn't interrupt business with a client, did I?"

"Oh no!" Ethan hurried to ease Dave's concern about Bash and ushered him over to introduce them. "You're not interrupting. This is my, umm... my, uhh...."

"*Close* friend?" Dave wasn't at all subtle about his whisper.

Ethan chuckled. He hadn't meant to trip on the words, but he hadn't been feeling like much of Bash's partner today. "Yeah. This is my boyfriend, Bash Bain. Bash, this is Dave Golding, my old cellmate."

Recognition dawned in Bash's eyes at last as he stood to shake Dave's hand.

"Caught yourself a lamb, huh?" Dave smiled with the dangerous sort of leer that Bash was also good at. If Bash hadn't been a werewolf, Dave might have bruised or broken something with the way he tried crushing Bash's fingers in his meaty paw, but Bash gave back just as good.

"More like he caught me. I suppose *Lamb* is a fitting nickname for our Mr. Lambert."

"Innocent as they come and sometimes in need of a good shepherd to watch his back. Might need to size you up a bit more, *Bash*, see if you're worthy. Only decent bloke I ever met in the clink was this kid. You decent?"

"Dave," Ethan reprimanded. Neither had released the other's hand just yet. "You don't need to do that. He's passed approval, I promise. Bash, do you think you could give us a few minutes?"

Bash's eyes snapped to Ethan with the same look he'd given him every time Ethan tried sneaking away lately. "You and your friend should definitely catch up, but perhaps—"

"I'll be fine."

The way Bash's gaze hardened said he wasn't going to be convinced that easily. At least he and Dave finally ceased the pissing contest and released their handshake.

"One sec, Dave. Have a seat." Ethan grabbed Bash's arm to drag him to the door for some semblance of privacy, hissing, "I can be alone for fifteen minutes with an old friend. He's human, and if he was enthralled, a lightshow of runes would have gone off when we hugged. Did you see anything?"

Bash's scowl said he hadn't. "The timing—"

"Sucks, I know. I don't like you being alone either, but we're still in the same building. So why don't you hit the bathroom, and then wait outside the door. Give me fifteen minutes. Nell and the others warded my office almost as insanely as the den. Dave's no threat to me. Unless you're having any *feelings* I'm not." Ethan almost flinched after he'd said it, because he wasn't trying to allude to last night.

He really wasn't.

Bash's look remained skeptical, and a flicker of wanting to say more seemed right on the surface. All he did say was, "Fifteen minutes." Then he slipped out the door.

"I don't like him," Dave said as soon as Ethan returned to the desk. "Won't even leave you alone? Seems controlling."

"It's not Bash's fault. We have a lot going on right now. The three of us will get a drink sometime when he's in a better mood." Even if Ethan couldn't drink the same things as them. "I'm sure you'll get along eventually. Bash paints *Warhammer* models."

"Yeah?" Dave was a closeted geek too, and while not gay, very protective of Ethan once he'd found out his orientation. "How long you been seeing this guy? You didn't mention a boyfriend in your letters. I wanna hear all about it."

For a long time, Ethan hadn't known what to say in his letters, since so soon after his own release, he'd become a vampire. But by now, he'd practiced his "safe for the masses" version of the story. Getting a job at a tattoo parlor, only to fall hard for its owner, an outwardly frosty but caring man, who'd then helped Ethan get his PI license. That had Dave a little worried Ethan was under Bash's thumb more than on equal footing, but Ethan assured him that what they had wasn't like that.

Other than the one-sided love confession last night.

Ethan didn't say that part out loud.

"I want to hear about you," he changed the subject. "This is a social call, right? You don't need a PI or anything?"

"Nah, nah. Got a job all lined up bagging groceries. Just for starters while I look for something better, but I figure it'll help me meet the neighbors, put 'em at ease."

For obvious reasons, Dave tended to intimidate people, but anyone who got to know him recognized the softie deep down. He'd win over those neighbors in no time.

"As soon as I got out, first thing I wanted was to pay ol' Lamb Chop a visit."

Ethan didn't mind the nickname, though he'd often wondered if Dave calling him that and his general protectiveness of him had others in prison assuming their relationship was different. "I'm happy for you. Did Leo have something to do with your early release?"

"Leo?"

Ethan had wanted to call Leo, but he was basically in protective custody, under surveillance with Kate's circle in Glenwood. He was getting blood bag donations just like Gordon now, since no one wanted to get close to him until Alexa was dealt with and they knew it was safe. "You don't have to pretend. I know my uncle probably had something to do with the nicest guy in prison becoming my cellmate."

Dave wasn't particularly adept at guile, so when his face scrunched in honest confusion, Ethan started to doubt his long-held assumption. "I don't know no Leo, kid. But I guess ya got me. I was paid off to keep an eye on you, and that same contact got me here."

For a second, Ethan wondered if it had been his dad, but Gordon couldn't have had anything to do with Dave getting out early now.

"Haven't met her in person yet," Dave continued. "Had a few calls, some money got wired. But hey, that don't change nothing 'bout my love for you, Lamb."

"Her?" Had Ethan missed something? No, Dave was human. And he wasn't enthralled.

"Said she was an old family relative or something. Knew your pop? Maybe that's where the uncle comes in. Not a real uncle but another friend? Coz she mentioned introducing your old man to some guy who'd helped you out before. Your old man passed away, though, didn't he?"

"Introduced...."

Alexa was Leo's maker. They already knew that. They also knew it hadn't been an accident, but that Alexa had caused Leo to frenzy the night he turned Gordon. She'd put all the right players in each other's paths.

Had she done it again?

But Ethan and Bash would have felt that something was wrong, wouldn't they?

"You're looking a little pale there, Lamb. Don't go holding this against me now."

"Dave." Ethan leaped to his feet. "It's too much to explain right now, but—"

A sharp sting in Ethan's neck cut off his words, and he learned for the first time that a bite from another vampire could still hurt.

He thrashed, but his arms became pinned to his sides as his attacker bit harder, sucking the blood from him so fast that Ethan's knees buckled.

Dave leaped to his feet too, foolishly ready to defend Ethan.

"*No need for that, Mr. Golding. Just watch,*" a pleased, purring voice said as a woman stepped out from behind Dave like she'd materialized from nothing other than the large man's shadow.

How? When? Ethan should have sensed something. The wards should have kept her out.

The vampire draining Ethan bit harder. He thought a chunk might be torn from his throat and he'd be left to bleed out on top of his desk, but the stranger kept drinking. Ethan was first and foremost a Focus. He could... he could... but he'd been too caught off guard. He already felt weak, and Bash wasn't there to help him. Ethan was at their mercy, both the stranger feeding from him with such brutal precision and the woman he recognized without having to know her face.

"Alexa."

"A name is just a name, little lamb." She trailed red-painted nails down Dave's arm as she stepped up beside him. He obeyed her thrall, frozen, watching, but his eyes betrayed he knew what he was seeing, and he looked terrified for Ethan's sake. Ethan had never seen his friend look terrified before. "Good for you. You know mine."

Ethan tried to memorize her appearance, even if he didn't expect to survive this encounter. She had an agelessness to her that was different from Gordon's, stretched out longer, with an ancient wisdom in her blue eyes. The long wavy hair was like Ethan's sketch, a rich auburn, her skin pale and body like an old Hollywood starlet with ample curves, hugged by a classy black dress like a high-powered CEO, and wearing a rectangular pendant made of white stone.

She didn't feel like anything. Ethan couldn't sense her standing there, no more than he could sense the vampire behind him. If he didn't know otherwise, he'd guess they were human. They were warded like Leo and Reggie had been to keep anyone from knowing they were vampires. But with Alexa, it seemed stronger.

"Please, Dave has nothing to do with—"

"You don't need to talk. Just listen." She betrayed no ounce of indecision or concern, no sense at all that she feared anything, ever. "I have a specific objective for our meeting today, Ethan. We're not going to kill you. I would much prefer to have you with me. That was always the goal. The world was different once, a better place when our kind controlled the top of the food chain. Hierarchies serve a purpose, to keep order and peace. Unlike some of my brethren from those ancient days, I always understood that shifters and humans serve a purpose too. As do people like you, the especially and uniquely powerful. Power simply needs to be culled at times, or at the very least, tempered, or everything is chaos, like the world we find ourselves in now. I merely wish to see a return to that more ordered, structured world of my youth."

"To enslave everyone," Ethan accused.

"You misunderstand. You rebel. And I can't have that. But since I can't currently enthrall you, *grandchild*, I need you to understand that if you get too much in my way, your precious Bashir, no matter how powerful he, you, or any of your friends may be, will suffer the same fate that our mutual friend is about to." She turned her gaze on Dave.

No.

Alexa became a blur, and Ethan expected to see Dave's throat slashed or guts spilled onto his desk. Nothing like that happened. Dave was left to his waking prison while a second pair of fangs bit into the other side of Ethan's neck.

His vision blurred, knees giving way completely. They were draining him, but they weren't going to kill him. They….

No, no, no.

Ethan saw a tear streak down Dave's face, watching what was happening to him. But he had no idea, no idea what came next.

"Please," Ethan said as the darkness encroached until all that remained were Dave's eyes. And then….

Nothing.

ETHAN GASPED, choking and spitting up the blood still being swallowed down his throat. He couldn't see clearly right away but knew he was on the floor of his office in front of his desk, with a heavy weight gathered into his lap.

Two swift knocks were heard at the door before it opened.

"Fifteen minutes became twenty, and we can't… afford…." Bash's voice trailed off as he entered, seeing the carnage Ethan had made of his friend.

Tears were already streaming down Ethan's face, mixing with the blood. Somehow, despite being frenzied, he must have started crying even before he came back to himself, knowing that the victim he had in his arms was Dave, who'd only wanted to be a decent man and a good friend. Circumstance and bad breaks had sent him to prison, but he'd finally gotten out.

Bash closed the door.

All Ethan could say through his sobs, hugging Dave against him and not wanting to look at his friend's mangled throat, was, "She was here."

Chapter 9

BASH KNEW he shouldn't have left Ethan alone, but he'd never expected this.

Alexa, right there, in Ethan's office. A second vampire too, one Ethan hadn't seen. They must have used magic to get inside, which should have been impossible, given the warding from when Bash first rented the space and the extra protection added since yesterday. She either had a powerful witch on her side or an artifact with more magic than a Magister. They'd never even seen her coming, but they should have.

He should have.

Now they had another mess to clean up, far worse than Robert's habits and falsified bookkeeping. People knew Ethan and Dave were connected, and now he was dead by his former cellmate's hands. Or rather, fangs.

Ethan wasn't taking it well. He hadn't stopped crying, a slow, steady stream, his gaze distant when Siobhan and Nell arrived with a crew of agents for cleanup. They'd asked Preston and Luke to watch Robert, but even thinking they'd been poised for anything, Alexa was ten steps ahead of them. They truly couldn't risk anyone being alone now.

Once they were back at the den, Ethan's tears still hadn't dried. Alexa hadn't merely made an example of him, but *to* him, proving she could get them to do anything, even murder a friend, who she'd set up from the beginning to cross Ethan's path.

"The good news"—Siobhan sat between Ethan and Bash on the living room sofa—"is Mr. Golding didn't leave much of a trail to your office. As far as anyone will know, he's just an ex-con who's going to skip out on parole."

Ethan winced, hunched over and hugging his chest. "But when he's reported missing, they'll look into his contacts. They'll call me or come see me and ask if I know where he is."

"And you'll say you don't," Bash said coolly.

Ethan's lips trembling without words finding their way past them only made the guilt Bash felt for this worse. He shouldn't have left him alone. He shouldn't have. He knew better.

"There's something else," Nell broached carefully, speaking gently from the armchair. "Given you mentioned another vampire was with Alexa, our first thought was to check on Leo and Reggie. Leo is missing."

"No." Ethan sprang upright. "Tell me he didn't hurt anyone."

"The guards watching over him were merely knocked out, no injuries. Everyone is fine, but Kate and Jude changed their plans to come join us. They're worried that if Leo is still in Glenwood, their pack might be in danger. It's possible he did stay in town, but it's also possible he's here."

Ethan sagged. Leo being spared, more than once now, had been for his sake, and he wore the guilt for what that might mean like a shroud.

"Glenwood has people out looking for him," Siobhan said, "and we'll have agents on the lookout here too."

Bash highly doubted he'd be spotted until Alexa was ready for her next move.

A portal opened behind the sofa, like an archway made of light, revealing Robert's office at City Hall. Preston, Luke, and Robert all came through it.

The pitying glances from Preston and Luke said they'd heard the news.

"No warrant for my arrest yet!" Robert declared, either not having heard or just with zero tact. "Saving-my-ass attorney Jay is staying at the office a while yet with that much more agreeable brother of yours, Bain. Naturally I'm denying the public funds part tooth and nail while they dig into it. Everything else is family values, blah, blah, blah. Got a good uptick from the gay vote, though. I'm fluid, by the way." He winked at an unimpressed Siobhan.

"Robert, we are in the middle of—" Bash tried.

"One more thing. My deputy mayor, the one who ratted me out due to vampire brain fog? Kinda half apologized but believes the records have to be true. It's the only way she can rationalize doing this to me. She definitely doesn't remember any fanger or whatever, not that I could point-blank ask, 'Hey, get hypnotized by any movie monsters lately?'

"Anyway, figured I'd have another crack at your old man downstairs, Rookie." He patted Ethan's shoulder over the back of the sofa. "Wanna come?"

"Thanks, Robert, but not right now. Been a bit of a bad day."

"Can't argue with that." He patted Ethan again.

Watching Robert simply walk across the living room made Bash tense at the thought of him being alone, even in the den, and even if that would only be true for five seconds before he descended into the cellar. Bash couldn't let what happened unravel them, and he didn't want to deny Gordon company when it eased Ethan's mind too, but they didn't even know what sort of magic Alexa was wielding to have accomplished what she did.

If she could cross the wards around the den just as easily, none of them were safe.

Luke hopped onto the arm of the sofa beside Ethan. "Hey, uhh… what *do* you want to do tonight, buddy? Movie marathon? *Mario Kart* tournament? Drive around checking out Christmas lights for the nineteenth time?"

"Twice," Preston countered. "We have gone twice, and to completely different neighborhoods."

"Aw, but it's your love of wonderment that makes me love *you* so much." Luke leaned up for Preston to kiss him, which he promptly did.

Their exchange only made Ethan look more stricken, and it was painfully obvious he was trying not to look at Bash. "What I'd really like right now is to go to the tattoo shop. Deanna and Rio were putting in a shift, right?"

"They're there," Bash said. "I had planned to call them in—"

"No, I'd really like to go. If we can?"

"Of course. Five minutes for me to finish debriefing Siobhan and Nell and we can go."

Bash pulled the women over to a corner of the living room, allowing Luke and Preston to better surround Ethan and try lifting his spirits. They were good at that usually, and it might have worked, too, if Ethan didn't look like he'd had enough of being around couples.

"I need confirmation the den is secure."

"It is," Siobhan asserted.

"So was Ethan's office, yet somehow Alexa got in."

She and Nell exchanged troubled glances, and Nell said, "We know Leo doesn't have his own magic, so it must be her. It's possible she knows some tricks around our warding that we wouldn't have thought of. The only people I'd have guessed were capable of that are me and Preston, but she is supposedly ancient. We know too little about her."

"I'm hearing a lot of negatives and speculation, and no solutions." Bash trusted them, but their best might not be good enough if disasters like this could happen. "Ethan and I didn't even get a blip of Seer premonitions to know what she had planned."

"We'll get creative," Nell promised.

"And my agents have Alexa's description from Ethan," added Siobhan. "It's not much, but any ageless-looking women with auburn hair, blue eyes, and a black dress get near the den, we'll be notified."

"We have other packs on our side," Bash reminded them. "Don't neglect what their Shamans and Magisters might recommend."

"One being Bari," Siobhan snorted.

"My brother can be very creative," Bash said.

The pair headed off, and Bash nodded to Ethan that they could leave anytime. For the rest of today, he owed Ethan whatever he wanted.

"BOSS. LEECH." Deanna focused on Ethan when they arrived at the Rogues Gallery. "How ya doing?"

"Call it a new low," Ethan said. Once again, the need to wear shades in the daytime was a blessing, because it hid how red the whites of his eyes must have been from crying.

There were other artists on staff, all shifters, one of whom had a client she was tattooing in the back, but the shop was otherwise quiet. It was modest in size, larger lengthwise than wide, with the typical classic tattoo art on the walls, as well as a few examples from each artist. Ethan's section of the display was sparse, but it did show both Rio's Bulbasaur tattoo and Bash's red moon.

"I'm really sorry, man," Rio said, not an artist himself, other than with floral arrangements, but he was behind the counter beside Deanna, seemingly playing cashier and appointment taker.

It figured everyone had already heard what happened, but Ethan was glad, since it meant he didn't have to explain. "Thanks."

"You wanting a shift?" Deanna asked. "'Cause it's been kinda slow for walk-ins—"

"I was hoping to *be* a walk-in," Ethan said. "I lost a friend today. I want to get something to commemorate him." He hadn't mentioned that to Bash. He hadn't said much of anything to Bash while they were alone.

This was all Ethan's fault. If he'd listened to Bash and let him stay in the office, maybe….

He'd been repeating that same what-if mantra since it happened.

"What'd you have in mind?" Deanna leaned closer. "Not a heart with his name in it, I hope, 'cause that would just be tacky."

Ethan laughed. Dave would have appreciated the joke. "What would you recommend for a guy built like a bouncer who played a monk in D&D, a cleric in *World of Warcraft*, and once quoted Nietzsche to me when I questioned whether making a big enough mistake to end up in prison was something I could ever recover from?"

"If I can paraphrase, Lamb: 'You try to justify the meaning of your existence with logic, you'll perish trying to prove yourself right.' Shit happens. Good and bad. Next turn could be a great one. Don't let this be a reason you're not worth something better."

He'd been right too, mostly. Sure, Ethan was a creature of the night living with people who could turn into animals, but he felt more at home in the den with Centrus City's shifter circle than anywhere else, and he still hoped the worst of what had happened to him could get better.

It had to.

"I got an idea." Deanna waved Ethan into the back.

"I'll be here," Bash said, which left Rio looking spooked, since Ethan didn't think he and Bash had ever been alone together.

Ethan knew where he wanted the tattoo—left arm beneath his shoulder—and took off his jacket to roll up his sleeve as soon as he sat down.

"Wanna know what I'm thinking first, or gonna let me freestyle it?" Deanna put on gloves and gathered what she needed to start cleaning and shaving the area Ethan indicated.

He hadn't witnessed much of her tattooing, but her area of the display wall was one of his favorites. Even classic familiar designs like hearts, quotations, or butterflies always had an added intricacy to them, like stained glass or impressive depth.

Ethan closed his eyes, trying to let his Seer senses guide him. He hadn't tried hard enough earlier before blindly leaving himself open to an attack. He and Bash being near each other was part of what made their visions stronger. Without him, Ethan hadn't seen Alexa coming. Bash had tried easing him, saying they probably wouldn't have seen her coming even if Bash had stayed. Alexa had unknown magic on her side, and she and Leo were warded to be basically invisible.

Leo. He hadn't always done right by Ethan, but he'd tried. He meant well. He didn't want to be caught up in this. He didn't want to do the things Alexa had controlled him to do for what was apparently decades. Ethan wished he could talk to him, but Leo didn't even have a phone for Ethan to try calling, left back in Glenwood with his foiled jailers. He hated knowing it had been Leo who bit him so painfully and helped set him up for the same horrible fate once set in motion for Ethan's father.

"Kinda need to start mixing up inks here, leech."

Ethan opened his eyes. Deanna was already finished prepping his skin. An exact image hadn't been conjured in Ethan's mind, but he knew he was going to love whatever Deanna came up with. "I trust you."

He hadn't been tattooed since he was human, and he couldn't say it hurt like he remembered, more like a buzzing tickle. Ethan knew he was being too quiet, but Deanna let him, not breaking the silence until she'd finished the line work and moved on to color—mostly reds, oranges, and yellows, which made Ethan curious, but he decided against peeking.

"Who's rocking the boat, huh? I'm guessing Bash."

"Boat?" Ethan supposed he had been watching Bash rather intently while she worked.

"Definitely Bash, then. Whatever idiotic thing he's done or is doing, be patient with him. He's never done this before."

"Done what?"

"Had a boyfriend. A relationship. Anything more than a night. Seriously."

"Oh. I guess I never have either."

The pit in Ethan's stomach sank deeper. Everything else was messed up enough, and there he'd gone, being too hard on Bash for *not* doing something. It had just hurt so much, being brushed off like that, like he hadn't said three words he'd never said to anyone else romantically before.

Maybe Bash had never heard them before.

"Yours and Rio's anniversary is coming up, right?" Ethan remembered Rio had started to ask him for advice before everything imploded. "Two months?"

"Same as you. Why? Shit, do I gotta do some grand gesture or something?"

"No." Ethan chuckled. "But Rio wants to. He feels bad he didn't do anything last month."

Deanna smiled, showing a softer expression than any Ethan would have thought the were-panther capable of when he first met her. "Never figured I'd go for a human, but I guess that whole Focus draw thing is kinda cheating."

"'Cause that's the only reason you like him?" Ethan teased.

"Please, have you seen that ass?" She paused in her needle work, which was good because Ethan's next laugh was shoulder-shaking. "Maybe I gotta knock his socks off first, then, huh? Ya know, surprise him."

"That's a good idea. And actually, remember what Bari told us— in great detail—about how he helped Maximus and Theresa with their anniversary?" The vivid descriptions had included the burly werewolf naked and tied to a bed. "Never seen Rio's face redder."

"*Yet.*" Deanna grinned.

They laughed. An hour ago, Ethan wouldn't have believed he could laugh so soon after what happened, about anything, but he knew Dave wouldn't want him sulking. What happened was awful, but the fault was Alexa's and only hers. He had to remember that. Dave's blood was still in him. He'd coughed up a little, but he could feel it, continuing to warm and strengthen him. He had to be strong for Dave's sake too.

"All set. What do you think?"

There was a mirror by each tattooing station, and Ethan didn't have to turn much to get a good look at the design Deanna had chosen. It was no bigger than three inches in diameter, but the detail made it look like it could fly right off his arm.

A phoenix, wings spread, split down the middle, half on fire and the other half ashes.

"It's perfect." Ethan sniffed, eyes growing warm with the threat of more tears, but these he didn't mind shedding.

When he showed the tattoo to the others, Rio swooned over Deanna's artistry, and Bash offered a small smile.

Naturally, once they arrived back at the den, with everyone else back too, *Bari* offered a running bear hug.

"Darling! You poor dear! If you need anything at all, just say the word and I will drop everything."

All Ethan wanted by that point was sleep—if he could manage it. He still hugged Bari tightly back. He should check on Gordon, but given

Robert had done so earlier, he elected to not put himself through having to explain what happened with Dave to his dad.

It was routine from there, quick debriefs and good nights, before he and Bash headed upstairs and dressed for bed. Or undressed for bed. Ethan kept his underwear on, but he didn't want to keep distancing himself from Bash. He wanted to be enveloped by him, and as soon as they crawled under the covers and Ethan looked at Bash with silent pleading, Bash knew just what he was asking for.

Ethan thought his tears had dried, but having Bash wordlessly gather him against him brought a fresh wave.

"I am so sorry that happened, Ethan."

"Me too. Me too." Though he had to wonder if Bash meant the apology for more than what happened with Dave. Ethan didn't want to push. He didn't need words. This was new for them both, and just having Bash hold him was special.

It didn't help Ethan find sleep, even after Bash had. He hated how the day's events kept replaying in his mind, but he couldn't help thinking of the connecting thread. Alexa had been the start of everything. She made Leo, set Leo up to turn Gordon, got Dave to watch over Ethan in prison. She'd planned it all to have Ethan exactly where he was now.

Had she influenced Decker too?

He knew Decker was into something shady, and if Alexa had her hand in everything, she had to have something to do with Decker being in Centrus. She had to.

He had a *hunch*, and he wasn't going to ignore it.

Ethan sat up in bed, looking down at Bash peacefully sleeping beside him. His new tattoo, fully healed without the effort and time he'd required as a human, made him think again of Dave, but this was about more than one man, one loss. Ethan wouldn't let anyone else be a casualty in Alexa's fucked-up chess match. Being more powerful or having larger numbers wasn't going to be what beat her. Being smarter was. And it was with every fiber of Ethan's instincts, normal and supernatural, that he knew to not try doing what needed to be done alone.

"Bash." He gently shook him.

"What is it?" Bash awoke groggily.

"We need to see Decker. Now."

Chapter 10

"WHILE I commend your caution," Bash said, gas station cup of coffee in hand to stay alert given the late hour, "what makes you so certain we need to see Decker now?"

They were outside Decker's apartment building, a modest-sized complex with twelve floors, tucked between a convenience store and a long building of mostly empty office space down the rest of the block. He and Ethan were around back among parked cars. Only a single streetlamp illuminated them, but their eyes could cut cleanly through the surrounding dark.

Bash's breath puffed visibly, while Ethan's gave no sign it existed. It likely didn't since he didn't need to breathe, but even when he spoke, no mist formed. Both could weather the cold like creatures built for winter, but vampires were more resistant, as if made from ice themselves. He never felt like ice to Bash.

Decker's apartment was on the fifth floor, but he was out, returning on foot, and Siobhan's agents were poised to notify them as soon as he headed inside.

Returning from *what* was part of what had Ethan on edge, but Bash wasn't as convinced of wrongdoing. Didn't mean he wasn't willing to let Ethan be paranoid.

"A hunch," Ethan said with a smirk.

Couldn't argue with that either.

Siobhan's agents had tracked Decker to the back entrance of a strip mall, which, given the late hour, was odd, but they hadn't documented anything incriminating. When Bash and Ethan headed out to meet them, the agents reported Decker was headed home, so they'd gone that way instead.

"*Blood Moon to Blue Moon, the harvest is ripe,*" Ethan murmured the prophecy. "Like Siobhan said, that's easy. *For the old queen to conquer by Cold Moon's night.* Also easy. Even the last: *As a united star they can hold back the morn.* We have to work together to defeat Alexa, fine. But the line before it…. What are we missing?"

"*Four corners connect where a fifth is born,*" Bash spoke the line for him. "Could mean a location, could mean people, could mean both, could mean something we haven't thought of."

"How can you be so calm about having another prophecy that could end everything?"

Bash held Ethan's gaze, trying to convey with a look all the things he wasn't yet able to say out loud. "Patience comes with the territory. I waited a decade for you."

Ethan's frantic eyes focused, centering and holding on Bash with the same heartfelt resolve and the twitch of a more genuine smile.

Bash's phone buzzed, displaying the text: *He's back.*

"I assume you weren't thinking of following him inside and knocking?" Bash turned the phone toward Ethan.

"He has a balcony."

"Five stories up. And unlike our assassin friend, I don't have wings."

"Maybe we don't need wings." Ethan took Bash's coffee cup and set it on the ground, then moved into his body with a twinkle in his eyes. "I've been meaning to try something. Trust me?"

Six weeks ago, Bash would have answered with a resounding "Never."

He nodded.

The world went topsy-turvy, a blur of darkness and the minor light from the backlot flickering until a new location presented itself. Bash and Ethan were on the balcony—five stories up.

"Speed has its advantages," Ethan said. He held Bash close, the area around them darker with the streetlamp far below. Ethan's vampire talents made Bash think of all the ways it meant Alexa was that much more dangerous, but all he wanted to focus on was the soft fullness of Ethan's lips.

A light turned on behind the curtains of the balcony's sliding doors, and he and Ethan snapped apart. Bash could see inside through the slit of the curtains. Decker had a studio, nice enough, but with no separation between rooms other than the bathroom and a few closets.

He tossed his keys onto his kitchen table as he entered, kicked off his boots, unzipped his jacket—

"Is that…?" Ethan's voice trailed off in an almost-gasp, clearly seeing through his own slit what Bash had made out too.

Decker's shirt had smears of blood.

Whether left unlocked or the lock was no match for him, Ethan threw open the sliding glass doors and sped inside with a billow of the curtains. By the time Bash had followed, Ethan had a stunned Decker by the throat, dangling above the floor. Ethan bore no fangs or yellow eyes, but if Decker had been more alert, he might have seen the impossible speed Ethan used.

"What the hell?" Decker sputtered.

"*Ethan*," Bash warned, smelling what Ethan hadn't yet recognized.

The blood on Decker's shirt wasn't human.

Ethan dropped Decker with the realization. "Why are you covered in cow's blood?"

"What's it to you?" Decker spat, rubbing his neck and furiously straightening his collar. "I finally, finally have a chance at a fresh start, and what, you want revenge? I'm not the one who put your ass in prison. You think I don't grieve every day for what happened to my son?"

"You… what?" Ethan stumbled backward.

"A man who almost went to prison for killing his son has just as tough a time getting decent working hours as an ex-con. I have a night shift with a butcher shop, okay? I get cuts ready for the next day's shift."

"You *what*?"

"Something broken up there?" Decker snarled. "It's a job. I got about three now, only way to pay for all the prep work I've been doing to take that contractor's exam."

"Which you would have taken at the local DLI office, I imagine?" Bash asked.

"Who's this guy?" Decker scowled.

"You're legit?" Ethan continued to compute what was happening. "Your job, jobs, are actually legit? You went straight?"

"Big shocker, I know."

"*Are you telling the truth*?" Ethan demanded with power.

"Yes," Decker answered monotone and then slipped right back into mildly annoyed at their breaking and entering. "You don't believe me saying it once? Of course not. You weren't wrong the first time, were ya? Want me to admit it? Johnny's death was on me."

It might have mattered that Decker was finally confessing, if anyone would have believed hearsay from the man who'd already gone to prison for falsifying evidence against him.

"But it wasn't on purpose. Kid came in during a job and got caught in the crossfire. I didn't shoot him because I wanted to. But I knew my wife would never forgive me, so I tried covering it up. She saw right through that, just like you did. I still got rid of enough evidence that you couldn't make it stick.

"Then you get caught trying to fake it anyway and went to prison instead. What do you think that did to me? Knowing some CSI lab rat thought low enough of me to risk his career and his own jail time just to prove what I did? I've tried everything I can to get back on track. I'm trying, even if I can't face my wife or little Rosie ever again. Shit, I send care packages every week they probably think are from you. If they knew I sent anything, Connie would just burn it all."

"You didn't come to Centrus for any reason other than a fresh start in a new city?"

"No. If I'd have known you were in town, I'd have gone to Shorehaven."

"*You don't know anyone named Alexa?*"

"No," Decker droned. "Who's Alexa? And what are you here for, huh? Gonna try framing me for something I didn't do this time?"

"No," Ethan said softly. "This was a mistake. But if that mess with the mayor clears up, I may have a connection for you if you have trouble getting certified."

"Just like that?" Decker's eyes narrowed.

"Just like that. I'm sorry. I was wrong about you."

"No, you weren't," Decker said with a little more self-loathing. "You weren't. But I am trying to be a man worthy of the freedom I got on that technicality. You willing to let me do it? We're even."

Ethan nodded for Bash to join him heading out the actual exit.

"Mr. Decker," Bash said.

"Mr. Mysterious."

Bash didn't say anything on the slow and very human trek down the steps of all five floors rather than using the elevator. Ethan needed the descent to regroup, and Bash gave it to him. Outside, Siobhan's agents waited, and once informed that Decker was no longer a target worth watching, they said they'd double-check the perimeter anyway and then help guard Bash and Ethan on their way back to the den.

While waiting, Bash and Ethan stood out front of the building, this time with a few extra lights around, brightening the still and quiet street.

"Why was I so certain?" Ethan asked. "I thought my powers were pointing me this direction, but they even tried warning me that I was wrong about Decker."

"They did?"

"Every time I tried drawing him, his smile came out kind. I couldn't get it right. Or I thought I wasn't getting it right. But I was drawing the real Decker without knowing it."

"He still killed his son."

"And if I'd done my job right the first time, he might have paid for that crime the right way. At least now he's paying for it in his own way."

Perhaps he was.

Bash had never had that sort of outlet for his abilities, the way Ethan's powers sometimes came out in his drawings. "Understanding the hunches and nudges from being a Seer doesn't always come easy."

"But I was so sure we needed to be… here…." As Ethan's words trailed off, his expression fell to something decidedly irritated.

Bash looked to where Ethan's eyes had narrowed and saw a billboard on top of the neighboring building, promoting something benign like VPN software but stating in big bold letters as its tagline: *Your real competition is distraction.*

"Do you think the universe has a sense of humor?" Ethan slumped against the building.

"Usually at our expense."

Ethan huffed and then chuckled before sharing a commiserating smile with Bash.

A small white speck landed in Ethan's hair. Then another. Then another. They both looked skyward at the sudden release of gracefully falling snow—first of the year.

Ethan held out an upturned palm to catch the flakes. They didn't melt quickly on his skin but still looked crystalline for a while, with all their details displayed. He looked almost otherworldly like that, more than he was, with a curtain of white between them and collecting more and more in his red hair like a halo. Ethan glanced over with a wider smile, and maybe he saw Bash as beautifully otherworldly too, something no one else could understand.

Siobhan's agents reappeared with a shake of their heads. No other suspicious activity.

"Come on," Bash said. "Decker won't be a distraction anymore."

ONE OF the bubbles of tension had finally burst, and as exhausted as Bash felt, he took some solace in that once he and Ethan had returned to the quiet den and climbed the stairs back to their bedroom without incident.

They undressed, snuggled close, kissed, and with part of the weight off their shoulders, it was easier to kiss again. And again. And *again*.

Bash held the back of Ethan's neck in a firm grasp, unwilling to let go, when lately, Ethan kept slipping through his fingers. Even one day without touching Ethan had made Bash hungrier for him, for Ethan's taste and the feel of his taut body. He had this way of moving, even when not intending to be sexual, that was fluid precision like a trained dancer. When he *was* being sexual, he was eros in motion.

Ethan's length twitched against Bash's thigh. He'd removed his underwear already like Bash preferred, and Bash hooked a leg between Ethan's knees to encourage the friction. Ethan's vampire speed came in bursts as he responded—a roll to be on top, a snap from horizontal to upright as his neck arched and he writhed in Bash's lap. Bash rumbled approval through a low growl, sprouting fur and fangs and gripping Ethan's hips. He wanted to be inside him, quick and messy, but saw an almost vision of what Ethan planned do instead even before he started.

A smirk overtook the young vampire's face, his small fangs peeking over his lips and eyes flashing gold. He reached up beneath himself, gathering precome to slicken his fingers that he began to slowly fuck himself with while propped on his knees and the balls of his feet. His long arms and the curve of his spine made the view unparalleled. Bash could see the tempting digits being swallowed up inside Ethan as equal tease and herald of what came next.

This was easy, fathomable, feasible. They'd started here, with flesh and lacking sense, even to their detriment, and returned here again and again. That didn't make it less special than the heartfelt confessions Bash avoided, because he wanted to return here, with Ethan and only Ethan—again and again.

He stroked his cock in Ethan's equally greedy view while waiting for his moment to replace those fingers. He let his claws graze the skin of his head, making him grunt and grumble, putting on a show as he was being given one, and tempting Ethan, as always, to be the one to break first.

"Bash... I'm so tight... even one day without you in me." He twisted his fingers up deeper.

Fuck, he was good at this. "Seems you need a refresher, then... and that pretty hole too."

"You gonna give it to me?"

"You asking?" Bash pulled on his dick slower, trailing the tip of a claw over his dripping slit.

Ethan shuddered and started circling a third finger around his hole as he thrust in the others. "Not yet."

Bash growled, real and warning and building in volume. He'd roar if he didn't want to risk alarming their neighbors, just to see if his Alpha sway could command the vampire capable of commanding him. A rumble was a start, and because he knew Ethan was interested in how his cock thickened in his larger stages, he gave over to the change.

More fur shimmered into being across his skin like a wave of silvery velvet, teeth and claws growing larger, ears tufted, and face nearly elongating into his black-nosed snout. But not quite, not fully a werewolf. That adventure would be saved, but this was enough for Ethan's eyes to witness Bash's cock nearly double in size the way his insides had felt the other morning.

"Fuck." Ethan thrust his fingers in faster, adding the third.

"Ask."

"No."

"*Ask*... and when I fuck you someday as the wolf you want, I may even let you come."

Ethan groaned an obscene whine of indecision only to furiously nod and pull his fingers away. "*Please*."

Bash slammed Ethan down onto his cock with the same speed as Ethan's vampire blur.

Ethan's howl was as loud as Bash's roar might have been, but at least that couldn't be mistaken for trouble. He rocked and writhed and hissed with a snap of fangs and fiercer flash of yellow eyes with every pound of Bash into him. It was wild and messy just like Bash wanted, and over too quickly because of it.

At least Ethan came first.

He whined again, with the cutest pout and scrunch to his brow and fangs digging into his lips as he spilled across Bash's stomach. Bash came inside him with a dig of his claws into Ethan's hips almost firm enough to draw blood, and Ethan stuttered out an extra spurt of spunk in answer. They sagged, surrendered, kissed with fangs clacking, and once Ethan had dragged himself away to get a cloth and cleaned them both up, they were human again, content.

They snuggled in the afterglow, no sense of how many hours might remain before their alarm blared, as Ethan whispered, "I really do love you."

Bash hated that he flinched. "Ethan…."

"It's okay."

"No, it's not. And it's not that I… don't. Being with you…." Bash snarled, teeth extending in his anger, but he shook them away. "Shifter culture says that someone's mate is meant to smell amazing to them."

"Okay," Ethan said hesitantly. "Do I smell terrible?"

"No," Bash huffed. "You smell… right."

"Then…?"

Bash pulled away to look Ethan in the eyes like he deserved, trying to collect what had been running through his mind since he first heard Ethan say those words, and why they were so difficult to say back. "Perfect mates, fated even, always sounded so romantic to me when I was a boy. But that's what my parents said they had, and my father drove my mother to an early grave. If I've learned anything from them and life, it's that there is nothing perfect about fate."

"But other than their abilities, we are nothing like your parents. And we are not going to end up like mine." Ethan pressed his forehead so hard to Bash's, he felt the thrum of Ethan's pulse. "I won't let Alexa do that to us. I won't let her make me do to you what I did to…." He sniffled back a surge of moisture from his eyes. "I'm sorry. I'm sorry."

No, Bash was. He hadn't even realized that Ethan was fearing a parental echo of his own.

As Ethan succumbed to his tears, Bash tried to kiss them away, knowing he couldn't make up for what Ethan had been forced to do only hours ago, and yet, if he could just say....

"Ethan...."

"Can we stay like this? I want to try to sleep, at least for a little while."

Bash blinked away his own tears before Ethan could see them. "Of course. Sleep. We'll figure this out. We will stop Alexa, whatever plans she has next. I promise."

He wished he could undo the pain of the past few days, past few weeks, and keep the good. He knew it didn't work that way, and the only thing he could truly hope for was to give Ethan a better tomorrow, a better next week, a better new year.

A better life.

Because he....

He....

He couldn't say it, not yet. He didn't want to say it now, not when Ethan deserved to hear those words in a beautiful moment instead of a sorrowful one.

"We'll stop her," he said again, kissed Ethan again, and held him close until Ethan fell asleep first.

Chapter 11

IT WAS good Ethan didn't need sleep, because even just the couple hours he'd gotten were enough to leave him refreshed when he blinked awake to the sound of their alarm.

Bash must have reset it at some point because it wasn't their usual earlier hour. Most of the others were gone when they went downstairs, but Preston and Luke were there, on the sofa, having a video call with Jesse on Preston's laptop.

"I'm going to grab some coffee." Bash kissed Ethan's cheek before heading into the kitchen, where Ethan could see Jay and Bari sitting at the table, everyone dutifully in pairs, with Jay working on his own laptop, having claimed the kitchen table as an office.

Ethan felt like he should do something. They hadn't had a full report of what everyone was up to today, but he could imagine them all hard at work, either trying to exonerate Robert, continuing to keep Dave's death under wraps, looking for Alexa and any signs of unrest, or taking whatever small solaces they could until they had answers.

Like Jesse cooing over Preston's new mouse.

"How is Gus-Gus doing?" she asked. From what Ethan could make out of her on the screen, the young teen still had several streaks of blue in her brunette hair and wore a goth kid level of eyeliner.

"He's Basil and Dr. Dawson's adopted little baby." Luke scratched the chin of the tiny mouse, Gus-Gus, currently perched on his shoulder while the pair of rat "parents" were on Preston's. "Just like we adopted you!"

Jesse gave a patented teenage eye roll to say she thought her parents were complete dorks. She brightened when she noticed Ethan behind the sofa. "Hey, Ethan!"

"Hi, Jess." He waved. Not wanting to interrupt their family time, Ethan moved out of view, debating joining Bash in the kitchen, at least long enough to tell him that he was going down to see his father. Assuming he wanted to visit Gordon this morning.

Ethan hadn't intended for Robert's addition to visitations to take the burden off him completely. He didn't want his dad to be a burden at all, but after what had happened with Dave, it felt different facing him.

"Everything all right, darling?" Bari joined Ethan near the exit into the foyer, still allowing clear views both to the family meeting on the sofa and to Bash and Jay chatting at the table. "Sorry, stupid question." Bari's expression looked more Bash-like when he scowled. "Want a bit of good news this morning?"

"Please."

"I'm a genius."

Ethan snorted. "That's hardly news."

"Obviously." Bari hung on Ethan's arm, always so comfortably physical. "But especially true with my newfound Magister skills. I had a brilliant idea to help with our warding issues. You've played those online games that Bash was always into, yes? Those massive multiworld whatever-they-are?"

"MMOs?" Ethan said through a chuckle.

"Yes, yes. And they have those nifty little ways of porting around the map based on a, um, stamp of return to where you want to end up."

"A hearth spell, sure."

"So, what if that stamp of return was on our partners in crime?" Hooking his arm more securely with Ethan's, Bari pointed into the kitchen at the partners in question. "Let's say Jay and I get separated and something happens to one of us. I get ambushed or just feel like something's off and need to get back to Jay without knowing port spells myself or being able to contact Preston. We'd both have emergency runes that, when activated, would port us to the other without any extra magic."

"That *is* brilliant," Ethan agreed. "But what if Jay was somewhere in mixed company? Like in the middle of a bunch of humans?"

"Thought of that too," Bari appeased. "We're working out the kinks once those two finish their call."

The call with Jesse did seem to be wrapping up, now down to the mouse and rats playing on the coffee table to Jesse's delight, much as she tried to hide any overactive glee, and then Luke said with a bit of his own scowl how he'd wished they could have had their first Christmas together.

"We still can," Preston argued. "There's more than a week to go, and I thought someone said we could easily thwart a prophecy in under that time."

"I did say that." Luke grinned. "And you're right. Call it a promise, pixie girl. We're gonna have you home for Christmas."

Ethan hoped that was possible, and the small sentiment of a family together at Christmas made him think of his dad again, alone in the basement, a prisoner, but through his own fault, thinking cruelty and control was how to bring Ethan back into his life.

And he kept making those same mistakes. Ethan wanted to see him, but sometimes he wished Gordon was far away and that he didn't feel guilty for not wanting to be around him.

"Robert did check on your father this morning," Bari said softly, maybe just that intuitive, or because when Ethan, Bari, and Bash were near each other, truth came easier.

Not that it was *easy* or always came to them clearly or like visions. Even now, Ethan was among the most committed of couples at the den, and despite being one of them, he wasn't sure what lay in store for him and Bash.

"Bari, how do shifters officially become mates?" Ethan asked. "Not like a normal wedding, right?"

"No, no, it's simpler than that," Bari allowed the subject change without comment. "More a declaration, like a proposal, but the act of asking and the other agreeing seals the union all on its own. I'm still having a wedding, though," he said staunchly. "Totally lavish, no matter how unnecessary!"

Ethan could picture it and looked forward to when that day came, even if he couldn't picture his own future as clearly. "Bash said mates smell amazing to each other in shifter culture. May I ask… what does Jay smell like to you?"

Bari's expression turned dreamy. "Would you believe this exact time of year? That holiday spiced smell from autumn into winter. Mm!" He leaned closer then and asked with a teasing lilt, "What does my brother smell like?"

Ethan had been wondering that since Bash said it. "There's a certain scent from humans that makes me think… food, I guess? With shifters, there's an extra layer to it, and I can tell which tribe you are, like a sense of your specific primalness. But Bash, he's… a tempting meal, the strength of a wolf, potent sex, all melded into one and dipped in honey that I just want to….” A growl built in his throat, fangs snapping free and eyes sharpening, which made it easier to catch how Bari’s eyes widened. “S-sorry!”

“Don’t be, darling!” Bari rolled his shoulders with an all-over shiver. “My! Are you sure you aren’t a poet instead of an artist?”

“I’m supposed to be a detective.”

“You are a lot of things, dear. We all are. No one’s meant to be one thing, and we are strongest when we embrace the whole.”

He was right. More than right.

Brilliant.

“You *are* a genius!” Ethan grabbed Bari’s shoulders in a firm squeeze. He was a detective. An investigator. But he kept thinking like a vampire, like part of this world, and forgetting he was part of the human one too. “Bash! Jay! Get in here!”

Preston and Luke had finished their call and turned at the exclamation as Bash and Jay hurried in, expecting another bombshell to drop.

And Ethan had one.

“We’ve been thinking of this all wrong. We keep expecting Alexa to use another artifact or something magical against us, and sure, she used something to get into my office, but her plays so far have mostly been through human means. Get Robert wracked by a scandal. Get Dave out on early parole, knowing he’d come to see me. Her pawns, her plays, have all been human.

“We need to use our human strengths too. Like Jay with the law, Preston with bookkeeping. And I already have something worth investigating that I let myself ignore.”

“What?” Bash asked.

“Dave told me money got wired to him. Alexa paid him to keep an eye on me in prison. She didn’t enthrall him. She used human methods then too.”

“Which means that transaction has a trail,” Preston caught on.

“And a trail we can follow,” Luke added.

Whatever else had been planned for the day, they first collaborated on finding that trail and following it to a source. Ethan was a good investigator, and with the others backing him through their various skills and connections, they were even more efficient. But Alexa was smart. She'd funneled the money they tracked to Dave's account through several obvious dummy companies and aliases.

The others eventually had to branch back to their original tasks—Robert still needed their help—but Bash did what he could to assist Ethan. It was nearly sunset, and Ethan feared they'd hit a dead end, when he finally found a connection that gave him considerable pause.

Because it traced to City Hall.

The watchdogs had all rotated by now, with Deanna and Rio on assassin duty again, Siobhan and Nell patrolling and checking in with agents, and the others having swapped partners so Jay and Preston could be with Robert at City Hall utilizing their skills, while Bari and Luke checked on the Shelter.

As Bash and Ethan made their way to City Hall on foot, Bash spoke on the phone with Preston. "Just letting you know we're headed your—you did?" Whatever Preston had told him changed the mood of the conversation. "That's good news at least. And explains the media frenzy."

Ethan looked up as they rounded the street corner, and outside City Hall, one of the tallest buildings downtown, was a zoo of news and police vehicles. He and Bash hunkered near the corner of the building instead of crossing the street.

"Yes, I know that back entrance well," Bash continued. He tilted the phone from his mouth to inform Ethan, "Preston confirmed the discrepancies he'd been looking for, proving the books were doctored. With Jay handling the legal side, it looks like Robert is going to be cleared. His deputy mayor, the one who ratted him out, is about to make a statement. That gives us a window to get inside if you want to poke around."

"Perfect, because she's who I wanted to poke."

Ethan had to take point. Bash wasn't a known figure to non-shifters in this city. Siobhan and Nell had been dubbed bodyguards, Jay and Preston legal counsel, so with Ethan's cover being the truth of him as a private eye, Bash was merely along for the ride.

They took the long way around the building, down a narrow alley, to a back entrance with the appearance of tight security and a camera, just like at the DLI office. Ethan assumed a dormant camera was true here too, but that also made him tense and glance around, awaiting another assassin or unexpected attack, given the similarities.

Nothing happened, not even a blip from his Seer senses, before
the door opened and Preston and Jay ushered them inside. Ethan almost
would have preferred a madhouse in the building, if only to feel more like
they could blend in, but the chaos was being kept to outside. Thankfully,
though a few workers going about their day gave perusing glances at
him and the others, most ignored them after noticing Jay. He was a well-
respected defense attorney in Brookdale and had been helping Robert
since the break of the scandal.

Not all the offices were on the main floor, several departments
taking up entire floors themselves on other levels, but the mayor's office
and other major personnel were meant to be easily accessible to the
public—except when the public was pissed or nosy.

"Who's taking the fall?" Ethan asked.

"We figured his deputy," said Jay, "since she'd shown signs of being
enthralled, but the trail from the doctored books led to her assistant."

"Who is swearing up and down he didn't do it." Preston snorted.

"Maybe he didn't," said Ethan. "Or if he did, he was enthralled too."

"Didn't get close enough to check. But yeah, probably."

They rounded a hallway toward the main offices, where several
more people were gathered, who Robert was addressing. Not press,
members of his staff, Ethan figured, while his deputy was outside giving
her statement.

"Have you gotten a look at the assistant's computer?" Ethan asked.

"Cops got to it first, but luckily for you, they didn't take the deputy
mayor's." Preston gestured to a nearby office door. "Just make it quick."

"Stay on Robert," Bash ordered, which the others clearly planned
to do, since they helped block any view of someone noticing Ethan and
Bash breaking and entering.

Once they'd closed the door behind them, Bash stayed beside it,
while Ethan hurried to the desk of Deputy Mayor Xandra Clarke. He
wasn't familiar with her, but then he'd only lived in Centrus City for a
few weeks. He'd never heard anything negative about her, and Robert
had been shocked that she'd betrayed him, which she hadn't really, being
enthralled.

That didn't mean she or her assistant weren't behind more than either
had been caught at, but right now, Ethan was focused on something else.

"What are you looking for anyway?" Bash asked as he kept an ear
on the door.

Ethan was no hacker, but what they'd already tracked was enough for him to know what to look for. "The trail from Dave's account pointed at certain City Hall subcommittee funds, which only a handful of people have access to, including the deputy mayor. Her being enthralled made it even more likely to me that she had something to do with Dave. If it wasn't her, we'll at least know the name of someone else connected to Alexa. I just need to know who accessed the funds at the time of the wire transfer."

The records Ethan needed to sift through were more numerous than he anticipated, and every passing minute was one less they had to have the office to themselves. Ethan stayed focused, while Bash gave occasional updates from Preston or Jay texting him. Like Robert retreating to his office, staff dispersing, more cops milling about, which could spell trouble, and then—

"She's coming. Are you—?"

"Got it." Ethan took a picture of the evidence with his phone rather than risk any downloads or print-offs. He closed out the windows to cover his tracks and returned the computer to sleep. "It was Clarke. Since she was enthralled, we just need to dig into how she might have encountered Alexa—"

Ethan was halfway around the desk when the door opened, faster than he'd expected given the forewarning. Bash looked equally startled, not having heard the person coming, but was thankfully hidden behind the door when it opened inward.

Ethan could talk his way out of this. He was a PI. He hadn't been caught red-handed doing anything illegal, and nothing save the photos on his phone proved he'd hacked her files. He had a million ready excuses.

And every last one turned sour on his tongue when he saw who came in.

"Alexa."

"Actually"—Alexa shut the door and grinned at Bash as if having already known he was there—"these days I go by Xandra."

ALEXANDRA CLARKE.
Xandra.
Alexa.

She'd been working with Robert the entire time, and he didn't even know it.

Bash wanted to throttle her, especially when he knew he couldn't. Not in the middle of City Hall.

"But you... you showed signs of—"

"Being enthralled?" She cut Ethan off. She was just as Ethan had described her. Mature but also ageless, with long auburn hair, fierce blue eyes, a perfectly fit and attractive politician in a classy dress, burgundy today instead of black, with a simple pendant necklace. "I'm sure there was plenty of that residue around me, but then, when the rest is covered by magic to shield someone, it's an easy mistake to make."

She walked toward Ethan, and Bash flinched. She couldn't do anything either. Could she? Would she? That he honestly didn't know made him quick to unsheathe his claws.

"Down, puppy." She glanced back at him. "I just gave a brilliant statement to the press out there. I'm rather beloved in this city at the moment. Because, oh dear, my assistant turned me against the mayor with falsified documents." She mockingly put a hand over her heart. "I couldn't be more upset. While I can't say I approve of Mayor Hedin's extracurricular activities, the truth is always my top priority."

With her false demeanor dropping, she continued toward Ethan, who backed away with a wide berth to curve toward Bash.

"Don't be too hard on those who should have recognized me from your descriptions, Ethan, but then, how detailed were they? And would it matter? For as you well know yourself, good shielding is meant to make someone forgettable—and, at least in my case, only to those I'd want to forget me. Naturally I was careful to not be too near any of your people while also around Robert. That nullification of spells is a useful but occasionally annoying trick when you can't control it."

"Where's Leo?" Ethan demanded.

"Haven't a clue." She shrugged.

Bash could see that Ethan was seething, phone clutched too tightly in his hand. They needed it intact, but worse, him holding it like that brought her attention to it.

"Why?" Ethan asked with a choke on the word. "*Why* did you make me do that to Dave?"

"I already told you. Your stubbornness keeps interrupting my plans. And here you are again." She glanced at Bash, back at Ethan, and then—

"Ethan!" Bash cried after the blur had already started, but her vampire sprint wasn't to slice open either of their throats. When the blur focused again, she was holding Ethan's phone, crushing it into a useless hunk like a soda can.

"Oh!" she exclaimed in mock concern, letting the bits of metal and plastic fall from her palm. "That's a pity. I hope you didn't have anything important on there."

Ethan backpedaled more swiftly to join Bash, and Bash reached out to tug him against him. Bash had only guessed she'd try something. He hadn't sensed it; he couldn't sense anything from her. Their powers were useless unless they learned how to cut through her shielding.

"If Robert was impeached, you'd become mayor," Bash stated the obvious.

She shrugged like before, like this was all so very trite and inconvenient. "Running the human side of things is as important as the rest."

"And you just gave some great soundbites as a future candidate."

"Ah, but good press isn't quite enough or quick enough when it isn't an election year, is it?" She leaned back against her desk, clicking her nails casually on its surface. "I've been patient for a very long time. I'm done waiting. The age of vampires will come again."

A threat. Robert wasn't safe. She needed him out of the way, and the scandal hadn't been enough. But if they got Robert near her, her protections should fail.

No, only enough that they'd be able to smell what they already knew, and maybe, maybe sense an action before she did it, but a Null would mostly affect her influence, not enough of her speed or strength. At least here, on her turf, they couldn't do anything, not yet. The only question was whether *she* would.

They had to get Robert out.

"Thank you for the brief statement, Ms. Deputy Mayor," Bash said and took Ethan with him as he fled out the door.

"Bash—" Ethan floundered at their escape.

"Not now. We get Robert, and we get out of here."

Ethan hesitated but quickly acquiesced to take point again, keeping attentions off Bash.

Robert was with Jay and Preston in his office, leaning against his desk much in the same way as they'd left Alexa.

"Get us back to the den. Now," Bash ordered before anything could be said. "And hope you aren't stopped by any counter spells."

"Counter… what?" Preston spun to face them.

"*Now*." Bash took out his phone and dialed Siobhan while Preston prepared the portal. "Siobhan, we need your agents at City Hall on the deputy mayor full-time from now on."

They stole away through the portal without incident, and most of what had happened was overheard by the others as Bash explained the rest to Siobhan as well. He reiterated for everyone at the den regardless.

They'd met the enemy, and she'd been closer than they realized the entire time.

Chapter 12

BASH HAD opened the floor for ideas since he was focused on Ethan, who kept staring at nothing, lost in his head. His chest heaved as he gulped down breaths he didn't need. Only maybe he did, if only to keep himself calm.

Once again, he'd faced Alexa with nothing to show for it.

Preston wasn't confident in retrieving anything from the cloud to make up for what had been lost on Ethan's phone. Usually he went out of his way to ensure none of the content from their devices made it to the cloud, but he'd still try. All that would do anyway was prove Alexa paid off Dave, but not for what, not why, not anything that could help them. Even if it did, jail time wasn't what they wanted. They'd hoped to learn who and where she was. Now they knew.

Or had known.

"Your agents *lost* her?" Preston exclaimed.

"Forgive them for not keeping up with ancient vampire speed," Siobhan groused back. "After she left City Hall, she rounded a corner and was gone. Though possibly worse is that they've encountered a few more assassins during patrol. No one's gotten in, just been politely asked to fuck off, but they're still being sent by neighboring cities."

"And our captive assassin?" Bash asked.

"Quiet but definitely scheming," said Deanna. "Metro City still denying they sent her?"

"Every time I ask. And now we know the viper we're facing is in our midst."

Silence fell. Opening the floor hadn't brought up anything but bad news and fidgeting.

They were a gathering of the same weary bodies that had been working hard all week. Only Bash and Robert were standing, several others having plopped down right on the floor like Siobhan usually did, including Ethan, near to Bash's legs but slumped, while Robert paced back and forth behind the sofa.

"Can't you just fire her?" Rio asked over the back of the couch.

"I can't fire Xandra. Alexa. Whatever!" Robert threw up his hands. "She publicly apologized. And she's amazing at her job. Plus, my approval ratings are terrible right now. I get any more flack or have something else blow up in my face, you can bet she's running against me next election, and she'll still get what she wants."

"Then what do we do?" Luke scoffed. "Ignore her?"

"She can't kill me in broad daylight."

"Only she already did with Mr. Golding," Nell reminded them. "We need to find out what she's after."

"We know what she's after," said Deanna. "Control of the city, both human and shifter ends of it, and getting a return to fangers on top."

"How, though?" Jay questioned. "How can she possibly accomplish that as things are now? The human side, fine. But even with magic, even with all her tricks and supposed plans, to take down all of us before we mount a counterattack, she'd need an army."

"No," Ethan said like an exhale, perking up and scrambling to his feet. "A family. Bash." He met Bash's stare with a spark of fresh resolve. "I need to see my dad."

BASH WASN'T letting Ethan go anywhere alone, not again, so he shadowed him all the way to the cellar door and asked Ethan not to cross the threshold.

Gordon was awake and waiting like usual, sitting on the bed, deep in thought. He smiled when he saw Ethan. "I was starting to worry. Not that Robert's company isn't entertaining."

"What do you know about Alexa?" Ethan demanded without preamble.

"Alexa?"

Ethan's arms shook from the clench of his fists. "My cellmate, Dave, told me she knew you, but because she 'introduced' you to Leo. I thought that meant how she made Leo frenzy and turn you, but then I started wondering if it meant more."

Gordon's expression didn't even flicker. "I never met Leo before he attacked me."

"That sounds like some very cleverly worded evasion, Mr. Lambert," Bash said.

His eyes flashed toward Bash like the pierce of a needle.

"Do you know what she made me do?" Ethan asked, betraying a waver in his voice. "Did Robert tell you?"

"Tell me what?"

"*Dave*. He was a good man. Maybe one of my first real friends. He told me Alexa paid him to keep an eye on me in prison, but that doesn't matter, because he was still my friend, for me, not because of money or magic.

"She helped him get out early, knowing he'd come to see me so she could use him as a warning. She had Leo attack me, start to drain me. She helped him too, until I couldn't stand any more. Until I couldn't fight them, but I knew what was coming. She'd frozen Dave with her thrall, and I knew, she made sure I knew, that once I frenzied, I'd…."

Bash didn't speak up to add anything, merely let Ethan trail off and compose himself, though he didn't need to finish the story for recognition to dawn on Gordon.

"I finally know what it must have been like for you, Dad. Waking up from that with a mouthful of Mom's blood and holding her lifeless body. Alexa warned she'd make me do the same thing to Bash if I didn't stop trying to fight her. And even though I am terrified of that happening, I am still going to fight."

Ethan's fists stopped shaking in one cold beat, his head lifting higher, like he'd seen the whole scene playing out while he described it. He matched his father's gaze, which finally showed a hint of sorrow and torn allegiance.

"What do you know about Alexa?" Ethan asked again.

Gordon's eyes dropped to the floor. "She's come to me before."

"So, you knew. You knew her name, who she was. You *knew* who we were dealing with, and you didn't say anything?"

"The world she can create for us will be a utopia." Gordon looked up again with a mix of pleading and fanaticism. "It was all for you—"

Ethan spun around to leave.

"Ethan!"

"You just keep lying!" he spat back over his shoulder. "Now I can't even trust you about our enemy? Then I guess I can't trust you at all." He continued up the stairs, leaving Bash to shut the cellar door, which he did with a challenging glare on Gordon the entire time.

He caught up to Ethan nearly at the top, where Robert sat on the steps and leaped to his feet.

"I was totally not listening. But uh, if it helps, Rookie, whatever he's done or lied about, he really does think he's doing right by you."

"It doesn't help," Ethan choked out and pushed past Robert the rest of the way up.

"Hold on, darling." Bari intercepted Ethan from wherever he'd meant to go. Everyone was around in various huddled clumps, either in the kitchen or living room, making the whole place feel suffocating once Bash joined too, but at Bari's soft tone, Ethan halted. "Preston and I thought of a marvelous addition to my hearth spell idea. We figure Nell is best to apply the runes, though, given her aptitude. Hold still a moment."

Nell had been holding Preston and Luke's wrists. Now she came over to Ethan and Bash to cast the same spell, grasping the right wrists of each of them. The runes she cast glowed opposingly red and green, and then green and red, before they dimmed. "Three taps on your inner wrist will port you to join your partner."

"So don't go banging them repeatedly on any hard surfaces unnecessarily." Bari winked.

The poke at humor made Ethan snort with a catch of his true emotions still on the surface.

"To counteract the threat of any humans witnessing someone appearing out of nowhere—" Preston came over with Luke in tow. "—once you've arrived at your partner's location, you'll be camouflaged to be invisible until you take your first step. That way you can assess your surroundings before making yourself known."

"That is a really great idea, from all of you." Ethan tried to smile.

"What's, um, up with your dad?" Luke asked. Bash would have shot a warning look at him, but they couldn't keep holing Gordon away, pretending he wasn't a danger.

"I thought he was another pawn like me," Ethan said, "with his own ideas that just happened to fall in line with Alexa's plans. But now, he might be working with her directly. We can't trust him."

"I'm sorry, Ethan," Jay offered.

Ethan nodded his thanks.

"However," Jay went on with a look of dawning realization, "we do know at least one other person with a connection to Alexa who maybe we can trust."

REGINALD EDITH Lancaster at your service," Reggie spoke with his English accent, tipping his sunglasses down to reveal a flash of yellow eyes—which was impressive considering his wrists were bound together with shackles etched over their entirety in runic wards.

Ethan hadn't seen Reggie since before they knew the Shaman of Brookdale was secretly a vampire instead of the werewolf he'd pretended to be. Ethan had been excited when he'd first learned the truth, since he'd known something about Reggie felt familiar, even with an advanced spell on him to mask his vampire nature with shifter scent.

Now Ethan knew it wasn't only because Reggie was a vampire, but because he had a vague sense of having met Reggie when he was younger—in Leo's house.

He bore a striking resemblance to a young Jeff Bridges, specifically "The Dude," with long brown hair and beard, wearing striped gaucho pants that might have been Zubaz, a V-neck undershirt betraying a sprinkle of chest hair, and a thick-knit cardigan sweater.

The shackles were built to both contain any magic he might try to use and to weaken his vampire strength. He couldn't take any bites out of anyone unless they let him. It would be nearly impossible to get something like that on other vampires unless they, too, offered their wrists willingly. If only Glenwood had something like that for Leo, he might not have escaped.

With Jay and Bari in Centrus, and Reggie already out of commission before he'd arrived, the Brookdale circle was down to three—Second Maximus, Warden Anjali, and Counselor Desmond. Jay didn't want any of them leaving their city when there were so few of them, so they'd video called in with Brookdale, giving Preston a clear view to portal over and retrieve Reggie himself.

"I, for one, missed you terribly." Bari swept forward to kiss both of Reggie's cheeks. "And to see you in chains! It's awful, darling, even if I know it's only a precaution."

"Nonsense! I adore chains, though usually under better circumstances."

"Robert Hedin." Robert pushed his way through to shake Reggie's hand, awkward as it was with them connected at the wrists. "Human mayor and very willing blood donor."

"Robert," Bash groaned, but Ethan had to chuckle.

The world might not be ready for all these men in one room.

"You must be the resident Null," Reggie said, "hot and cold at once and impossible to define. Like his and hers lube working in tandem."

"Oho, a man with good taste," Robert said. "Or a taste for something good? 'Cause if you ever need a nip there, Reg, I am well initiated at being *sucked*."

"Okay—" Bash tried again.

"Having experienced that myself," Bari joined in with hearty comradery, "I completely understand. I even like to watch." He glanced at Jay, who he'd once seen fed on by Reggie, and Bari had been fed on by Ethan.

Jay didn't seem pleased at the reminder.

"I'll stop." Bari crossed the expanse separating them and attached himself to Jay in apology. "Sorry, dear."

"Guess we all know who my partner is for this buddy system." Reggie offered his elbow to Robert. "Unless you're spoken for, love?"

"Oh, I am always open."

"I do hope there's a back door." Reggie quickly turned to Bash. "Into the den, of course. I hear you need help with some creative warding?"

"Among other things," Bash said, "and yes, you will be sticking with Robert. But Robert, do not directly touch the shackles, understood? They'll hold so long as you don't."

"Not the shackles." Robert blatantly eyed Reggie from head to toe. "I can do that."

"While I trust them to do their job, if they fail, as a Null, you're the only one immune to his charms." Bash grimaced as soon as he said it.

"I certainly hope not," Reggie cooed.

With most having had their fill of innuendo, the gathering of forces started to disperse, leaving Bash and Ethan alone with Reggie and Robert. They all had tasks to perform—more patrols and check-ins and planning to be done, both magically and tactically.

The four sat on the sofa, with Ethan and Reggie in the center. The flood of sexual tension had washed a little of Ethan's anger and grief away, but now all he could think about again was how his father knew more than he'd admitted and was still keeping secrets.

"I heard you've been briefed on what's happened," he said to Reggie. "Now that my dad confirmed he's met with Alexa before, I know I need to push him. Find out what he knows. Leo's out there somewhere. Alexa's in the wind. She'll show back up to work tomorrow, I'm sure, but she's otherwise a ghost. I thought finding her would make everything clearer somehow. Instead, we have a fuller house and fewer answers. We know it was a risk to bring you here when you're one of her fledglings, but we were hoping you might have some insight."

Irreverent as both Reggie and Robert could be, both knew when to be serious, and Robert held back, merely listening as Reggie addressed Ethan. "I wish I had better news for you, love, but I'm afraid I still have no memories of Alexa. A few have come back to me about Leo. I even think I remember meeting you once when you were a boy."

"Me too."

"But as for my sire, it's a blank space. I didn't even know to be concerned that I couldn't remember who made me. I simply never thought about it. Definitely her will at work. I remember Leo was always better at resisting. I can picture him arguing, fighting with... well, that blank space. Must be why he started to remember things about Alexa when prompted, and I still can't.

"What I can help with, however, is my knowledge of magic and magical artifacts. There are several lost items and techniques that explain how she might have superseded the wards at your office. To prevent the same from happening here, I know a few layering tricks that literally nothing other than a Null crossing them could counter." He grinned and leaned into Robert on his other side. "Just be sure to stay behind me, love."

"No problem there." Robert leered. "Though I do have a question myself, Rookie. You have some rune thingy on you and your pops to prevent him from controlling you, right?"

"That's right."

"Can't you use something similar to prevent Alexa from controlling Reg?"

"Only if she ever so sweetly held still while someone placed it on her," Reggie explained. "But fair question."

"I keep waiting for her to walk into the den," Ethan admitted. "Just appear with Leo beside her and...."

"She won't do that," Reggie returned to a softer tone. "I may not remember her, but I don't care how strong or ancient she might be, or what magics she has at her disposal, she won't put herself at risk by barging into your territory. Too many unknown variables. She'll bide her time and wait for you to do exactly as she needs without her ever having to cross your threshold.

"Not to be a downer or anything!" He swiftly brightened. "And I absolutely still recommend adding layered wards. Of course, I may have to teach your Preston and Nell how to do so, considering…." He lifted his bound wrists.

"Given your nullifying partner and time being of the essence…." Bash reached around Ethan to tap a specific rune on Reggie's shackles intended to only respond to him or Jay. The shackles opened and dropped into Reggie's lap with a multicolored fizzle. "Only while you're placing new wards. Then they're going back on."

"You also realize that darling Robert here will have to stand several paces away from me while I cast anything." Reggie sounded both skeptical and grateful of this show of faith.

"Then do so quickly and don't lose sight of each other."

With a gleeful squirm, Reggie rolled to his feet, leaving the shackles behind, and hefted Robert up as well, dragging him toward the front entryway and main staircase. "Top to bottom, love?"

"Always." Robert eagerly followed.

"The assassin is in the last room on the right!" Bash called after them, and Reggie waved a hand over his head to indicate he'd heard. "I'm not sure which I'm going to regret more, offering him leeway or those two being introduced."

A stray string of tinsel chose that moment to fall from the lighting fixture above and landed on Bash's head. Ethan laughed, even more heartily than from the excessive flirting. He plucked away the glittering decoration and kissed the scowl from Bash's lips.

"I know this is difficult for you because of your father's involvement," Bash said when they parted. "You don't have to talk to him again tonight if you don't want to. We're doing enough."

"He'd probably just lie to me again anyway."

"Maybe. Maybe not. If there wasn't a way for us to win this, we wouldn't have prophesied that we can."

Ethan often forgot to think of it that way. There *was* an answer; they just needed to find it.

The whirlwind of everyone working on various next steps eventually returned them to the living room and kitchen. The non-vampires needed to eat, and several of the others began working on a meal so they could take a break.

Robert and Reggie weren't among them.

"Anyone see where those two ended up?" Ethan asked once he realized.

"I think they went to find that back door," Nell said. "My back door!" She flushed at the continued poor wording. "The separate cellar door that leads into my workshop," she tried one last time.

There was both a way into Nell's area of the basement from inside the den, separate from the cellar holding Gordon, and an entrance from the exterior of the building. Bash seemed to have the same thinking as Ethan, and after grabbing the shackles, they headed for the workshop.

It made up the larger portion of the basement, and once down its interior stairs, was seen as an almost-replica to a new-age magic shop that Nell ran in town. A mix of technology, runes, and potions like an ancient apothecary all wove seamlessly together, both in Nell's efforts as Shaman to protect the pack from exposure and to provide healing.

There was no sign of Robert or Reggie.

A gasp sounded from across the room, and Bash tucked Ethan behind him with a sweep of his arm. Ethan grabbed Bash and swept him back instead. He was the vampire, after all.

Bash didn't argue, and Ethan led the way through the dimly lit workshop. Faint noises like pain or struggling could be heard up ahead. Ethan picked up the pace, keeping Bash's hand clasped in his to drag him along. The exterior door was near, up a longer set of steps and leading to a door that not only had runic protection but a modern keypad.

The noises grew louder the closer they got to the steps, and Ethan let his fangs grow, feeling fur sprout into being on Bash's arm as they crested the corner and started to bound upward—

"Geez, don't you make noise?"

Robert pulled from Reggie's embrace, revealing a shimmer of red on Reggie's lips from how he'd been slowly and seemingly sensually feeding from him, given that the glassy look in Robert's eyes was clearly from more than blood loss.

Ethan groaned and let his vampire aspects dwindle. Robert and Reggie were up near the landing. The outside door was still closed and glowing with what must have been renewed wards.

"If you're finished—" Bash began.

Robert snorted.

"With the *warding*—these are going back on." He stormed up the steps to get between them and placed the shackles on Reggie, touching that same specific rune to lock them in place.

"Kinky," Robert said.

Ethan was definitely ready to call it a day and had a feeling everyone else was too.

Chapter 13

JAY WAS glad he'd been of help with Robert's case and that, as a team, they'd gotten him cleared of all charges, but even with Reggie added to the cause, he couldn't shake that their efforts might not be enough, not when the enemy was closer than they'd ever anticipated.

"Don't you start looking like you get hunches now." Bari plopped down beside him in bed, both down to their underwear and exhausted after another long day.

"Well, I do sometimes feel left out." Jay smiled at him.

"Trust me, inclusion in this case isn't better." Bari kissed him, pulling him close and out of his own head. He was good at that, even though Jay knew Bari could get lost in his thoughts too.

When last Jay was in Centrus City, he'd stayed at a hotel. He had to admit, staying in Bari's room was better. Technically, it was just another guest room at the den, but it was Bari's, often saved for last to be given away to boarders, Jay had noticed, since it had been Bari's room growing up. At least that was the impression he'd gotten without fully asking.

The Freddie Mercury poster on the closet door may have had something to do with his guess, aged and a little worn at its edges like it had been there for twenty years.

There were enough rooms for Reggie to have his own, since they'd elected to have him stay in case he remembered anything about Alexa. His room would, of course, be locked and warded while he was unaccompanied, but if Jay's guess was correct about the nature of Robert's whispering to Preston, Reggie wouldn't be alone for long.

Jay was happy for him, even if it would only be a friendly romp. He knew it had been a long while since Reggie had felt like he could be intimate with someone. Before Bari, it had been a long time since Jay had wanted to be with someone either—not including Bashir—and the first time he'd had a partner he knew he never wanted to leave.

"I hope you're not too depleted after another lengthy day of diligent work," Bari whispered, reaching between Jay's legs with a promising squeeze.

Their closeness wafted over the pleasant scent of jasmine that solidified what Jay had long since confirmed. This was his mate. This was his always. "I'm never too depleted for you, Bari." Jay kissed him back, rougher now, and rolled them to pin Bari to the bed, growling between their mouths.

Bari squirmed and rumbled back with the tinge of a whimper. He flailed to adjust his position beneath Jay's weight—and the sound of something falling to the floor was heard. "Oops," Bari said when Jay lifted off him at the noise.

He'd rolled them a little too close to the edge of the bed, and it seemed Bari had knocked something from the end table.

"Sorry, darling. You make such an animal out of me." Bari smirked and reached over the side of the bed to retrieve what had fallen.

A small wrapped box.

"I'll take that!" Jay seized it and scrambled over Bari to shove it into the drawer.

"Keeping secrets from me?" Bari teased as they adjusted so that Jay was on the side closer to the end table.

"Christmas presents are supposed to be secret, aren't they?"

"It's for me?"

"That would be telling part of the secret."

Bari laughed, but despite the complete failure of Jay trying to cover, he didn't ask for more. "I can't wait till Christmas." He pulled Jay closer again, kissed him, and yielded beneath him when Jay retook control.

This was why Jay was never going to let him go, because no one else had ever felt so right.

IT WAS probably jewelry. Oh, Bari hoped it was jewelry. Jay did have a keen eye, and since most of what Bari had gotten Jay for Christmas was fresh articles to jazz up his wardrobe, it would mean having something to wear together on their next date night.

Bari desperately wanted to shake the box. But no, he would behave, no matter how insanely curious he was.

He didn't want to *behave* at the moment, though. Jay was showing his Alpha side, the take-charge, fully in control, had Bari at his mercy side. While they swapped roles on occasion, which Bari also loved, he'd never had a lover dominate him so completely, and he relished every moment he was under Jay's command.

A nip at his throat made Bari moan and release some of his own inner wolf, silver fur sprouting, fangs lengthening, and eyes aglow as they sharpened in the dark. He'd keep his aspects just a little bit less than however much Jay unleashed, a small sign of his submission and utter surrender to Jay's claim on him.

His underwear was shoved down as Jay bodily lifted him and flung him closer to the center of the bed. How he'd managed to do both was an even greater turn-on—his speed, his strength, his clawed hand palming Bari's prick and stroking firmly while he caged him with his hovering body.

Bari played into it, giving little pleas of desperation for his Alpha to go easy on him, when he absolutely wanted Jay to go hard. Parts of him were definitely hard already, Jay's own underwear shoved down for his already moistened slit to prod Bari's hip with rolling thrusts. He took his time stroking Bari. Then he slowed his rocking too, clearly intent on drawn-out rutting that wouldn't bring either of them to the edge too quickly.

Jay growled and bit into Bari's throat to mark him. Then he nuzzled there, licked the marks, and sucked his skin.

"*Ahhh….*" Bari thrust up into Jay's grip, enjoying the occasional graze of claw tips that sent little tingles through his body. He wrapped his arms around Jay's back and felt that his fur had sprouted too, a beautiful brown that must have painted them as the most stunning contrasts when writhing together.

Maybe he'd invest in a mirror for their bedroom ceiling back home.

Home—because Brookdale was home now, city and den and his shared room with Jay. That was home, and though Bari knew he would always have a home here too, the one with Jay was where he wanted to build the next chapter of his life.

"Ah!"

The first collision of Jay's cock with Bari's ratcheted up the heat between them, Jay's hand twining around them both to let their fluids mingle and build upon each other. Jay lifted his head from Bari's neck.

He was between Stages Two and Three like usual in the bedroom, almost to the point where his face broadened into a snout, and fur covered his ears, including the crooked one that Bari most adored.

He showed his worship of it by running his fingers along its tufted tip.

"I love you, Bari," Jay said in a sensuous rumble.

Bari was never going to tire of hearing that. "I love you too."

Jay kissed him with a swoop downward that made Bari yelp and then giggle a little too. He squirmed as Jay stroked, and the friction and wetness between them built and built, starting to crescendo—until Jay promptly slowed and removed his hand to rock Bari's hips back instead.

Oh yes. There was no need to rush toward a messy end when they could get even messier other ways. Bari arched his neck and spread his thighs apart, presenting himself to his Alpha. His love.

His mate.

He was keyed up and left on edge where he might have burst, but he calmed himself to wait, just wait, as Jay aligned himself to push his thick, pulsing cock inside him.

Oh yes. No need to rush at all.

THE SOUNDS coming from the next room were growing increasingly more vocal, with Bari's unmistakable voice crying out in pleasured moans and rumbling whimpers.

Luke was getting a little hot under the collar listening—if he'd still been wearing a collar. He was down to boxers and having a really hard time not shoving a hand beneath his waistband.

"*Why* is our room next to theirs?" Preston groused as he exited the bathroom.

"You don't think it's kinda hot?" Luke asked, admiring how hot his mate currently was too, with long dark hair loosed from its bun, wearing boxers as well and a too-big borrowed T-shirt of Luke's.

Preston glared as he removed his glasses to set on his desk for the night.

"I'm not saying I'd want to see them! Well…."

Preston smacked his ankle from the foot of the bed, but he couldn't hide the twitch of a smirk. His smack undid some of the tinsel from around the footboard, and he paused to resituate it, squinting a little to get it right, since he'd already removed his glasses.

As usual, their room was an explosion of decorations even more pronounced than the rest of the den. At other times throughout the year, the room had a few favored pieces up from all sorts of holidays, but when it was the actual holiday of any kind, that one took over, and Christmas was the most flamboyant.

Luke didn't think he could see the paint on any of the walls, it was all so covered in snowflakes and Santas and colored bulbs. It was a good thing he wasn't the insomniac type, because strings of lights around the windows and hung in loops from the ceiling were on at almost all hours. He actually found it cozy, which he knew was true for Preston too, who'd grown up with such strict parents, he'd never gotten to experience the fun side of holidays.

Even some of Preston's prized action figures and other geeky memorabilia had added Christmas elements to them—including a manger scene made of the nests for Basil and Dr. Dawson and the new mouse addition of Gus-Gus. In place of an actual Joseph, Mary, or baby Jesus, Luke would swear the rats had tucked Gus-Gus in, wrapped around him on the bedding shavings made to look like hay.

When Preston finished with the tinsel, he turned around to pet the rats and mouse good night.

"Ohhh, Jay!"

Fuck, Luke was horny, having to hear that.

"Urg." Preston went to his side of the bed, looking like he might knock on the wall. Then his eyes squinted again, narrowing between Luke's legs. "Are you hard?"

"What's the best answer to that question?"

He huffed and crossed his arms, averting his gaze with the faintest color in his cheeks.

Luke groaned to draw Preston's eyes back to him, stretching in a manner that, oops, caused his boxers to shimmy down, and he maybe helped with a pry of his thumb beneath the waistband to pop it over the head of his cock. It sprung free, glistening with precome.

Preston's eyes slid to it and then darted away again.

"You're blushing."

"Because of the surround sound next door."

"Uh-huh. And maybe coz it's making you hard too, but you don't wanna admit it." Luke could see the evidence of that, the slowly growing bulge between Preston's legs. "Kinda makes me think of our first sexy time in this room. Remember?"

Preston's eyes slid back to him, and Luke ran a hand down his thigh purposely more and more center, causing his cock to bob in answer. "I know what you're doing," Preston said, maybe inadvertently saying the exact words he'd used those ten years ago when he first saw Luke naked.

Luke responded the same way too, stretching his thumb outward from his thigh to graze the length of his cock. "And what am I doing?"

"Ah! Ahhhhh!"

Preston stifled a laugh after the eruption next door and admitted defeat, because he dropped down onto the bed and yanked Luke's boxers the rest of the way off.

Luke spread his thighs to let Preston settle between them. "I'll never forget how much it meant to me to find you," he added a bit of sentiment to his seduction, which made Preston blush darker all these years later, "even if I can be an idiot sometimes."

Preston leaned forward to kiss Luke. "Good."

LUKE LAUGHED. "Thanks, *Han*. That's practically an 'I know' to an 'I love you' confession."

"I stand by my answer," Preston said but then amended, "and I won't forget either."

"Even when *you're* an idiot sometimes?"

"I didn't admit to that part."

"Jerk!" Luke laughed again.

"Oh really?" Leaning forward once more, Preston got in snug between Luke's legs and let more of his weight sink down, squishing Luke's full-mast cock between them. Preston's got squished a little too, but he wasn't the bare one, and he positioned himself low enough that the tip of his cock bucked up against the base of Luke's. He dragged himself higher slowly so that the fabric of his boxers and the hardness of both their cocks on either side of it swelled from the friction.

"*Fuck*." Luke panted. "Jerk… definitely a jerk."

Preston huffed and nipped at Luke's jawline, letting his rat teeth extend.

Luke purred, writhing up against him and making Preston's breath start to hitch, just enough that he was taken by surprise when Luke grabbed him around the waist and flipped them. He pinned Preston's arms back and thrusted his hips down like a rutting beast.

"*Ohhhh!*" It was seriously hot and made Preston's moan escape him louder than intended.

Served their neighbors right.

Not to be outdone, especially when their sizes and strengths were equally matched, Preston suctioned his mouth to the line of Luke's throat until his grip loosened. Then he twisted his hands free, grabbed Luke's wrists instead, and flipped them right back the other way. He let one wrist go to shove his own boxers down and rutted into Luke with the same abandon.

"Fuck… fuck!"

Bari and Jay probably heard that too, but Preston didn't let up, pinning Luke's other wrist again, though he hardly tried to fight him anymore. Their dicks clashed together until the wetness between them was as good as any lube.

Lube. Yes, he definitely wanted more than clumsy grinding and started to slow them.

"*Pres*," Luke whined.

"Patience. I don't think you're going to be complaining for long."

Sitting up on Luke's hips, Preston kicked away the tangled remains of his boxers and lifted the T-shirt over his head to toss it aside. He shifted higher, so Luke knew exactly where he planned to sit next. He paused to summon a tiny portal beside him. Its partner opened inside their end table drawer, and he reached through it to pluck out the bottle they needed.

Luke marveled up at him, not only for the display of magic, he knew, but with the devotion only a true mate could convey with a look. Slitted cat eyes and whiskers were in Luke's expression, and even the faint hint of his tabby stripes that Preston would never tire of. Not five years from now when they'd raised their daughter to adulthood. Not ten or twenty or a hundred more.

This was the only home he wanted.

"I won't forget," Preston said, pressing the bottle into one of Luke's palms, "even when *I'm* an idiot sometimes."

Luke beamed adoringly. "I love you, Magic Man."

"Good," Preston said again, and again, Luke laughed. "I love you too."

Luke retracted his claws and slicked his fingers with the lube. He slicked his cock too, and then coaxed Preston to sit so he could fill him.

Preston hoped the ensuing minutes had them both panting and moaning so loud that Bari and Jay knew to be more courteous next time.

ONCE ETHAN and Bash had finally retired, the last thing Ethan wanted to think about was, well, anything other than the soothing touch of Bash's embrace, their legs coiled and hips met and moving.

Their coupling was slow and quiet, without the usual indulgent teasing. Ethan was ready and wet when Bash slid in, not needing to be stretched with more than a few pumps of Bash's tip to ease the way. Ethan liked indulgent teasing, pushing each other's boundaries, driving each other to the brink and beyond. This was nice too, just clinging and thrusting and letting the crescendo draw out in the silence, broken only by their gasps and occasional moans.

Like Robert and Reggie in the stairwell.

Although he also thought he might have heard some distant voices from other rooms.

Ethan's eyes would meet Bash's, sometimes green against brown, sometimes yellow against glowing bronze, but with a look in Bash's gaze like he might, maybe, this time, say the words. He didn't. Ethan didn't say them again either, but he felt that they were shared between them in what wasn't said aloud and knew he could wait to hear those words spoken.

As soon as the light woke them the next morning, they started in again, a few minutes before their alarm. Ethan would have welcomed a repeat of the night before, with writhing, slow kisses, and barely a tuft of fur or fangs sprouted between them. They almost made it too, with Ethan's hand on Bash's cock to guide him in....

When the phone rang.

The *house* phone, the landline that, to Ethan's knowledge, only had a receiver here in Bash's bedroom and down in his office.

Bash reluctantly answered. "Bash Bain." His eyes widened at the voice, which Ethan could hear but wasn't sure he believed who it belonged to until Bash handed him the phone.

"Hello?"

"Ethan, my boy."

"Leo?"

Chapter 14

ETHAN SAT up on the edge of the bed, gathering the covers into his lap, though his arousal had swiftly dwindled.

"Where are you? Are you with Alexa? Are you okay?"

"I don't know," Leo answered and could have meant it for any of those questions.

Bash sat up behind Ethan, close at his back, listening.

"Did I hurt anyone when I left Glenwood?" Leo asked shakily. That had been days ago, but he asked it like he'd only just surfaced from a long, terrifying nightmare.

"No, you didn't hurt anyone in Glenwood," Ethan assured him.

"Elsewhere?"

"You don't remember?"

"I... I'm in Centrus, but I'm not certain how I got here. I don't remember seeing Alexa, but... I don't know."

Ethan didn't want to put the burden of what happened on Leo, how he'd helped Alexa force Ethan to kill a friend, but he also didn't want to lie. "I'm so sorry to tell you this, Uncle Leo, but I think she got you to break free from Glenwood. She had you come here. She made you do something terrible."

He explained but kept as light on the details as he could. He didn't blame Leo, he wouldn't, but he heard the hitch and frustration in Leo's breaths as he listened.

"I'm so sorry, Ethan," Leo said once all was told. "She'd made sure I'd forgotten her, kept in my periphery all those years, controlling me when she needed me and leaving me in ignorance when she didn't. Once I remembered her, I started remembering more, other times she'd enthralled me as my sire. It is a powerful connection, a maker and their fledgling. Only the power of a Focus could hope to break it, like how I can't control your father.

"However...."

Ethan felt Bash's hand on his shoulder squeeze in expectation.

"Power channeled through multiple generations could change that."

"What do you mean?"

"Because of your unique and growing power as a Focus and Seer, your father eventually failed at controlling you, but if Alexa controls me, with her added power, I might have the strength to control Gordon, and then he—"

"Would have the strength to control me."

"You wouldn't be able to overcome it this time, not even with Bashir or his brother near you, or your other Focus friend, not with four generations of a vampire bloodline supporting her will. She'd be able to use your boosted abilities to control the entire city, and eventually more, just like she wants."

"Then why didn't she try that the first time," Ethan asked, "when Dad was mounting his takeover?"

"Robert," Bash said, loud enough for Leo to hear.

"Yes," Leo agreed. "She may have allowed Gordon's attempt just to see if it could work, but she couldn't risk playing her true hand knowing the mayor might nullify everything."

"And she couldn't kill Robert then," Ethan deduced, "not until she knew she had a foothold for mayor. Leo…." He clutched the phone tighter. "I wish I could tell you to come here, but I can't risk that it wouldn't be a trap she's set in motion."

"I'd never ask that," Leo said. "It's best that I stay away. I just needed to hear your voice, to know you were all right."

"I am. But you stay safe too."

"I was on a street corner when I came to, but I've gone to where your father used to stay."

"Our old house?"

"No, that belongs to someone else. It's an apartment. I was helping him with rent all these years, so I knew where it was and that it'd be empty. It's dusty but still in his name. I didn't want to stop the payments, hoping he might come back to it someday."

Ethan had hoped for so much too, that his father would shed his haunted ambitions and twisted thinking. "Thank you."

"I'll call again if I learn anything. If I… if anything happens that I can call about. I tried your cellphone, but—"

"It's trashed. This works fine."

"I am so sorry for what she made me do to you. That I could harm you... I can't believe it, I don't want to believe it, but she's made me do so much else. I'm glad I don't remember. I love you, Ethan."

"I love you too, Uncle Leo."

Ethan let the receiver drop, clutching it tightly before he hung up.

"You realize the timing of Leo calling now could be a trap in itself," Bash said, "to give us false information, false hope—"

"I know. But if he's right, we need to keep Robert safe and take Alexa down before she finds Leo again."

The alarm went off, and Bash rolled away to silence it.

Ethan shifted on the bed to face him. "After the fallout from the scandal, I think Robert will be taking a mental health day from City Hall."

"Agreed."

ONCE THE conversation with Leo had been relayed to the others, Preston and Luke mentioned Leo having said something similar in Glenwood, that Alexa might be able to control Gordon through him, and Reggie corroborated that it was possible, making it even more likely to be Alexa's endgame.

Bash couldn't say he liked what Siobhan's agents had to report about Alexa's whereabouts. She'd resurfaced as expected, arriving back at City Hall for her usual workday as deputy mayor, though they'd never actually seen her arrive at or leave her supposed place of residence before she popped back up on their radar.

The address they had for Alexandra Clarke might not be the only place she was staying, but knowing she wasn't there now still gave them somewhere to investigate.

"That building has some serious security," Siobhan said, "and records indicate that *Ms.* Clarke has her place wired to the nth degree with a state-of-the-art alarm system."

"Human means," Ethan muttered.

"Even more reason to see inside," Bash said. "Preston—"

Only just then Preston and Luke got a call about unrest happening at the Shelter.

Then Siobhan and Nell got several new border reports about other potential assassins.

And Deanna got an alert about the tattoo parlor having a break-in, and the shifter who'd opened wasn't sure if it was related to the recent insanity or just some foolish thieves not knowing whose business they'd broken into.

In a heartbeat, the inhabitants of the den were halved, and Bash and Ethan had no one to accompany them to Alexa's.

"We could—" Bari began, but Bash held up a hand to squash that idea.

"I need you and Jay to stay here and keep watch over the den. Robert can't be left alone with a caged assassin, Gordon, and our... wild card." He indicated Reggie, among the last of them still at the den, currently gathered in the living room.

"This is too coincidental." Ethan shook his head. "All this happening at the same time?"

"You think Alexa had a hand in it?" Jay posed. "An attempt to clear out the den?"

Robert immediately looked spooked and didn't shy from clinging closer to Reggie. "Maybe you boys don't run off and leave me vulnerable, huh? You can wait for the others to get back."

"If we do that," Bash countered, "we might miss our window to get inside that apartment and figure out what sort of power Alexa's wielding."

"But how are we supposed to disable a security system we know next to nothing about?" Ethan asked.

"Well...." Reggie raised his shackled wrists like a student volunteering an answer in class. "Given the expertise of this particular wild card, you could bring me. It just so happens that I know another layered rune trick that can help. Magical EMP. Set me loose for a few brief moments like before, boyos, and bam, I can get you in."

Bash did not like that one bit, even if Alexa's plan of vampire succession didn't require Reggie to work. But until they knew what they were dealing with, they had to act on what they could.

Thankfully, Reggie's penchant for wearing cardigans and kimono-like cover-ups made it easy to hide his shackled wrists from the casual passerby. It was a nice building, with a doorman in the lobby who didn't let strangers simply use the elevator to pay unannounced visits.

Ethan made quick work of him.

"We live here."

"Happy to see you again, sirs. Go right up," the doorman responded mechanically, and they did so without being stopped.

That part of the security was easy, but once they reached Alexa's door, it was Reggie's turn. Bash released the shackles like before, with him and Ethan boxing Reggie between them should he suddenly seem of less sound mind. The shackles didn't prevent Alexa's influence, if she even knew Reggie was in town, but at least when they were on, Bash and Ethan didn't have to worry about him trying something.

He first checked for wards and expressed his surprise at finding none. "Strange. She must have some powerful confidence in her technology." He rolled up the sleeves of his kimono and pressed a palm to the door.

A rune unlike any Bash had ever seen imprinted on its surface. It resembled a dispelling rune but was encircled and had a distinct pattern around it within the sphere, like connected circuitry. The rune pulsed, disappeared as if seeping into the apartment right through the door, then pulsed back bright white, only to fade to gray and fizzle.

"Poor man's EMP." Reggie gestured for Bash to continue inside. "Or that of a brilliant magician."

Before entering, Bash secured the shackles again, to a responding sigh.

"I am so looking forward to being done with these," Reggie said. "Feels like a bloody hangover every time, and I hadn't experienced one of those in ages." He grinned, peering over the top of his sunglasses.

How many ages, Bash would have to ask sometime.

Inside, Bash was immediately struck by how normal the apartment looked. It was nice, stylish, and proved Alexa's wealth without being ostentatious. The entryway went straight into a large master bedroom, where Bash assumed a master bath was located as well, or into the main living area, where a wall of windows looked out over the city and a skylight filtered more light from above.

"Search for anything useful," Bash said. "We can split up, but try not to stay out of eyeline for long. I want to be out of here in less than fifteen minutes."

Reggie nodded his intent to start in the bedroom, while Ethan went for the office area in the far corner beyond the living room. Bash continued at a slower pace, taking in the full square footage before checking out the last area in an arch around where the guest bathroom was located next to a tucked-away kitchen.

Occasionally, someone would call out that they'd found something, but nothing of real note. It was too tidy to be deeply lived in, maybe more a safe house or side dwelling. Most interesting in the kitchen were recent newspapers, folded open to stories pertaining to City Hall, its workers like *Xandra* herself or Robert, and stories both positive and negative on projects being undertaken in the city. All very expected from a deputy mayor.

When Bash joined Ethan, who had the most to sift through with the office area's desk, he'd found similar clippings, as well as detailed campaign tactics, but also energy-saving ventures, crime rate statistics, methods for reducing the homeless population by getting them jobs and places to stay rather than forced migrations.

"She actually has some pretty good ideas floating around this place," Ethan grumbled.

"Opportunistic zealots often do," Bash said. "They have to hook the people with something tangible before the inevitable dictatorship kicks in. If she truly wanted to help, she wouldn't care about being the one in charge, only whether she could get people to listen to her good ideas."

"Says the man in charge." Ethan smirked. "I'm not saying I want to hear her side. It's just easier when the bad guy only has bad ideas. I'd say I wish I could check the computer." He tapped the monitor that was dormant from Reggie's spell. "But I honestly don't think anything will be on there." He opened a final drawer in the desk, and in it was a small wooden box with the rune for fertility etched onto its cover, like a greater than and less than sign crossed with each other to create a diamond between them. The rune was often used to reference the full potential of a person—or their magic.

Ethan set the box on the desk and opened it. Within was a small carved idol of a priestess, made from white polished stone. The idol held her hands up centered over her chest as if she'd been holding an object, like a book, because there was a rectangular gap as though a piece was meant to be slotted there.

"Reg—" Ethan cut off as he looked up and must have realized Reggie was still out of sight. Before he and Bash could exchange any sense of alarm, Reggie appeared with a shrug.

"Nothing of too much note in there, other than an extensive wardrobe and far too many windows." He adjusted his sunglasses. "Even for a vampire, she keeps it brisk in here, don't you agree?" He then tightened a silk scarf around his neck that hadn't been on him before.

A slightly less extensive wardrobe now, apparently.

"Do you recognize this?" Ethan asked, holding the idol up.

"I'm not sure…. It does bear a ring of resemblance. Looks like it's missing a piece. If memory serves, it's something like a conduit to use for casting stronger spells, but I'm afraid I don't know more than that or what the missing piece might mean."

"Whatever it is, Alexa has it on her."

"You're certain?" Bash asked.

"I remember, both times I saw her, she was wearing a pendant this color and shaped exactly like the missing piece. The funny thing is"— Ethan replaced the idol in the box—"the person who'd probably know more about this is Leo. He's an anthropology professor and well-versed in shifter artifacts."

"But not the only one," Bash said with a creeping grin. "In case you've forgotten, we have another expert back at the den."

Ethan brightened. "*Bari.*"

IF ETHAN ever forgot how close it was to Christmas, returning to the den was a stark reminder, coated in Christmas cheer like Santa's workshop had been pressure washed onto every surface. That was truer than ever when they returned to find that some of the others had beaten them back, because Preston was with Jay, putting presents under the tree.

"Don't we save that for Christmas Eve?" Bash asked as he, Ethan, and Reggie trailed into the living room.

"Hush," Preston said without looking up. "Santa came early, and you're grateful."

"Love, I am rarely grateful when anyone comes early," Reggie joked, adjusting his sunglasses.

Luke entered from behind them with Robert and Bari, all clearly having come from upstairs with their own armfuls of gifts. "We, um… didn't want to forget later."

Or be dead before they could.

Ethan hated that he thought that and took a few of the presents from Luke's armful to help him.

"Did you go through everyone's rooms for those?" Bash asked.

"Don't be cross, brother." Bari breezed by to onload his gifts. "I've seen your unmentionables before when going through drawers. I was mostly only embarrassed by what hangs in your closet."

Ethan chuckled, while Bash rubbed his forehead in an almost facepalm.

"Where'd you get that one?" Jay snatched a smaller present from Robert's pile and clutched it to his chest.

"Your room." Robert shrugged.

When Bari turned from unloading his presents beneath the tree, Jay whipped the small package behind his back as if to hide it, then seemed to remember it was wrapped and walked it over to the tree himself. Bari didn't seem to notice.

"How were things at the Shelter?" Bash asked Preston.

"Nothing we couldn't handle."

"What about you guys?" Luke questioned.

"We found something." Ethan opened the photos he'd taken of the idol on his new cellphone and passed it to Bari, who immediately marveled at the images and fell into appraisal mode. Besides being a Magister now, Bari was a museum curator and currently had access to a secret shifter vault at the museum in Brookdale. "Reggie knew a little, but we were hoping you might know more."

"A magi doll!" Bari exclaimed. "Marvelous! Think of it like a proto ying-yang, meant to represent balance, specifically of magic and lack of magic. I'm surprised Alexa would leave it behind if it's the source of her power."

"Unless even just the small piece missing is enough," Ethan suggested. "I saw her wearing it. Do you know what it is? What it might be capable of on its own?"

"Hmm… I know the piece that's missing is meant to symbolize the cost of magic, to show the give and take of power and how something must be offered in order to gain, but if there's specific purpose to using that piece on its own, I have no idea. *Yet*.

"Finally, a task worthy of me!" he declared and clutched Ethan's phone to his chest. "I mean, a shame my expertise is needed, of course, but still exciting. I'll get right on it. As soon as we finish the last batch of presents. Send me those." He slapped the phone back into Ethan's hand and grabbed Jay to accompany him upstairs.

Luke didn't follow this time, so there couldn't be many presents left. Ethan saw some of his own beneath the tree, though not his gift for Bash, since that was too large to wrap. It almost made it possible to forget that they had a ticking clock to catastrophe.

"Can one of my presents be to dispose of those deplorable things?" Bash sneered at the porcelain statues in the corner of the living room.

"I love Mr. and Mrs. Claus!" Luke defended. He'd clearly been infected by his mate over the years. Ethan also thought the figures were a little unsettling.

Gus-Gus chose that moment to scurry over the statues to get closer to the presents and tree, but Preston scooped him up and placed him on his shoulder.

Meanwhile, Reggie was taking a rather obvious sniff at Robert and visibly shuddered. The human aroma could be intoxicating, but Ethan had gotten good at ignoring it.

"Aren't you festive?" Robert stroked the end of Reggie's pilfered scarf, which was a Christmassy mix of red, green, and gold.

"Like it? I was debating gifting it to one of my patients, but perhaps I'll keep it. These can have so many more uses than being tied around necks." He dusted the end over Robert's wrist.

"Patients?" Robert questioned, leaning closer and coaxing another obvious sniff. "Right, right, cause the Shaman handles any shifter cure-alls. What's the worst you guys get, fleas?"

"Oh, you know," Preston played along, "worms, rabies, the plague."

"Actually, Reggie's a regular miracle worker," Jay said as he and Bari returned with the final batch of gifts. "It's nearly impossible for couples from different tribes to conceive, but he's been working on helping change that."

"Altruistic and brilliant to boot," Robert praised, playing with the end of the scarf again, which made Reggie shudder *again*. "Be still my beating cock."

Luke snorted.

"That actually is really cool, Reggie," Ethan said, though it took a moment for Reggie's gaze to move from Robert to Ethan.

"Miracles do happen, love. Especially with the magically inclined like Focuses, Seers, and Nulls, oh my. If you'll recall those creation tablets, the story was that the original births of such powerful people came from mixed coupling, allowing for the rebellion against vampire rule and why they tried outlawing it."

"*They*, but not you, having been there personally?" Preston asked.

"Goodness, no! That you would even dare assume I'm so ancient wounds me deeply," Reggie scoffed.

"But so many of us having that type of magic now," Ethan said, "and all in close proximity, must mean more of us are being born regardless."

"Right you are, love. Not to diminish my own efforts, but it seems nature is finding a way. With the resurgence of people like you, dear boy, it might also mean that those like you will have the easiest time conceiving within mixed couples again. Not to say you might get your Alpha pregnant anytime soon, but what a fascinating experiment that would be!"

"You can experiment on whether I can get pregnant anytime," Robert purred.

"Well, if it's for science."

Bash sighed deeply at the continued inuendo-off.

"So wait," Luke said, "a mixed-tribe couple, or even a shifter and human pair, have a better chance at conceiving if one of them is a Null, Seer, or Focus?"

"Don't tell Deanna that." Preston snickered.

"Tell me what?"

Deanna and Rio walked in, causing a wave of silence, since, after all, Rio was a Focus.

"*What?*" she demanded.

"Later. Work comes first." Bash gestured for her and Rio to follow him into the kitchen. "I need caffeine—and your report."

Ethan turned to help the others finish organizing the presents. As much as it already looked like Christmas in here, the addition of gifts completed the picture and warmed Ethan's heart, which he assumed was Preston and Luke's goal.

"It's really quite sweet, those two," Jay said quietly with a nod at Reggie and Robert, in their own little world of whispers and hinting touches. "Reg acts like the biggest flirt, but I found out recently it's more bark than bite."

"It's definitely all bite with Robert." Ethan chuckled. "But wow, really?"

"Secretly being a vampire among wolves, he admitted he didn't feel comfortable being with anyone, since he would have had to lie. Robert might have been his first in... I don't even know. So I think it's sweet, even if it's only a fling for them. Though a little less sweet being in the room next to theirs." He grimaced.

"Nonsense!" Bari turned to them with a wink. "I found it inspiring." He held the small gift Jay had fussed over, and in the few seconds he had it before he set it somewhere new beneath the tree, Jay's eyes widened to twice their size.

Speaking of size, that little box was a very telling one if Ethan's guess at its contents was correct.

"Uh, it's not Reggie and Robert's room next to yours." Luke snickered.

Preston turned a little red at the admission, and he and Luke exchanged knowing and possibly embarrassed looks with Jay and Bari, confirming whose room *was* next to theirs.

"What's up for the rest of today, boss?" Deanna asked as she, Rio, and Bash reentered, Bash having poured himself some of the morning's leftover coffee.

Bash contemplated the question, scanning over the many inhabitants of the den. "Exactly what we're doing. Any objections to a quiet night in?"

Siobhan and Nell called to make their report and explained they'd decided to relieve some of the agents for the evening and show more circle presence on the streets, but everyone else was very much down for a night of vegging—which, for Bari, included research into an artifact.

What made the night truly feel like the sort of normal, comfortable holiday get-together Ethan had been craving, surrounded by Christmas decorations and good friends, was Deanna and Rio making a tray of hot chocolate. Though, from the smell, it was more alcohol than chocolate, with whipped cream drizzled with bourbon caramel.

"Booze it up, kids!" Deanna announced as she set the tray on the coffee table. "Now, am I throwing in *Diehard*, *Gremlins*, or *Cobra*?"

They decided on all three but started with *Cobra*, planning to leave *Diehard* for last.

Bari and Jay snuggled in an armchair, with Bari half watching the movie, half fussing on his phone doing research. Robert and Reggie had the other, and Preston and Luke had claimed their usual corner of the sofa, with Deanna and Rio down from them. Ethan didn't mind being relegated to the floor between Bari and Jay's chair and the sofa, so long as he could do so with Bash against him, hands clasped between their thighs while Bash sipped from his mug of boozy hot chocolate.

Across the coffee table, Robert and Reggie were definitely not watching the movie. Reggie kept sniffing Robert with little shivers and adjustments of his scarf and sunglasses. The shackles didn't help any, and Ethan wondered how the pair had done anything intimate last night with them in the way and Robert not allowed to touch them—and then absolutely did not want to know.

The sunglasses part was strange, though, since Ethan was used to Reggie peering over the top of them while flirting, but he'd been touching them a lot since they got back, intent on keeping them from falling from his eyes.

"I feel a bit guilty imbibing when you can't join in," Bash whispered and then took another sip from his half-gone drink.

"I don't mind." Ethan snuggled closer. He'd long since removed his own sunglasses, the lights dimmed in the living room to set the ambiance for the movie. "It just means you'll taste sweeter later." He snapped his teeth at Bash's cheek and then kissed it. "Thanks for this."

"A silly Stallone movie?"

Ethan chuckled and hugged Bash's arm. "This is what I wanted for this time of year, my first Christmas in my new life, with my new family." He cringed after saying it, which Bash frowned at when he noticed.

"Except you wish your father was here."

"Only if he'd earned it. But Leo too. And Jess. And Siobhan and Nell not having to patrol to keep the masses from possibly mutinying." Ethan chuckled again. "I know we have responsibilities."

"No, *I* do. And my circle does. You don't. You can be my kept boy for as long as you want." Bash kissed Ethan with a quick swipe of his tongue between Ethan's lips that tasted like chocolate and whiskey. Even if Ethan didn't crave normal sustenance anymore, he still smacked his lips in approval.

"As long as I want, huh?"

Bash's teasing expression softened, their faces closely met as they whispered in the dark, with the glittering of Christmas lights all around them. "I wasn't planning on otherwise, even if I fail sometimes at expressing that."

Ethan kissed Bash this time. He knew. He also knew how much he loved this life, even being a vampire, because he loved these people, this home. He loved Bash. And he wasn't going to let anyone, not even his vampire great-grandmother, take that away from him.

He glanced at Bari and Jay, with Bari unabashedly in Jay's lap, in a giggling faux argument about whether Stallone's character, Cobra, was a virgin or not before boffing the female lead.

Ethan turned to look at Deanna and Rio, closest to them on the sofa. They were leaned into each other, heads touching, hands clasped much like Ethan and Bash, and otherwise cuddling their mugs to their chests, enraptured by the movie as much as each other.

Preston and Luke were similar, with the addition of Basil, Dr. Dawson, and Gus-Gus snuggled together too, on the back of the sofa behind them.

Reggie and Robert were….

Gone.

"I've got it!" Bari announced, back to his phone research. "And, oh dear, the idol isn't only about balance, but a lesson in overuse of magic." He snatched up the remote to pause the movie. "With the one piece missing, it can increase magical output tenfold, but it's dangerous. Often drains the caster. When the pieces are together, it's harmonious, allowing someone who's maybe had a mental block for their magic to finally show their true potential. But how the missing piece balances that is by being a Null rune.

"By itself, it's the same as a true Null, able to negate magic it touches or that's cast on its user, only they can choose what they negate. Alexa enthralling someone, no problem, but she's a completely undetectable blank slate that no other magic can work on, and no one can sense."

"No wonder she wants Robert dead," said Preston. "She's her own Null."

"Where did they go?" Ethan sat up taller.

"Hm?" Deanna glanced at the empty chair and snorted. "Where do you think?"

That made sense, a given, easy to imagine them sneaking away and for what purpose after the extent of Reggie's sniffing and shuddering in the wake of each whiff.

And the glasses adjusting. And scarf fiddling. Neither of which should have been weird, but Ethan couldn't shake the faint feeling, slowly growing in his gut, that something was very wrong.

"We're going to look for them," Bash said before Ethan had to. "I'd rather be paranoid than right."

They hadn't seen where Robert and Reggie went, so they started by heading toward Nell's workshop, only as soon as they passed the main cellar door, Ethan called Bash back.

"Wait. I can smell them here." He paused only a moment before throwing open the door and hurrying down the steps to discover—

Robert and Reggie engaged in the same intimate embrace as the day before, pressed up against the closed door of the cellar prison.

Ethan stopped at the halfway point down the steps, as Bash caught up to him and whispered:

"Paranoia it is. They just found a different dark corner to…." But he trailed off, likely for the same reason that Ethan remained worried.

There was a specific feeling that being near Robert evoked. A confliction of emotions, turmoil, indecision, something almost unsettling but also oddly comforting. Despite Robert being seemingly enraptured in Reggie's arms, with Reggie's face buried in Robert's neck, that feeling was too faint, fading, like he was losing consciousness.

Or dying.

Reggie's head snapped up as he noticed them. His sunglasses had fallen down his nose, revealing the unmistakable sight of red frenzied eyes.

Chapter 15

BEFORE BASH could blink, Ethan was down the last steps. He snatched Robert from Reggie's arms, and Reggie hissed and snapped at Ethan in anger at his lost meal, clearly feral.

Bash leaped to intervene, shifting to Stage Two to help hold Reggie back.

Robert fell limp to the floor, Bash and Ethan's combined efforts needed to pin Reggie against the cellar. Robert wasn't moving, but they couldn't do anything until Reggie calmed.

As the blood he'd drained from Robert raced through his system, he slowly did, returning from his frenzied state, with red eyes turning amber and then, finally and thankfully in only a few blinks, yellow.

"What?" Reggie squinted in confusion.

Ethan released him as swiftly as he'd charged, dropping down beside Robert. "Robert? Robert, come on!" He patted Robert's cheek, but Robert's eyelids didn't so much as flutter.

Bash slammed Reggie against the cellar with a clang, retaining his fangs, claws, and sprouted fur long enough to growl, "You were perfectly well-fed yesterday. What happened?"

"I... I-I don't know! Robert?" Reggie looked down at him, running his tongue over his lips with dawning horror.

The scarf around Reggie's neck was coming loose, the one he'd stolen from Alexa's. Bash tore it off him, revealing for a split second a pair of puncture wounds that healed from the renewed nourishment of fresh blood.

She'd been there. Alexa had returned to the apartment while they were there and drained Reggie to the brink of frenzy without them even noticing. She must have enthralled him to not remember, to not notice his growing hunger until it was too late. Robert's nullification didn't negate the thrall if Alexa used it like hypnosis and turned Reggie into a damn sleeper agent.

"Robert!" Ethan shook him harder. Robert was breathing, but too unsteadily.

"What did she make me do?" Reggie lamented.

Bash wanted to slam him back again, but there'd be no point. He hadn't been in control, wasn't to blame, and so Bash let his shifted traits fade.

Ethan hefted Robert's body up and opened his mouth.

"What are you doing?" Bash asked.

"Four vampires are in Centrus besides Alexa. *Four*. Me, Reggie, Dad, and Leo. And a fifth born, all from Alexa's bloodline."

Four corners connect where a fifth is born

Ethan bit into his own wrist to start the flow of blood.

"He won't be a Null anymore," Bash said. "A Seer, Focus, other magic users, can be vampires, but not a Null."

"He won't be one if he dies either." Ethan held his wrist to Robert's mouth, allowing the first few droplets to spill inside. If he wasn't too far gone, all they needed was for him to drink.

As more drops touched Robert's tongue and slid down his throat, he began to, first with a faint swallow, and then latching on to Ethan's wrist to suck out more. He never opened his eyes, but he drank and drank until Ethan's eyelids drooped and Bash was ready to intervene. Only then, right on the brink, did Robert fall slack, like a marionette with the strings cut.

He had no breath now, but Bash could hear the rapider beat of his heart, and the old sensations Robert used to arouse were gone completely—a Null no longer.

"He'll wake frenzied," Bash reminded Ethan.

"I know." Ethan gathered Robert's limp body and stood with him cradled in his arms. "But since he's not a Null anymore, we have the perfect place to put him."

Pounding came from inside the cellar, and a very muffled cry. "Ethan? Anyone? What's going on out there?"

"What the hell is happening?" Preston's voice called from the top of the stairs.

A collection of curious heads peered down at them, having heard the commotion.

"Get down here. Circle meeting," Bash said and moved Reggie aside to open the cellar door, revealing a startled Gordon on the other side.

IT HELPED that Gordon backed away to give Ethan room to enter, seemingly in shock as he stared at Robert in Ethan's arms.

"Robert? Ethan, what—"

"No more bullshit, Dad," Ethan snarled. He placed Robert on the bed. Other than Robert's strong, changed pulse, he looked as though he might have died after all. He had, in a way, changed forever from how he'd been born.

Ethan hated that he'd been forced to do it, unable to ask if it's what Robert would have wanted, but in that moment when he'd feared Robert was seconds from dying and the thought of turning him crossed Ethan's mind, he realized it was the only thing their prophecy could mean.

He hoped that would be enough for Robert to not hate him over it.

Ethan turned from the bed as Bash stepped into the cellar, bookending Gordon between them. The others hung back, a tight clump outside the door, all trying to peer in. Ethan might have laughed at seeing the shimmer of energy in Preston's hand in the shape of a machete like the day they first met, but any humor was drained from him, just like the blood Robert took that had left him woozy. Ethan would need his own replenishment soon, but first things first.

"You knew about Alexa," Ethan continued. "Met with her. You knew she was Leo's sire. You even believe in her cause, but she is not some savior. She tricked us again, forced us to walk into the line of fire, and made Reggie frenzy and try to kill Robert right under our roof."

"He's...." Gordon stared at Robert, seeing the lack of breath, but perhaps not yet smelling or sensing that Robert wasn't human or a Null anymore.

"Not dead, but he's not going to wake up in the best mood."

The truth dawned on Gordon with a look of nausea crossing his face. As always, Ethan hoped it was a genuine expression, but he needed more than flickers of remorse.

"You knew about Reggie too, didn't you?"

"What?" Gordon glanced at the door, and Reggie, haggard-looking and unlike the carefree figure Ethan usually knew him to be, entered the cellar to stand beside Bash.

"If you want me to listen to you, Dad, then tell me the truth," Ethan demanded. "All of it. And maybe this time, I'll believe you."

Gordon pivoted, positioning himself to better look at them all, but focused most on Ethan. "I didn't know I was a Focus when I was human. I honestly don't know if your mother knew she was a Seer. But Leo could tell what I was since he didn't have the ability to enthrall me.

"It was later, after I had Leo take you away, that Alexa came to me. She knew what I was too, knew what you were, and had plans for us, great plans, that would make up for all that had gone wrong."

"It can't, Dad. It hasn't," Ethan insisted. "The ends don't justify whatever means she thinks will make this world better. She's manipulating you. She had you manipulate me."

He nodded, and his gaze fell to the floor. "She gave me the idea to turn you, whispered in my ear, convinced me I could have you back if I gave you the world. Even if I failed, I just had to be patient and she'd bring you back to me. And if I failed, like I did, if I could get to her, I was supposed to, but otherwise, I was to keep you occupied.

"But she never told me… she never said she'd do to you what she did." A cringe squeezed a few tears from Gordon's eyes, and he looked at Ethan with a quiver in his lip. "Making you frenzy and kill someone you cared for. Threatening to do it again with the person you love most." He turned his gaze on Bash.

That had been a touchy subject between him and Bash, but it was true, and Ethan wanted so badly to believe the emotion and regret he saw on his father's face. To believe that this, finally, was the truth.

"To do it to Reggie too, another of her children like Leo…." Gordon clenched his fists as if close to erupting, anger mixing with his grief that Ethan had rarely if ever seen from his father, whether from childhood memories or since they'd reunited. "She swore she didn't want any harm to come to my family. She *swore* that what I did to your mother was an accident she hadn't meant to let happen."

"Alexa will do whatever she has to in order to reach her goals," Reggie said with a haunted tone that said he knew that well now even if he didn't remember everything.

"Yes," Gordon agreed. He released his fists and stepped toward Ethan, a slow approach, and stopped with a few feet still between them. "Please believe me that the one thing I never wanted was for you to experience what I did with your mother."

"Then help us," Ethan said. "And not as an excuse to escape and turn to her side, but for real. We can't beat her without you, Dad. The prophecy I had about how we win this said: 'four corners connect where a fifth is born.' That's us. It has to be us. Me, you, Reggie, Leo, and Robert. Her bloodline needs to be what stops her. We just need Leo now, and I know where he is. Then we wait for Alexa to come to us."

"Um…," Luke hesitantly called from outside, peeking his ginger head around some of those taller than him. "Then what?"

"We do what she did to us," Reggie said, echoing Ethan's thought exactly, "only we don't stop until she's nothing but a husk."

"And we're trusting *him* as the linchpin?" Deanna nodded at Gordon. "Like, willing to let him loose? Because, no offense, leech, but I'm still not liking your pops all that much."

"I know it's a risk," Ethan admitted, "but I honestly believe this is how we win. Dad?"

"I'm with you," Gordon said, though when he tried to take a step closer, Ethan answered with a lurching step back. Not yet. He couldn't forgive or forget yet, and much as Gordon looked pained by the rejection, he nodded.

"While I don't know if I like being used in a prophecy," Reggie tried pulling on a little of his more jovial tone, "I'm with you too, love. There are a few memories starting to resurface that I owe Alexa for."

"Not to be a buzzkill," Bari called from outside this time, tall enough to be more than a disembodied voice, "but we literally just found out that direct magic won't work on her, and without Robert being a Null, having joined the Type A drinking club, if you all get close to Alexa together, can't she just take you over like she planned?"

"Yes," Ethan said, because he'd thought that much through too. "And we're going to let her. We're going to give her exactly what she wants. I have an idea for how we beat that, all thanks to you, Bari."

"Me?" Bari squeaked.

"If just one of us can get close enough to remove the Null rune from her neck, it's all we'll need. Trust me."

"One last—though probably *not* last—problem, if we manage to kill Alexa," Preston put in, still holding his conjured machete at the front of the cluster at the door. "How are we going to handle *that*"—he pointed at Robert—"and his deputy's sudden disappearance with the human side, the press, the fallout?"

"I know how," Bash said with a scheming smirk. Some dissension from the others was expected, but Ethan was grateful that Bash hadn't been among them and trusted him enough that this would work. "I think our caged assassin might finally have a use.

"Feed him when he wakes," he said to Gordon, nodding at Robert's still motionless form on the bed. "We're going to need a few days to prepare for this, but if you're really with us, the next time we open this door, both you and Robert can walk out of it."

"YOU EXPECT me to help you?"

Bash stood before their imprisoned harpy eagle assassin, who sat on the bed of the room they'd been keeping her in, just the two of them, facing off alone. Bash had even brought in her weapons as a good-faith gesture, though he hadn't yet handed them over.

She'd been more than well cared for, the room having its own bathroom for her to bathe and use the facilities as needed, and Deanna or someone else in the household having brought her food and water since day one. They'd even given her extra clothes to switch out and taken her laundry away to get washed.

She was currently wearing one of Rio's graphic T's, this one stating *I'm with Stupid*, but with the arrow pointed down.

Clearly a purposeful choice on Rio or Deanna's part.

"I expect you're getting rather antsy about your stay with us," Bash said. "So, if you agree to my terms, despite your Alpha's refusal to admit she sent you, I will let you go. And if you feel we have done enough to eliminate the real vampire threat—"

She opened her mouth to interrupt.

"You don't need to say *all* vampires are a threat. I know that's how you and many others feel. I also know that there are three packs now who have come to accept the vampires who have proven they are not."

"All capable of being worse threats if I understand correctly that this Alexa can take control of them and turn them against you."

Fair. Bash hadn't held anything back when explaining the situation to her. "Meaning, if we kill Alexa, that threat is gone. Forever. And if you're willing to help once we've accomplished that, you and your pack won't have to worry about three packs with five vampires on our side paying a visit to your city."

Her posture was impeccable, a regalness to her like an Alpha herself, only she still managed to sit up straighter at the threat. "You also expect me to believe that shifter culture is a sham, that we weren't the original inhabitants of this world but merely a side effect of human experiments to become vampires?"

"You don't have to believe me. It's true. Shifters being up our own asses, wolves in particular, because we're supposedly superior, is not only a waste but a reflection of the very species you're so set against, since vampires did it first. But that doesn't matter. That is the past. I'm concerned with the future, and while my priority is my pack, it, and the packs I trust most, include vampires. Take it or leave it."

"I'll have to see your success first. No promises that I'll lend my skills to the aftermath unless you deliver Alexa's head."

"Done." Bash hadn't expected more. He threw her knife and spear with its hidden chain in its hilt onto the bed and turned to take his leave. "We don't intend to fail. Enjoy the last few days of your... vacation."

He wasn't going to waste more time on her now that he had an answer. She was an outlier but devoted enough that he believed the odds of her coming through for them were worth the risk that she wouldn't. Trained assassins knew how to make someone's unexpected death look exactly the way they wanted for human authorities and the public.

Bash nodded to Deanna and Rio, who'd been keeping watch in case he needed backup, as he exited. He went straight for his own room, hearing the last few words from Ethan on the phone with Leo as he entered. If Leo was already compromised, he couldn't be told the whole plan—neither could Reggie or Gordon, since they'd be enthralled by Alexa first and might give away the truth—so all Ethan could tell Leo was for him to go with the flow once they joined him.

"He'll be ready," Ethan said after hanging up the landline. "How'd your part go?"

"I'll still keep a close eye out for a talon in my back, but she's in. How are you feeling about all this?" Bash sat beside Ethan on the bed.

"It was my idea."

"And it's a brilliant one, but it also means you might feel the press of your father's thrall for real for the first time since all this started."

"I know. And I hate that, because when I'm in it, I am so certain that I want what he is telling me to feel. But I have to risk it, no matter how... well...."

"Dangerous, possibly suicidal, or at least the largest risk any of us have ever taken?"

"Yep." Ethan snickered. "We fail, we're fucked."

"We're not going to fail." Bash took Ethan's hand between them. "Because we prophesied how to win, and that is exactly what we're going to do."

Ethan smiled, a bright and beautifully genuine smile that spoke of a depth of affection he'd admitted to Bash several times now.

Then he did it again.

"I love you." Ethan quickly covered Bash's mouth with his free hand, preventing any possible response. "And I'm going to say that again when this is over. Okay?"

Bash's heart ached for the patience and faith Ethan had in him. It wasn't an ultimatum, but an opportunity to do this right. Bash had no doubts that Ethan was what he wanted, that this family of theirs and all its strange members was a better one than any he could have asked for. It scared him to think of all the ways he could lose it, but what he'd begun to realize was that it scared him more to have any regrets if he did.

Bash nodded, and Ethan dropped his hand, replacing it with the press of his lips.

Chapter 16

IT SEEMED almost quaint that they were poised to finally end this not on the night of the Cold Moon, with minutes ticking down to do or die, but several days ahead of schedule—the night before Christmas Eve.

Though this wasn't exactly the *family* gathering Ethan had been looking forward to.

"This is bitchin'!" Robert exclaimed, leaping up onto the base of the lamppost on the street corner where they were about to cross and spinning around it like Gene Kelly in *Singing in the Rain*.

Hating Ethan hadn't been an issue since Robert was loving every minute of this.

They'd debated disguising themselves for the walk to Gordon's apartment where Leo was supposed to be staying, or even using their speed to get there faster. In the end, they'd decided a leisurely stroll was best, since the point, if Alexa wasn't already with Leo, was to get her to notice them.

Xandra had continued to be seen in public and working as deputy mayor. Robert hadn't been. They'd played it up too, sending in messages on his behalf to City Hall and to the press that the events of the scandal had shaken him enough to require more time away.

Some speculated he was drowning his sorrows in more BDSM, some thought he might be poised to step down as mayor, while others were on his side that private lives were no one's business but their own, and he had every right to be upset. For Ethan and the others, they'd simply hoped Alexa believed Robert was dead, maybe Reggie too, and that they must be panicking, struggling to decide what to do next.

Until tonight, when they were ready to make their move.

"*Robert*," Ethan chided, tugging him down from the lamppost so they could cross the street. They were Ethan, Robert, Reggie—no longer shackled—and Gordon. "We want her attention, but we still need to be vigilant. You're not a Null anymore, remember, and your role is most important."

"Yeah, yeah, but the trickle-down economics of vampire bloodline magic can't fully screw us until we're with your uncle," Robert droned, like it was all hardly important compared to the burst of energy in him, the power, speed, and enhanced senses. Ethan had been enamored by some of it too, those first few nights, though maybe not as much given the shock of discovering that shifters and magic and vampires even existed. "I got it, Rookie. I'm enjoying my death sentence!" He spread his arms and took a deep breath of air he no longer needed. "Whichever way that might end up."

He hadn't bothered with a winter coat, saying he wanted to feel the chill in his bones, if it even managed to seep through his preternatural skin. There had been more snowfalls since that night at Decker's apartment, but while a few drifts had been made by plows, the sidewalks had been cleared enough to not require boots, even if someone not wearing a coat might still draw attention.

Ethan had gone simple, in a button-down, jeans, and warmer jacket. Reggie was in his usual "The Dude" attire, though for the first time since Ethan had known him, he'd forgone his sunglasses. Gordon mostly mirrored Ethan.

He'd also been shadowing Ethan ever since they let him up from the cellar. At least he respected Ethan's requests to not get too close. Ethan still feared his father was too indoctrinated by Alexa to truly see reason and might try betraying them, but he wanted to believe and therefore didn't push Gordon away either.

"So, Reg…." Robert skipped in front of their line of related fangers to take the other end beside Reggie and looped his arm with Reggie's too. "What are your policies on vampire orgies—"

"Love, please!" Reggie leaned into him with a cackle. "Not a man easily tied down, I take it?"

Robert grinned at the unintentional, or maybe intentional, double entendre.

This left Ethan walking alone beside Gordon, and he shifted a little at the proximity, the strangeness of being on the street with his father. Despite the past several weeks of knowing Gordon was alive and trying to reconnect, it still felt surreal when he'd grown up assuming he was an orphan.

"It's on the first floor," Gordon said softly. "My apartment. Easy to reach."

"You said that already, Dad," Ethan answered.

"Ah. Well, I chose it for the convenience since it's not as if I had to worry about muggers. But I didn't kill anyone, if you've wondered. If you've worried about that. Perhaps that's the one good lesson Alexa instilled in me. When she first came to see me, after Leo took you away, she said to be especially careful to never kill, for my own protection, just as much as shielding runes kept me hidden."

"We're not hidden at the moment," Ethan said, glancing about and catching the occasional scent of human, or the less frequent scent of shifter, which was almost always accompanied by a curious—and fearful—glance back.

They wouldn't attack. Even with four vampires boldly out in the open, the policy of "kill fangers on sight" was no longer allowed. The entirety of the pack had been warned to not confront any vampires they might encounter, whether actually a threat or on their side. Some might doubt that Ethan and the others were with the pack, like they had when Ethan was first introduced to it, but none did more than raise their heads or allow a brief flash of their eyes.

"No, we're not hidden." Gordon stared forward, a wistful look on his face as he led the way, just a half pace ahead of the others, allowing Ethan to look at his face without their eyes meeting.

Robert and Reggie were talking hushed now and practically giggling, but Ethan had noticed when Robert first stumbled up the cellar steps, back to sensible thought from his frenzied newborn state after being fed, how edgy and uncertain Reggie had been. He was the cause of Robert having to be turned, even if Alexa had forced it, and it clearly eased Reggie's guilt that Robert didn't seem to care.

They'd needed those few days between then and now to crash-course Robert on how to control himself and not accidentally attack someone who smelled good, but he'd taken to it all like he'd been meant for this change since day one.

"Do you remember the first time we took a walk together at night?" Gordon asked.

"I don't know."

"Your mother had dropped us off at the movies. I forget why she didn't come along or which movie it was. She was supposed to pick us up later, but you begged for us to walk back instead because it was a full moon."

Ethan looked skyward. This moon still had a week to go before it would be full.

"You had no idea yet that your love for science and a desire to understand things would lead to pursuing investigation and law enforcement but proceeded to tell me everything you knew about the moon in rambling, brilliant detail." Gordon smiled, a huff of amusement leaving him at the memory.

Ethan didn't remember that night, but given how beat up his old astronomy book had been, he wasn't surprised he'd had an early fascination with the very celestial body that had been dictating the course of his life these past few months.

"I always only ever wanted to see that same passion and happiness on your face. When I set my plan in motion and turned you, I honestly didn't anticipate that Bashir's involvement would become what it did, but it seems fate had other plans. Even now, I just want you to be safe and happy. If you never again had to fear—"

"Dad, please, don't try to tell me it all would have been easier if you'd won back then and I'd chosen you over Bash."

"That wasn't my intention, but I suppose that is what happened, isn't it? You chose Bashir."

Ethan's gut clenched because he'd hated having to choose at all.

"I forgot how important it was to let someone choose for themselves after choice was taken from me," Gordon continued. "That's not an excuse for my actions, Ethan. I know my good intentions aren't an excuse either. I'm just...." He glanced back, a slide of his eyes to capture Ethan's in a matched gaze. "I'm sorry. I'm so sorry. For all of it."

Ethan faltered, hearing the right words, for the right things, that he hoped had been said for the right reasons. Then he picked up his pace again when he started to fall behind.

His father didn't say more, didn't hold his stare or ask for anything in return, least of all forgiveness, but merely continued forward too.

"No, no, no, but like, if you can go fast enough that someone can't even see you, can't you also... slow things down?" Robert was saying with an increasingly louder and sensual tone. "Oh! What about back-to-back stamina recharge, like—"

"Robert, love, you are insatiable." Reggie clung to Robert's arm, looped with his. "There is more to vampirism than rough animal sex. Although it had been so long for me, I forgot how fun that part is."

"Then we better kick ourselves some vampire queen butt, baby!" Robert declared. "Because I am ready for the after-party."

In his snickering and shaking of his head at the pair, Ethan almost missed that Gordon had stopped. As Ethan and the others noticed, they too stopped and turned to face the building before them.

"Good thing it's time, then, Robert," Gordon said. "We're here. Apartment 103."

"Remember, she's likely expecting us." Ethan took point, moving closer to the doors, already knowing the building code to get inside without having to inform Leo that they'd arrived. One thing they needed to be certain this worked was to at least see Leo before everything unraveled. "She also probably knows we have a plan in mind to foil whatever she has waiting for us. We just have to hope she doesn't guess what the real plan is."

From there, entrance into the building and the short walk through the lobby to the first corridor of apartments almost went by too quickly.

Reggie was the one who knocked.

Leo looked terrible when he answered, the most worn and distraught Ethan had ever seen him. He seemed smaller with how he slumped, thinner too, his blond hair mussed and blue eyes haunted. His disarray, and how the professor look he was known for was down to a rumpled button-down and slacks, might have made him look older, but it surprised Ethan how young he seemed.

"Leo, love!" Reggie embraced him, taking hold of his wrist between their bodies with a tight clutch. "I'd forgotten your face. It's been too long, brother."

After a moment's shock, Leo sank against Reggie and hugged him just as tightly back. "Reginald. I'd forgotten you too."

They released each other, allowing the rest of them to file inside the apartment. Further anguish marred Leo's face with contrasting relief when he saw Ethan, and they hugged too.

Robert, not having met Leo, offered a small wave, and when Leo and Gordon's eyes made contact, they shared a stiff, quiet exchange that ended in mutual nods.

"You shouldn't have come," Leo said. It was a nice if modest apartment, a studio, with minimalist furniture and all the curtains drawn. "We shouldn't be doing this, whatever you're thinking."

"Is she—?" Ethan started, but *she* answered before he could finish.

"Here?" Alexa stepped from the shadows without so much as a whiff of her presence before she spoke. "Yes, I am."

Leo and Reggie groaned, hunching over in immediate pain with teeth gritted as she bent them to her will. They stood up hardly a second later with dormant, stoic expressions, unable to fight the thrall with her being so near, as she stalked forward, wearing a red dress tonight, which seemed both fitting and cruel.

Ethan refused to fear her or be overcome with doubt, even when Leo turned his gaze on Gordon, and despite Gordon never having succumbed to Leo's thrall before, he groaned and bent over like they had, the power of the vampire line giving Leo the strength he needed to overcome a Focus's resistance.

"If only we'd realized back during the first rebellion that we could overcome such power through the power of our own bloodlines, we might never have lost our empire. But ah, all for the better. The new world we can rebuild will be even better."

"I missed what it feels like to have you boys together," Alexa cooed, unafraid as she stood between Reggie and Leo and reached up to cup both their cheeks like a doting mother. "I had many fledglings once, most killed over the years by shifters thinking us vermin. But you were always my favorites. Reginald, my dear witch, and Leopold, while nothing special in many respects, always able to just barely resist my thrall, only to inevitably succumb."

Gordon grunted louder and clenched his eyes shut with an awful grimace. It froze Ethan to see his father in pain, but he had to remember the plan. This was the right way, to make Alexa think she could win before they proved her wrong.

"I wouldn't have even needed Reginald to be here, you know," Alexa continued, almost daring Ethan and Robert to make a move. "But every action you took gave me more opportunities to play this smarter. Why walk into that den of yours when you kept bringing what I needed to me? And here you are again."

"Ah!" Gordon's knees buckled, and he dropped to the floor, panting and snarling, until it suddenly stopped and he, too, stood up with that vacant expression and turned his eyes on Ethan.

"Now!" Ethan cried as he pulled his phone from his pocket, on a video call to Bash, who'd been waiting for his signal.

Portals popped into existence all around them—

And then fizzled out before anyone could jump through.

"Was that your plan?" Alexa stepped toward Ethan, placing her in the middle of their circle. "Get me alone and have all your friends port in to attack at once and catch me off guard? Not bad. Only even magic like that can't be used near me if I don't allow it." She touched the pendant hanging from her neck, the simple white rectangle that matched the stone of the artifact they'd found.

The pressure Ethan hated struck him like a punch, and he dropped to his knees. It was so different than any time Gordon had tried imposing his will on Ethan before, worse than even the first time when Ethan hadn't known to try resisting. The phone tumbled from his hands. It was all-encompassing, like a warm blanket enveloping him and asking so very sweetly that he merely listen.

My beautiful boy, she can give us everything we ever wanted.

"No!"

Gordon didn't mean it. He didn't really want that anymore. It was only because Alexa was making him think it.

A vision flashed before Ethan's eyes of Centrus City like a paradise, humans aware of their shifter masters, just as humans and shifters all served vampire lords. When blood was needed, necks were offered freely, and mixed couples could mate and have children as they pleased.

So long as newborn Seers, Focuses, and rarest of all, Nulls, were watched carefully to determine their use—or killed at risk of their numbers growing.

"*No*," Ethan gritted out firmer, hands forming into fists and pressing into the floor as he fought the potent sway.

"It would be so much easier if you didn't resist," Alexa said over him as if from an altitude high above, "but try all you like. You will succumb, and despite your disobedience and the frustrations you've caused me, I won't punish you again. You can keep Bashir and your friends. After all, with our powers combined, they will kneel before us and beg to serve."

"I give, geez," Robert spoke up with blatant disregard. "No need to do any of that when you get to me. I love this new me! I know I wasn't part of your original plan, Xandra, *Alexa*, great-great grandma, apparently. But no hard feelings for trying to kill me, huh? Truth is, I really dig the whole being-bitten thing." He was circling her, and she looked so very unconcerned. "Do you?"

He lunged, biting deep into Alexa's shoulder, and the pressure on Ethan stopped. Robert tore the pendant from her neck and tapped three times on the rune on his wrist, porting him instantly to the rune's twin— with Alexa in tow.

ETHAN'S PHONE being on helped prepare them for the moment when Robert and Alexa blipped into existence.

Bash sprang to Stage Two, snarling with claws extended, knowing how precarious a timeline they walked to make this work, and everyone else was ready with him.

They were in the alley behind the tattoo parlor, circled tight around where they knew the others would arrive, and not for one moment willing to let Alexa escape. So long as she hadn't finished taking over Ethan, once her presence left her children, the distance between them would have severed her thrall. Now they just needed to do this one fledgling at a time, backward from how she could control them, and they'd have her down before she stood a chance.

Four corners connect where a fifth is born

They'd almost gathered in the cellar, or even at Ethan's childhood home, but when they considered how all this connected, it began for most of them right there in this alley.

By the red moonlight.

Ethan blipped in next, still tethered to Bash, invisible at first, only to appear like a phantom with his first step, lunging at Alexa to join Robert.

Most of the others had switched partners, ensuring each vampire had someone to port to. Bash, Luke, Deanna, Preston, and Siobhan were the tightest circle around where Alexa was being drained. Robert had ported to Luke, Gordon would appear by Deanna, Reggie with Preston, and Siobhan had the match to what Reggie should have placed on Leo with an immediate embrace and hidden clutch at his wrist.

Ethan would have explained to the others by now what they needed to do, only Robert having known ahead of time what the runes were for, since they hadn't put one on Reggie when he first arrived. They'd still stagger their arrivals, having Reggie come next, not being a direct part of the bloodline from Alexa to Robert.

Farther from that tighter circle was Bari on one side of their huddle protecting Rio, who was adding his Focus energy to everyone he could. On the other side, Jay protected Nell, who'd cast a shield around them to lock them in so that even if Alexa got free, she wouldn't get far.

Bash almost shifted to Stage Three when he saw Alexa starting to struggle free from Robert and Ethan's hold, only for Gordon to pop in next. If he wavered or betrayed them, they were done for, but he bit into Alexa like the others, higher on her neck than where Ethan had her shoulder.

"Pres!" Luke cried, and Bash whipped his head to the left where Luke stood beside him.

Several rats were scampering past Luke's feet, headed for the vampires. Bash snapped his attention to Preston next, whose blank expression proved his guess right.

With only the power to enthrall a single shifter, Alexa had chosen the right one—the Rat King who could summon others to her aid. The rodents were already climbing up Robert, making him squirm and kick as he tried to keep his bite latched tight.

"Rio!" Luke called for added help and then broke the circle to grab Preston by the collar and kiss him.

Preston gasped and blinked awareness the moment the kiss ended. "The hell? We're supposed to be in a fight here!"

"You needed it!" Luke argued.

The rats scurried away without Preston's control on them, and in came Reggie, grabbing Alexa's arm so harshly, he nearly jerked it from its socket, and bit into her wrist.

"*Stop!*" she tried commanding him, the first of them she directly could, but though he faltered for a moment, she was too weak now to keep her hold on him.

She sank to the pavement, and none of them stopped from viciously draining her.

Leo was last, slow in the step that brought him into view. Slower still as he lowered to his knees in front of her and took her free arm. He never once looked away from her eyes as he bit into her wrist like Reggie.

Bash could feel the tension within their bubble of support lessening, sensing that they had won.

Then Alexa laughed.

"We beat you!" Ethan ripped his fangs free from her shoulder long enough to snarl, blood staining his lips and teeth. "You didn't win!"

The light was dimming in her eyes, yellow, but then not even fading to amber or red but straight to the blue of her human form. The others were laying her back as they finished draining her, and she seemed to look on them with fondness, maybe even pride, as she managed her last words.

"Didn't I?"

There was no denying the smell of vampire then, but also, suddenly, of decay.

Alexa was gone.

Nell dropped the shielding around them, with a gust of cold winter air blowing in. Slowly, everyone released their shifts, Deanna having gotten especially close to Stage Three with a rip in her shirt. The vampires who'd all had their fill of ancient blood wiped the stains from their mouths, as the one person who'd been left outside the shield came forward, arms crossed, not having fled to freedom like she could have.

"I suppose this is something," the assassin said, expertly hiding any true emotions she might feel. "Fine, then. Authorities will find the body in a manner that points at some very specific radicalists we're aware of in your city—not at your mayor or any of you." She nodded to Robert, who was getting to his feet with aid from Reggie. "We'll be sure to plant enough evidence so it looks as though they're targeting Mr. Hedin next, which will help him look uninvolved. The rest is up to you, Mr. Bain, and your… vampire mayor."

"You still sound skeptical," Bash said.

"I wouldn't be good at my job if I wasn't. But because of that, when I report this to my Alpha, she'll believe me, maybe even about our true history. Just don't give us any reason to change our minds about leaving you alone." She smirked just enough to instill her threat, and then moved toward Alexa's corpse, which her line of progeny looked more than happy to have taken away.

Ethan crushed a hug to Bash's chest so abruptly, Bash lost his breath and didn't really witness the congratulations passed among the others, though it was difficult to miss the cheers and Luke's resounding "Booya!"

Once released from the hug, Bash smeared away the last traces of blood from Ethan's lips and kissed him.

Shuffling alerted them to Gordon approaching, smiling but looking like he didn't want to overstep where he might not be welcome.

Ethan crushed him in a hug too. "Thank you, Dad."

It was over.

EVERYONE MOSTLY crashed when their tasks were through, a week's worth of tension finally relieved. Maybe two months' worth, really, Bash thought.

Before he knew it, the next day's Christmas Eve bled almost seamlessly into Christmas Day, playing out as he'd hoped for his pack, for Ethan, for all of them, without anything else to worry about other than sharing food and presents and holiday cheer.

Kate and Jude, the Alpha and Second from Glenwood, delivered Jesse back to the den in person on Christmas morning, and she launched at Preston and Luke, nearly bowling them both over. Neither were much taller than she was, after all.

"Told you we could do this in one week instead of two!" Luke laughed.

Kate and Jude also relayed that they'd been able to track the idol Alexa used as once having been in Leo's collection, just like the creation tablets. Also like them, Leo had apparently donated the idol to Brookdale to keep it safe, but after escaping Glenwood, he'd broken into the Brookdale Museum and stolen it back from the secret shifter section before going to Centrus. The idol was familiar to Bari because he'd once catalogued it himself.

Bari then dove into deep discussion with Leo and Reggie about working together to keep a closer eye on shifter artifacts in the future— such as the idol itself, the missing piece having been retrieved from Gordon's apartment, along with Ethan's phone.

As festivities continued, it hadn't escaped Bash that Ethan hadn't yet said "I love you" again, not that first night before they fell asleep or on Christmas Eve or today. There was no distance between them, no pulling away, but rather, Bash realized Ethan was waiting for something else.

He'd said he'd say it again when this was over, and it wouldn't truly be over until the prophecy's due date passed.

On Cold Moon's night.

Jay's Christmas present for Bari certainly didn't help with the anticipation, since it seemed he was ready to move from engaged-to-be-engaged to simply *engaged*.

Ring and all.

"It's perfect!" Bari exclaimed after a jubilant "Yes!" and Jay sliding the ring onto his finger, which was a fashionable yet blingy conjoined pair of bands, each alternating between gold and diamond-lined braiding.

Preston and Luke had their first Christmas with Jesse. Ethan had his first with his father in over twenty years. Siobhan got a new coffee mug with a surface like scales and the handle shaped like a lizard tail. Nell got a beautiful custom-made dress stitched together from differently colored fabrics, which Bari must have had a hand in. And Rio opened a present that turned out to contain handcuffs, which made the poor man blush the color of the Christmas lights, until Deanna pounced and dragged him out of the room.

Robert and Reggie passed around eggnog that Robert had apparently been saving, and even though he could no longer enjoy it, he still wanted to share—and anyone who tried it promptly responded with a choke from the level of alcohol.

For the most part, Gordon kept to himself, understanding that not everyone trusted or liked him very much, but he had formed a bond with Robert, and now Reggie too, that would probably last an entire afterlife given the blood that bound them. Even Gordon and Leo didn't have ill will toward each other, and eventually, the vampires all ended up in a cluster while Leo and Gordon traded childhood stories about Ethan, much to Robert and Reggie's delight and Ethan's embarrassment.

Gordon would be staying at the den for a while, no longer in the cellar but still under observation. Eventually, however, he'd return to his apartment and remain part of Ethan's life.

Bash was happy for them.

Ethan did mention, once he'd escaped the "tales of Ethan's awkward years," that he wanted to visit Dave's grave when they could. And his mother's. Once those somber thoughts were said and set aside, Ethan nodded for Bash to follow him out of the living room, and they headed upstairs.

"I don't want to be away from everyone for too long," Ethan said along the way, "but your present is up here."

"Really?"

"Not *that*. Though that is definitely also on the table for later." He pulled Bash into their bedroom and had him stand centered facing the door to Ethan's closet.

"I hope you don't mind having to wait for your present," Bash said.

"You already got me something," Ethan countered. "The new art supplies and sketchpad."

"This is something extra that I just decided on. But I think it best saved for next week."

Next week meant it would fall on the night of the Cold Moon, and the importance of that wasn't lost on Ethan, who smiled. "I can wait. Now close your eyes."

Bash did so. He heard Ethan open the closet door and then knew Ethan had flipped some sort of switch to turn on lights, because he could see the brightness of red, green, and gold through his eyelids.

"Ta-da!" Ethan declared, and Bash opened them again.

The interior of the closet held a table that took up almost the entire space, displaying what Bash could only describe as a *Warhammer* Christmas village.

While the display itself had been painted, the figures had not, primed for painting and configured to fit the theme, but clearly left for Bash to paint himself.

"Preston wanted to set it up downstairs," Ethan said, "but that would have spoiled the surprise! Besides, I figure this way, your goal can be to finish painting them all before next Christmas, and then we can add it to our own Christmas village downstairs. I know you haven't had much time for your geeky pursuits lately, but I'm going to make sure you take time next year."

"It's perfect," Bash said, unintentionally echoing his brother's response to an engagement ring. He knew his voice was even a little choked as he added, "Thank you, Ethan."

"Everyone added touches, so it wasn't all me, but it helps not having to sleep sometimes."

Bash drew Ethan to him, gathering him in his arms so he could thank him properly with a kiss. "It's wonderful. So much so that I'd like to take advantage of that *other* gift you said was on the table."

"Later." Ethan chuckled. "But thank you."

"For what? Wanting sex or not yet giving you your other present?"

Ethan smacked Bash's chest but then leaned into him again and said seriously, "For what you chose to do *by the red moonlight*, and everything that came after."

They kissed, and maybe got a little heated while caught up in the moment, but eventually returned downstairs. Although Bash was fairly certain he heard some interesting noises coming from Deanna and Rio's bedroom before they made it to the landing.

Bash was glad Ethan didn't mind waiting for his real Christmas present, because he had something very special in mind, something he'd promised Ethan combined with something he owed him, and on Cold Moon's night, the third full moon they would spend together, he was going to give Ethan both.

Chapter 17

BY COLD *Moon's night*, Ethan thought, glancing through the shades of his office window as the sun began to set. He had a date with Bash to keep, and he'd done plenty of work today.

Bash had asked him before he returned to his private eye duties if he wanted a new location, given what had happened here, but Ethan loved this place and the effort Bash had made to give it to him. He didn't mind being reminded of what Alexa made him do, because it also reminded him of how much they'd overcome and made him think of Dave and the good times that outweighed the bad.

Since the sun was still partially out, Ethan fit his sunglasses onto his face before grabbing his bag and any files he might want to look over through the weekend—he was taking New Year's Eve off—and headed out for the quiet walk home.

It had been nice not having to be around someone at every moment of the day the past week compared to the week before, but he also sort of missed the added time he'd had with Bash. Being connected at the hip for so long made him even more eager to see Bash at the end of each day.

Alexandra Clarke's body had been found far from the tattoo parlor with nothing to point at Robert or any of the actual people involved, just as the assassin had promised. Ethan wasn't sure how he felt about things ending on this chapter of his life with planted evidence, given that's how he'd started down the road that led him to Centrus City, but every rule needed some exceptions, even if the law wouldn't see it that way.

Robert had given a good speech at the discovery of *Xandra*'s death, lauding her skills, her service to the city, and promising a crackdown on the criminals supposedly responsible, putting himself back into the good graces of the public after his scandal. For the most part.

"You may not like that I go hard in the bedroom, but you can't deny I'm also hard on crime."

Of course, part of the reason Bash had helped him get elected was that a Null was the perfect politician, liked and disliked in equal measure, and useful if Bash needed him. Having a vampire in office was still useful, but Robert was maybe becoming more liked than disliked now, which they'd decided to take as a blessing. So long as he didn't enthrall anyone without good reason or before first passing it by Bash and the circle.

They'd also made sure that the deputy mayor's assistant didn't see jail time for those doctored documents. He'd been proven innocent, but they didn't throw Xandra under the bus, since her being responsible might add suspicion on Robert concerning her death. It would just remain an unsolved mystery.

The sun was almost set once Ethan reached the den, meaning he was right on time to meet Bash and decided to slip in quietly so no one would delay him. Bash had told him to meet at dusk down in the cellar for his belated Christmas present. That area of their basement was finally in the process of being turned into the wine cellar Bash had always intended it to be, with the furniture and all signs that it had once been a vampire's cell removed. Gordon was staying upstairs now until he moved out.

There was also a nifty little spell Reggie had cast on the ceiling as a parting gift before he returned to Brookdale, creating the illusion of a skylight that showed the actual sky above. It made it a beautiful space that would make a nice getaway spot once Bash decided how he'd refurnish it and fill it with wine, having said he might add an armchair and bookshelves for a reading nook—or maybe a place to paint his minis.

Ethan could hear some of the household members in the kitchen, so he zipped into the cellar at vampire speed. The lights were on, and he expected to see Bash at the bottom, already waiting for him. He didn't appear to be there, though. Bash had told Ethan not to bother changing after work, so he'd tucked his jacket into the front closet with his sunglasses in the pocket, wearing nothing fancier than one of his work button-downs and a tie.

He'd almost expected to find a candlelit dinner set up inside, even if he couldn't join Bash in eating or drinking, but the cellar looked empty, the door left open to invite Ethan over its threshold, but with no other signs as to what Bash might be planning.

The light was on inside too, but it was dim, leaving most of the room cast in ambient glow from the magical skylight. The Cold Moon was already out, shining down on Ethan and growing brighter as the sun finished setting.

Which was when he noticed something new in the cellar with him, as the moonlight shimmered across metal against the wall.

Shackles connected to chains hung from the ceiling.

The scent of honey-dipped sex was Ethan's only warning before he sensed a presence rushing in behind him. He smiled, keeping his back turned to allow the *trap* to play out as Bash wanted.

Bash slammed him into the wall with a growl at his ear and warm breath tickling the base of his neck. "You know what happens when someone foolishly trespasses on a werewolf's territory, don't you?" He was half changed, at least to Stage Two, given the grumble in his voice and faint brush of fur where he touched Ethan—and also naked.

"Death on sight?" Ethan asked, trying to put a tremble in his voice, but it was difficult to hide his smile.

Definitely naked, he thought, as the hard line of Bash's chest and thighs and cock pressed against him. "Unless you can prove to please me other ways."

"I'll do anything."

"You will. And I will take everything I want." He spun Ethan around and slammed him back again. The door to the cellar was closed now—hopefully with a "do not disturb" sign—and Ethan's cock throbbed.

Best present ever.

The primal look in Bash's eyes, fangs glinting, a curl at his lips, naked body lined in beautiful silver fur, even more silvery under the Cold Moon's light, was as enticing on its own as Bash fitting the shackles onto Ethan's wrists. The chains were set high enough that the binding forced Ethan up onto his toes. Bash hadn't even undressed him yet, though he had a feeling that would change in swift, brutal fashion.

Bash yanked Ethan forward with a grasp at his tie. "I think I'll fuck you raw to start, no prep, then again with my cum as lube, and again and again, until it's dribbling down your thighs and you're stuffed full to bursting."

Fuck, Bash needed to talk dirty more often—and yes, do all those things.

Ethan tried to play into the fantasy, to make his expression fearful as he begged, "Please."

"Oh, you'll be saying that many times before the night is over. And if you satisfy me, maybe I'll let you come when I'm through with you, and the best you can hope for afterward is being kept down here for me to use again any time I want."

"*Fuck*," Ethan couldn't help saying aloud, practically squirming as precome soaked through his underwear and slacks, dribbling down his thighs already like that promise of several rounds of release.

The knot of his tie was undone with a few tugs from a single claw, the article tossed behind Bash before he lashed out with both clawed hands to tear Ethan's shirt open. The scratches left behind were a pleasant sting for a vampire, barely bubbling with any red before they healed. One less shirt for Ethan, though. Oh well.

Almost acting offended by the shirt's continued presence, with part of the tails still tucked, Bash tore it open again, until it was two shredded halves, baring Ethan's chest and part of his shoulders.

"You please me so far, but let's see how you taste."

"Ah!" Ethan hadn't expected a gentle kiss but wasn't prepared for the ferocious bite into his neck, right at his pulse point, harsh enough to make his knees grow weak. He sagged, struggling to keep lifted on his toes, and felt an ache in his shoulders and a stronger pulse between his legs.

Bash licked long and hot at where he'd bitten Ethan, the tender lapping helping to heal there too. He tore Ethan's belt off next and shredded his slacks and underwear more swiftly than the shirt. When Bash plucked Ethan's shoes and socks free, having his bare toes to balance on was actually easier than the toes of his loafers.

The beginnings of a growl rumbled through Bash as he looked upon Ethan's naked body. "It seems you like being captive and roughly treated." He dragged the back of one clawed hand down Ethan's neck and chest, slowly turning the hand as it neared Ethan's hips so the claw points dragged over the skin and threatened to prick his shaft when they reached between his thighs.

"N-no, I...."

"No need to pretend. Maybe you trespassed on my territory because you want this." Bash pressed up against Ethan, and with his captive hoisted taller than usual, Bash's cock slid right between Ethan's thighs beneath the base of his sac and bobbed upward in greeting.

Ethan shook his head, falling into the performance easier now, with his arousal growing. He fixed his face into a desperate, fearful display of hidden want and bit his lip.

Bash hefted him up the wall, with hands beneath his thighs to spread his legs apart. "Moonlight," he whispered with a nuzzle at Ethan's cheek, and Ethan understood, not that he had any intention of using a safe word to escape what Bash had planned.

He nodded, and not a second later, Bash had his head aligned and slammed upward into Ethan's dry hole from tip to base, utterly impaling him.

Ethan whined, mouth dropping open from the shock and sudden fullness. He loved the burn he could take as a vampire, relished it in a way he never could have when human, and swallowed Bash in deeper with a familiar stretch and inhale of all that glorious girth.

There was no need to wait for Ethan to adjust, and it better suited the game that they didn't. With Ethan lifted up the wall, the ache on his shoulders soothed as Bash pounded into him with the sort of brutal rhythm that would have bruised him in his old life. The wall dug into his skull and shoulders with every thrust, harder, faster, chasing an initial orgasm for Bash that Ethan knew would not be the last, far from it, because Bash clearly intended to do just as he'd promised.

He came with no attention given to Ethan's weeping cock, spilling inside him with a flood of heat. But he didn't stop or pause for even a breath. He kept pumping into Ethan's spent hole, eased by the natural lube, and throbbed larger inside him.

Ethan's eyes snapped to Bash's face. He was shifting further, beyond Stage Two, with more fur sprouting, body growing taller, bigger, just like his cock felt bigger, and the structure of his face changed too— into the snout and maw of a fully shifted werewolf.

Ethan howled, head dropped back at the bright full moon, as if he was the werewolf between them, because *fuck*, in this form, Bash was big. He felt massive, putting blinding pressure on Ethan's insides.

Then Bash slowly, agonizingly so, slid out, letting Ethan feel every inch of him, to be certain he understood how much there was, because the retreat never seemed to end. Bash kept pulling out, more and more, until Ethan seriously couldn't believe he'd taken that much, only for his vision to go white when Bash slammed it all back in.

Ethan went limp, given over to the chains and Bash's hold on his hips. If he could have reached down to touch his stomach, he imagined Bash up in his rib cage, he was so full. He moaned, as long and drawn out as that slow slide of Bash out of him, because holy Christ, it felt amazing.

Bash pulled out again, just as slow, slower, like he wanted Ethan to experience as much torture from the loss of him before he viciously rammed in again.

"*F-f-fuck...* oh fuck, please."

Bash went even slower, and the thrust back in caused Ethan's head to bounce off the wall.

"Please... please...."

Slower.

"Fuck, oh *fuck*, I can't, *please*."

Slower, and so ruthless with the next slam in that Ethan thought the chains might rip from the ceiling.

He sobbed, feeling the wetness of actual tears on his cheeks. How Bash could go even slower, Ethan couldn't fathom, but he managed.

A growl rumbled from Bash on the next sharp thrust. Ethan was being fucked raw by a werewolf and loving every second. He rarely got to appreciate Bash's Stage Three form, since the few times he'd seen it were when he was first shown the stages in this very cellar, the other times during fights, to be discarded as soon as the battle ended. To truly see him—while having his mammoth cock inside him—was mind-boggling.

Bash came a few slams later, and it felt like two, three times as much cum as the first round.

Ethan's cock still hadn't been touched.

Bash didn't stop this time either. Ethan could feel the fresh release spilling out of him like Bash had pledged, oozing from his tender, harshly used hole, even as Bash continued to use that cum as lube to fuck him again. He was still all werewolf and didn't bother thrusting after a while but gripped Ethan's hips harder to pump him up and down on his dick. Ethan was a rag doll at Bash's mercy, a cock sleeve to be used and abused.

Why the fuck hadn't they done this before?

Ethan's own cock ached to be allowed release. He didn't know how he hadn't come yet from the intensity of Bash's harsh treatment and the insistent slams on his prostate. His cock must be in shock, insides overstimulated so that all he could do was take and take as Bash continued to relentlessly fuck him.

In his stupor, Ethan gazed up at the full moon again and wept, seeing the first signs of new snowfall, even with the moon glowing through the clouds that had formed. He loved this man so damn much, and they were definitely doing this again in the future if Ethan survived the first time.

He almost thought he hadn't when the third round finished with so much cum flooding into him that the excess had to be creating a pool beneath him on the floor.

Finally, Bash softened, but when he slid out, he did so with the slow, agonizing speed of the first time he'd let Ethan feel the breadth of this cock. When it was out, Bash dropped Ethan's hips and let him hang, and hang he did, because he couldn't possibly try to lift himself onto his toes when his legs felt like Jell-O.

He was raw and empty now, his hole and cheeks and thighs absolutely drenched in cum. He may not need to breathe, but he panted regardless, so spent and yet still so hard and ready for more.

Bash roared with an Alpha's command for him to meet his gaze, monstrous and glorious, as he dropped to his knees.

Ethan tensed, toes digging into the floor now as he squirmed at the sight of that maw drawing closer to his throbbing cock. He wouldn't. He couldn't. But even if he couldn't suck Ethan down his throat with so many sharp teeth in the way, he could lap out with that long, textured tongue.

It coiled around Ethan's cock almost from head to base, for a wet, hot lick.

"Ohhhh…." Ethan went limp again.

Bash licked and licked and twirled that werewolf tongue until Ethan was sopping and so close to coming. Claws returned to his hips to steady him as Bash kept going and going, but it was when he licked a bit of his own cum from Ethan's thighs that Ethan spilled, right onto Bash's tongue.

Fuck. It felt as if just as much cum had left Ethan as the amount oozing out of him, and he honestly felt dizzy.

Bash leapt to his feet, hoisted Ethan up the wall, and slammed back into him.

"Fuck!"

Bash was hard again. He was fucking hard *again* and began to mercilessly repeat the last performance. Ethan could do nothing but take it, the intensity even greater after finally being allowed to come. He felt his mind drift away, lost in a sea of bliss, as his werewolf boyfriend fucked him through a cumload of previous rounds until he'd swear he saw God in the face of that moon looking down on them, curtained by the falling snow.

After Bash came a final time, he shrank from his Stage Three form all the way to human and sucked Ethan into his mouth properly until Ethan came again too. Ethan's whole body tingled, rendering him useless for anything other than small whimpers from orgasm aftershocks.

Bash stood, gazing at him with affection pushing through the fantasy of a brutal captor.

"Did I... please you?" Ethan asked, smiling again from sheer dopamine overdose. "Will you keep me instead of killing me?"

"I think I might. Especially because...." Bash cupped Ethan's cheek with a gentleness he hadn't yet displayed during the performance and leaned in close enough to rest their foreheads together. "I love you, Ethan."

Ethan gasped. All this, and Bash managed to outdo himself even more by beating Ethan to what he'd intended to say again himself. "I love you. I love you so much." Ethan strained to capture Bash's lips, and he wasn't denied.

They kissed and kissed, while Bash opened the shackles to ease Ethan from the wall and held him close. Though Ethan's face was sticky from tears, and his lower half drenched in shared fluids, he'd never felt more at ease than under the Cold Moon's light.

"I'M EXPECTED to wear this?"

"It looks good on you! And it was a gift from Bari."

Bash had a difficult time considering it a "gift" when the note it came with read: *Because I hate seeing our body look basic.*

The shirt wasn't terrible but was an altogether too bright shade of mint for Bash's tastes, with one almost entirely black sleeve that branched outward with floral-like curls and coils toward the buttons, where the designs got sparser until they stopped, leaving the other side of the shirt plain. Very Bari rather than Bash, even with darker green accents on the underside of the collar and cuffs. Bash had refused the accompanying black brocade pants.

"I like it," Ethan said, plastering himself against Bash, which was a much better something to have on him. Ethan also wore a gift from Bari, his shirt peach floral with accents in green that, while it did match nicely with Ethan's red hair and green eyes, seemed a bit too purposely intended to match Bash. Couples did not need to match.

"Yours looks better."

"We can switch."

"No."

Ethan giggled. "Then stop complaining. It's New Year's Eve! And you told Bari you'd wear it."

"He and Jay aren't even going to be here."

"I have a feeling he'll know if you break your promise."

He would. Even before he inherited their mother's Seer abilities, he would have.

"Come on," Ethan chided, but at least he kissed Bash before leading him from the bedroom.

The den was less full than it had been, back to the circle six, plus Ethan, Rio, Jesse, three rodents, and Ethan's father, who wouldn't be staying for much longer. Robert was still there so much of the time, however, he may as well have moved in too. Leo visited often enough, but at least he'd gone home to Glenwood.

Bash and Ethan froze in the hallway. Deanna and Rio had also entered it—and Deanna was wearing a dress. Had Bash ever seen her wearing a dress?

"Shove it," she said before comments could be made. It had a "little black dress" vibe but with a gothic flare, including a see-through shrug with bell sleeves.

Rio was wearing a floral shirt too. Bash's twin could clearly not be stopped until he'd given wardrobe makeovers to the entire circle. Heavens knew how Jay's pack was faring and whether Bari had risked attempting to dress Maximus yet.

"You look great!" Ethan said.

"Doesn't she?" Rio gushed.

Deanna might have blushed but hid it by dragging Rio ahead of them down the stairs. As they passed, Bash had the strangest sensation of a tickle in his gut.

Must be his phone buzzing.

Take pictures! Bari had texted, along with a selfie of him and Jay smiling wide—and the engagement ring conspicuously managing to make it into frame. Bash showed the picture to Ethan, who laughed.

Bash also had a message from the Alpha of Metro City, who'd finally admitted she sent the assassin and wanted to plan a visit for early next year to confirm all she'd been told. Fine by Bash. It seemed the truth of shifter origins would spread through the packs and cities after all, but any more surprises or takeover attempts and Bash wasn't going to be cordial.

The Christmas decorations were still up, added to with a few streamers and signs in blue and silver in honor of New Year's, which clashed horribly with the Christmas colors. Nell breezed by as they entered the living room, wearing the dress she'd been given at Christmas and twice as many bangles and other adornments as usual.

"Happy New Year's Eve!" she called.

"The *hell*?" Deanna barked ahead of them.

Siobhan was dressed like any other day, in comfortable pants and a black tank top. "What? We didn't specify a dress code."

"Even the alley cat is wearing a dress shirt, for fuck's sake!" Deanna hooked a thumb across the room.

Luke was indeed looking rather smart in a button-down, although Bash was pretty sure there were cartoon cats hidden in the pattern. It was probably the best Preston could manage, himself wearing a more classic white button-down and black vest. Even Jesse was in a party dress.

Music played, and snacks and drinks had been set out for those who could imbibe them. As for those who couldn't, Robert was chatting with Gordon.

"I'm just saying, 'you only live once' doesn't apply to us! You're on round two, Gordy. You should be getting out there." Robert patted Gordon's shoulder.

"I'd say round three." Gordon chuckled. "But I don't think my first act of trying to return to a semblance of normal life should be entering the dating pool."

"I know plenty of eligible women. Men too—"

"Robert, leave my dad alone," Ethan said. He and Bash joined their cluster, and someone—possibly Siobhan—pushed a glass of champagne into Bash's hand. "I thought you'd be ditching us for the Brookdale circle's New Year's party to see Reggie."

"I can do both! Gotta love that yo-yo trick of your brother's, Bain." Robert tapped his wrist, careful to not do so more than once. Apparently his and Reggie's runes now connected to each other for frequent rendezvous. The spell couldn't send someone back to where they'd come from after a trip, but both being vampires and Reggie being a witch made it fairly easy to travel between cities. "And come on, Rookie, I'm just trying to get your pops to loosen up a little."

"What's important to me," Gordon said, "is that, despite my best efforts to ruin things, what I really wanted was for my son to be happy, and he is." He nodded gratefully at Bash. "It's just a shame we can't share in the champagne."

"I've been testing that." Robert looped an arm around Gordon's shoulders, and Bash saw Ethan shake his head at what was to come. "All done smart, thrall used for brief nibbles on people who are then healed and made to forget, blah, blah, rules, but feeding from drunk people totally tingles your tongue and gives you that same old rush. Just get your Alpha to knock back a glass at midnight, Rookie, at the same time you're knocking back him, and you'll see. Then *we* each need the same." He squeezed Gordon against him and called out to the larger gathering. "Who's volunteering?"

"Back off, bitey," Deanna grumbled. "I only ever gave blood bag donations. No fangs are ever piercing this neck, or mine are gonna rip out your throat."

"Anyone?" Robert pointedly ignored her. "Anyone at all?"

Between having Ethan at his side and his chosen family all around them—even if Bari and Jay were enjoying their own party a city away—Bash had to admit, the way this year had turned out seemed just about perfect.

"You know, it's funny," Rio said, "but with that 'fifth born' line in the prophecy, I kept thinking someone might end up pregnant."

Deanna laughed but seemed to have a twinkle in her eye. After all, Bash had eventually warned her about what Reggie said.

There came that tickle again, and when Bash glanced at Ethan, seeing a growing smile on Ethan's face, he knew they were both sensing the same thing, almost like another *Focus* was in the room.

Which was why the stomach drop that assaulted Bash next felt like a slow-motion nausea attack, as if all sound went low and garbled and everything might as well have frozen—the universe ensuring he knew something else was coming.

Bash looked at Ethan again, whose face betrayed he'd felt the same. It wasn't like the slowly encroaching dread from before their vision of Alexa's demise, but it was a warning that the consequences of all they'd been through, the decisions they'd made since Halloween, still had fallout yet to come.

The doorbell rang.

They weren't expecting anyone, given it was New Year's, after dark, and not a place where casual callers came around. Bash and Ethan must have been broadcasting their concerns because everyone turned to them in a moment's quiet, before Deanna broke it, saying:

"What the fuck now?"

She followed Bash and Ethan to the door, everyone else hovering near the entrance into the foyer to be certain this wasn't a defend to the death sort of surprise. A peer out the peephole showed... not what Bash expected, but he was still on guard when he opened the door.

The young woman was dressed simply and looked like she could use a shower and a meal, with a single knapsack slung over her shoulder and a wariness in her eyes that betrayed she was as nervous as them. One whiff toward Ethan helped her relax, and Bash didn't need to breathe deeply himself to know why.

A vampire.

She looked young, not that that meant much, maybe twenty when she'd been turned. She seemed gaunt, like she'd been barely getting by feeding, and Bash worried her eyes might be amber or closer to red if they changed from the glassy gray they appeared to be now. She didn't give off any threatening aura but was hunched and fussing with her hands.

"I don't know if this is something your kind does, but given what I've heard about your pack and the company you keep, I had to try." She glanced again at Ethan for a long, held moment and then focused on Bash. "Asylum?"

That they no longer killed vampires on sight but had welcomed several into their pack, and knew others from surrounding cities, was clearly spreading.

"Get in here," Deanna called between them, a far cry from how she would have reacted a few months ago. "Right, boss? It's a full-blown pandemic."

That had always been the fear, that vampires were a plague and even one was too dangerous to let live inside a pack's city, but with that proven to be true only as much as any human or shifter was a threat, it didn't feel right to turn her away.

"Come in," Bash agreed. "If you need a drink, we can provide, but this is expected to be a bit of a rowdy New Year's Eve party, just to warn you." He opened the door wider to admit her.

That feeling that something was coming wasn't just her. It was her as the start to a very likely flood. They'd changed the game. Vampires were welcome, and any that might still be out there, not killed by other packs or hiding in small towns and far-off places, had somewhere to go.

"Do you think this is what Alexa meant?" Ethan quietly questioned once their guest had been led upstairs to settle in. "That she still won? A vampire is mayor. There are vampires in multiple cities with close ties to those packs' circles, and now this, asylum, with more vampires coming out of the woodwork. In some ways, it is a return to the past."

"For better or worse," Bash said, "even if this was in part what Alexa wanted, she's not here to see it. I for one plan to carve out our future exactly the way we want." He kissed Ethan to seal the promise.

So they had a new boarder for the time being. Their abilities would warn them if something bigger was on the way—usually—and until that happened, Bash wasn't going to let anything interrupt ringing in a new year.

"Ready for the countdown?" Ethan asked later, just before midnight, with the others all clustered around them in a loud din, their new guest included, and with Bari and Jay on a video call showing their circle in the background.

As Bash stole another early kiss from Ethan before the inevitable one when the countdown hit zero, he wondered what their next prophecy might bring, what the next year might bring, when there was no riddle of an unknown Halloween night to haunt him, like it had for ten long years.

For now, he just hoped to spend the next full moon and many more after it in the same arms as he was tonight.

"I'm ready."

"Ten... nine...."

Keep reading for an excerpt from
Acsquidentally in Love
by K.L. Hiers!

Chapter 1.

SLOANE BEAUMONT sighed, regarding the cheesy Halloween decorations scattered around the house with a disgusted pout. They were absolutely hideous. Green pimpled witches leered at him while twisted jack-o'-lanterns grinned brightly alongside nimble skeletons dancing across the walls.

The worst were the tentacled cartoon fiends stretched out on the mantle, and Sloane smiled wearily as he recited their names, "Yeris, Salgumel, Galmelthar, Shartorath, Bestrath...."

All old gods of an ancient faith, reduced to ugly cardboard cutouts at a Halloween party.

He could still remember his mother pressing jasmine flowers into his pillow after a nightmare for Salgumel to bring him more pleasant dreams. His father would wear amber when they went fishing so Yeris would bless them with a good catch. On the rare occasion that his parents had a fight, they would burn lavender incense and pray to Shartorath.

Up until their untimely deaths, they had always been dedicated followers.

They had been Sages.

"What's wrong?" a concerned voice asked, snapping Sloane out of his thoughts.

"Sorry," he said, smiling when he saw it was his best friend and the host of the party, Milo Evans, peering worriedly at him. "Just not really in the mood."

"It's Halloween!" Milo cheered, clapping a hand on Sloane's shoulder. He was broad and bearded, dressed up as Han Solo for the evening's festivities. "This is, like, a super cool holiday for you, right?"

"Something like that," Sloane replied with a strained expression.

It wasn't easy for people to understand. All of Sloane's life, his parents were the only Sages he had ever known. The religion was considered archaic, a joke to some, and had made him the target of relentless childhood bullying. Sages worshipped gods they believed descended from the stars, their rituals structured around the seasons and the movements of celestial bodies.

Sloane's mother had told him the gods all went to sleep ages ago, and that was why their following had begun to dwindle. People no longer believed in Azaethoth or Gronoch, even though all of their gifts to mankind remained.

Gifts like the power of magic.

Most people believed magic came from the natural world now, explaining it through science and attributing it to unseen energies that could be measured within the elements. If there was a spiritual attachment, it was given to the new god, the Lord of Light.

When the old ways began to fade, the Lucian religion took its place. Instead of dozens of deities, there was only one to appease, and it was now the dominant faith for practically the entire planet.

The Lord of Light condemned the old gods as blasphemous and obscene, and Sloane remembered all too well when Lucian children would tell him how he was going to burn in some fiery pit for being a nasty sinner. Even as an adult, it was isolating. Granted, no one was telling him that he was going to roast in holy flames for all of eternity, but it was hard for anyone else to understand when he got upset.

He couldn't explain to Milo that this all felt wrong to him. This wasn't Halloween; this was Dhankes. This holiday was about praying to the dead, cooking feasts, and giving thanks to the gods, not dressing up like robots and cowboys while gorging on candy.

"Is it because of your parents?" Milo asked hesitantly. "Their death day is right after Halloween, yeah?"

"Yup," Sloane said with a grim smile. "It's been almost twenty years since they were murdered, and I still…." He paused, shifting awkwardly. "The holidays are always hard for me, but especially this one. The dead are supposed to be able to hear our prayers tonight, and I keep thinking—okay, this one, *this* will be the Dhankes that I can finally tell them I caught the guy who killed them. And another one goes by and another and I still haven't found him yet."

"Never gonna give up, are you?" Milo smiled affectionately.

"Nope. I don't care what the police say. The case is not closed. It wasn't a magical ritual gone wrong. I know what I saw."

"Crazy guy in a robe with a glowing dagger?" Milo recalled.

"Yes," Sloane replied begrudgingly.

"Look," Milo said gently, "I believe that you believe you saw whatever you saw. But I've gone over the case, like, a million times with you, remember?"

"Before I got fired?" Sloane cringed.

"Using department resources without permission can kinda do that. But there was no evidence, magical or otherwise, that anyone else had ever been inside the house. I'm CSI, remember? I should know."

"So my testimony was just the rambling of a hysterical child," Sloane grumbled.

"Hey," Milo said, holding up his hands defensively. "I didn't say that. I just mean… maybe it's time to let it rest, you know?"

Sloane scrubbed his hand over his face with a long sigh. He'd put everything he had into getting justice for his parents, but he was no closer now than he'd been when he first started.

"You're gonna go home, aren't you?" Milo asked forlornly.

"Probably," Sloane said with a grimace. "Look, I'm really sorry. I appreciate the invite and everything—"

"Seriously, does talking about your parents and all this Halloween stuff, uhm, bother you? You can tell me and I will totally shut up if it'll make you stay."

"I can't have a serious talk with you while you're dressed like Han Solo." Sloane laughed, playfully tugging at Milo's vest. He knew his friend didn't mean to offend him, but he wasn't in the mood for a heart-to-heart.

Not tonight.

"Hey! Wait until you see my date!"

"Slave Leia?" Sloane guessed.

"I'm gonna marry this woman." Milo sighed dreamily. "I know it's only been a few weeks, but Lynnette is seriously, like, the perfect geek lady. And hey, she's got a pretty good-lookin' brother. He's coming with her. Just saying!"

"Mmm, planning double dates already?"

"I'm merely suggesting that you wait, like, five minutes for them to get here, have some delicious punch, and meet him," Milo pleaded, giving Sloane his absolute best puppy dog face. "Pretty pleeease?"

"Ugh, come on."

"Look, man. I worry about you," Milo said, dropping his voice again. "All you do is work. When was the last time you had a freakin' date?"

"Ehhh, probably not since we were in college?" Sloane admitted bashfully, which was over four years ago. "I'll meet this guy, but I'm not making any promises."

"You'll love him," Milo assured him. "I gotta go check on the punch and make sure it's alcoholic enough to provide the proper amount of lubrication for social interaction."

"Sounds like fun." Sloane chuckled, patting his friend's back. "I'll come help you test it, how's that?"

"Best idea ever."

Sloane downed three cups of heavily spiked punch and was already working on his fourth when he finally noticed the time. It was almost eleven, and he still had a candle to light before midnight.

Lynnette had appeared in full slave Leia regalia, golden bikini and all. Introductions were friendly, though brief. She was very beautiful and gave Sloane hope that perhaps her brother would be as well. She said her brother was running late but promised he would be there soon. All of Milo's attention had been focused on her ever since.

Sloane couldn't stop looking at his watch, deciding that "soon" had already come and gone several times over. He couldn't wait any longer. He decided to make a quick exit and darted toward the door.

So speedy was he in his escape attempt, he accidentally smacked right into a guy in a devil costume on his way inside.

"Oh, hey!" The devil laughed, grabbing Sloane's shoulders to steady him. "You okay?"

"Shit! Sorry!" Sloane sputtered, blinking stupidly as his eyes focused on the most gorgeous man he had ever seen. He was tall and athletic with a mop of curly red hair. Sloane was immediately lost in bright green eyes that twinkled beautifully and bewitched by a killer smile that accompanied an absolutely flawless face.

He'd blame the drinks, but this guy was perfect. The fact that he was dressed as the devil seemed fitting because Sloane definitely thought this was a fellow worth selling his soul for.

"I mean it, you okay?" the devil asked sweetly, holding on to Sloane as if he might still topple over.

"Fine!" Sloane replied quickly. "Just, uhm, trying to get out of here. I'm so sorry!"

"What's the hurry?" the devil asked with a shy smirk.

"I have to go light a candle for my parents," Sloane said, hoping the unusual answer would prompt the stranger to let go of him, even though having his hands on him was very nice.

"Oh! You're a Sage?" the devil asked instead, obviously interested.

"My parents were," Sloane explained, surprised that the stranger didn't seem put off yet. "Very devout. I'm not really anything, but I still make sure to light a candle and leave out some food…."

"Make sure that candle is lit in a doorway facing west." The devil chuckled. "I have a great recipe for colcannon if you're interested. Guaranteed to please the gods."

"Wait, *you're* a Sage?" Sloane blinked in disbelief.

"Mm-hm," the devil said with a little smile, finally letting go. "My whole family is Sagittarian. Sages for countless generations."

"Wow," Sloane gushed, honestly excited to meet another person who shared his family's faith. "You must hate Halloween, right? It's such a freakin' rip-off!"

"I prefer to think of it as a 'very heavily inspired' holiday," he said carefully. "People don't mean to be so offensive, and it keeps traditions alive that are thousands of years old. The meaning is lost, yes, but the act itself becomes immortal. There is something beautiful in that."

"You really think so?" Sloane was still skeptical.

"Of course. Sure, lighting up carved gourds isn't quite the same as lighting a candle to guide the dead back home, but the ritual persists to this day."

"It's a night for the dead, and we all still light candles," Sloane mused.

"See?"

"I suppose I never thought of it that way…."

"And hey," the devil said, gesturing to his costume. "The dressing up is pretty fun! Who are you supposed to be? Let me guess—Chad Warwick, *American Horror Story*?"

"What? No!" Sloane laughed, fussing with his hair and glancing down at his sweater and jeans. "I'm not actually dressed up as anyone. I don't, you know, do that. Although I have been compared to Zachary Quinto a few times…."

"Gives you a lot of options for costumes," the devil said with a grin. "You could pull off a pretty awesome Spock. Just a thought, maybe for next year."

"I will take that into consideration." Sloane chuckled, surprised at how much he was smiling. "Maybe the Halloween traditions aren't all bad, but the little cartoon old gods are still really ugly."

"No argument there." The devil laughed with his pleasant, smooth voice. He extended his hand, saying, "I'm Lochlain Fields, Lynnette's brother."

"Oh! You're Lochlain! Hi, Lochlain!" Sloane replied dopily as they shook hands. "I'm Sloane Beaumont. It's nice to meet you."

"It's nice to meet you too," Lochlain said, blushing faintly, probably from Sloane's exuberance. "Sorry I'm so late. I had something to take care of before the party. Milo has told me a lot about you."

"I hope all good things." Sloane realized his face was starting to heat up too. Lochlain was really attractive, and he struggled to find something to say to fill the silence. "Right, so, Lynnette is a Sage too? Milo didn't tell me."

"Religion isn't something Lynnette discusses very openly. Most people assume she's Lucian. Uh, so, Milo said you used to work together? Are you in magical forensics too?"

"Not exactly." Sloane chuckled nervously. "I'm a private investigator now, but I used to be a detective with the Archersville Police Department. I was mostly doing cases for magic enforcement."

"Taking DNA samples from voodoo dolls? Chasing down ancient cursed objects?"

"Mostly chasing down unlicensed magic users," Sloane said, shrugging. "Not really that glamorous."

Just as being licensed to drive a car or own a gun was the law of the land, anyone who wielded magic was required to register and pay for a license. There was also rigorous testing to determine what discipline a person would be registered under. Sages attributed the different types of magic to their various gods with dozens of possibilities. Using the structure of elements provided by the Lord of Light's teachings, the modern system designated a person's abilities as fire, air, earth, or water.

This was too elementary for Sages, whose beliefs couldn't reduce magic to such simple categories. An element like water possessed too many varying presentations—like ice for Yeris, the god of the ocean and its freezing depths, or healing for Galmethar, a god associated with the life-giving substance for his kindness and restorative abilities.

There was also a very rare discipline that encompassed all the elements, including very advanced spiritual abilities, that the Lucians called divine. The Sages called it starlight, a power they believed was given by the very first god and father of the universe, Great Azaethoth himself.

"I take it you're registered, then?" Lochlain asked curiously.

"Yeah. Ever since I was a little kid," Sloane replied dutifully, trying not to sound like he was bragging. He had shown a natural skill in magic from a very young age. "I was five, actually."

"Really?" Lochlain was clearly impressed. "And what discipline did a five-year-old have a proficiency in?"

"Well—" Sloane paused, smirking as he answered. "—as my mother would say, I was touched by starlight."

"Blessed by Great Azaethoth himself, very nice." Lochlain nodded, seeming even more impressed, as that gift was revered as the most powerful of them all. "I'm blessed by Yeris's Tears. So is my sister."

"Water," Sloane said, noting how a Lucian would explain Yeris's blessings. "That's what you're registered as?"

"Mmm. Not quite," Lochlain said mysteriously, a bashful smile curling his lips.

"Wait. You're not licensed?" Sloane gasped loudly, quickly lowering his voice. "Seriously? You know that's crazy illegal!"

"Only if you get caught," Lochlain said playfully.

"Lynnette is unlicensed too? Wait. Is she?"

"We're Sages," Lochlain replied with a smirk. "I bet your parents weren't registered either. Magic isn't meant to fall within some ill-constructed government regulations. It's a gift from the gods, our natural right as descendants of Azaethoth."

"My parents *were* registered"—Sloane pouted—"although I know they didn't like it, especially my mother. They didn't use much magic at home that I remember. Mostly stones or herbs, uhm. But seriously, you know that's super dangerous."

"Maybe I'm a dangerous sort of guy," Lochlain teased, although the way he was blushing made it hard to take him seriously.

"You're really a rogue witch?"

"Maybe I'm just a rogue," Lochlain replied slyly. "Why? Gonna arrest me, Sloane?"

Or just dying to get some cuffs on you, thought Sloane's alcohol-riddled brain.

"I think I can keep a secret," Sloane said with a shy grin. Then he glanced at the time and exclaimed, "Shit, I'm gonna be late! I really have to go, but it's been super great talking to you."

"Would you like to go out some time?" Lochlain blurted like he was afraid he'd lose his chance.

"What? Like on a date?" Sloane smiled brightly, trying not to sound too excited.

"Exactly like a date."

"Wow, yes, absolutely!" Sloane said, fishing out his wallet and offering one of his cards. "Here."

"Sloane Beaumont, private investigator," Lochlain read out loud, smirking as he traced the symbol stamped in the corner. "You have the Sage's Cross on your card?"

"My mother said it would bring me luck," Sloane said with a little shrug.

The Sage's Cross was an arrow tilted skyward, representing the Sagittarius constellation. The Sages believed those stars led to a hidden place called Zebulon, the home in the heavens where the gods were said to have descended from.

"I agree, because I think a lucky someone is gonna get a phone call tomorrow," Lochlain said. "You have yourself a good night, Sloane."

"Bye, Lochlain. Yeah. Good night!"

"Night. And hey! Happy Dhankes."

"Happy Dhankes." Sloane laughed, waving as he left, head held high.

He hadn't connected with someone in a long time, especially not someone so gorgeous, and yet who was also somehow as awkward as Sloane was with his flirting.

As he cranked up his car, he knew he was a little too drunk to drive, closing his eyes and coughing into his hands. All of the alcohol in his system magically came up in a neat and tidy little ball of liquid, floating in his palms. It was a handy little spell he had learned when he was in college.

Sloane rolled down his window and chucked it outside, not able to shake his happy smile the whole drive over to his office. He didn't like going home to an empty apartment, and an offering to the gods could be anywhere personal. Right as he was about to pull in, however, he realized he had nothing to offer.

Making a quick turn, he doubled back to an all-night grocery store and grabbed a blueberry pie. He hauled butt back onto the road, hurrying to make it to his office again before midnight. After letting himself in, he quickly searched his desk for a candle. He knew which direction west was and set the candle in one of his windows. It was supposed to be in a doorway, but his door was on the wrong side, so this would have to do.

Sloane lit the candle with a snap of his fingers, reciting quietly, "Though souls stir in the slumber of stars, breathless but bright, surrender forgotten flesh and dream once more."

He stood back, watching the flame catch the wick and cast a somber glow around the room. He picked up the pie and left it out in the hallway with a mumbled, "Hope the old gods like blueberry."

His mother would have scolded him for using any baked good that wasn't made from scratch, and his father probably would have told him that blueberries were totally offensive to the gods somehow. Thinking of his parents, having lit that candle more for them than for anyone else, made him suddenly miss them with a great aching sorrow.

He made sure the door was locked and returned to his desk, pulling out a bottle of rum from the bottom drawer. He wished he didn't have to start over after cleaning up for the drive, but he needed to drink again to cure his sober state of mind. This was going to be another holiday without them, one more Dhankes where he couldn't pray to them and tell them he'd found their killer. Milo's suggestion to let it go made his heart ache. He had already sacrificed so much, he couldn't possibly give up now.

It was miserable. It was hard. And by all the gods, it was lonely.

Allowing himself to feel a flutter of interest when he glanced at his phone, Sloane wondered if Lochlain really would call him tomorrow. It had been so long since he'd gone out with anyone, maybe it was time to try and do something for himself.

Immediately feeling guilty for even considering it, he once again wished his parents were with him, if only to tell him what to do, if he should finally give up and live his life. He watched the candle burn, tears glistening in his eyes. The flame flickered briefly, and he hoped it was somehow them telling him everything would be okay.

The flame flickered again, but Sloane was certain he was reading too much into things.

Smiling sadly, he drowned his sorrows in the rum until his head hit his desk and he passed out into a deep sleep. He slept there all night, waking to a curious chewing sound. Groggily lifting his head, he was startled to see Lochlain sitting in front of him, eating the blueberry pie.

"What… what are you doing here?" Sloane asked, jerking up and rubbing his eyes. He swore he had locked his office door. "Did you think I wouldn't answer if you called?" He laughed lightly.

Lochlain kept munching, pulling out Sloane's business card and laying it on the desk between them. He tapped the Sage's Cross as if that was a sufficient answer and went back to eating.

Sloane frowned, looking over Lochlain carefully. Something about him seemed different, but he couldn't quite place it.

He was also horribly hungover, wishing he had been in the right fraternity to learn some anti-hangover magic. His sobering spell was useless at this point since his body had already absorbed all of the alcohol. Ugh.

Maybe he was imagining it, but there was a wicked shimmer in Lochlain's eyes that he hadn't seen before. The way he sat in the chair with his legs kicked over the arm was full of youthful mischief and yet totally commanding at the same time.

He exuded confidence, perched smugly as if he owned every inch of the office and everything in it, Sloane included, which wasn't at all like the man in the devil costume Sloane met last night. He was dressed more casually now, normal, but the way he gazed hungrily at Sloane made him worry that Lochlain wanted to gobble him up like the pie.

It was way too early for this shit.

"Look, Lochlain," Sloane said with a short groan, "it's really cool of you to stop by, but I had a really long night—"

"Not Lochlain," he replied curtly between bites, wagging a finger at him.

"Not Lochlain?" Sloane repeated dumbly.

Not-Lochlain shook his head, working on the last slice of pie. He'd eaten the entire thing, licking his lips coyly at Sloane and making him shiver down his spine.

Every bone in Sloane's body was telling him that something was wrong. Brainwashed, cursed, possessed, the possibilities were endless.

He casually traced a protection sigil on the edge of his desk, asking politely, "Then who are you?"

Not-Lochlain snorted as if greatly amused by the question, tilting his head and winking. The top of the desk suddenly cracked right through the middle of the sigil.

On his feet in a flash, Sloane gasped and stuttered, "Wh-what the freakin' hell was that? How, how did you do that? Who the hell are you?"

"Azaethoth," he purred in reply, his tongue seductively licking every last crumb of pie from his long fingers. "Mmm. The Lesser. Named after my great-great-great grandfather."

Sloane was stupidly entranced by that tongue, asking hesitantly, "Azaethoth the Lesser? As in... an old god?"

"Mm-hm," he hummed, lewdly sucking on his thumb. "If you're more comfortable, you may address me by this vessel's name."

"But you're not... Lochlain?"

"No."

Sloane stared back down at his desk and the fractured protection sigil. He didn't know of any mortal magic that could possibly be powerful enough to break that spell. But there was no way this guy was actually a god.

There were no gods, not anymore.

"And why exactly are you here?" Sloane asked warily.

"You're a witch, yes?"

"No," Sloane replied. "I mean, I'm registered, but what does that—"

"You follow the old ways?"

"I guess? Look, what is going on—"

"This vessel," Azaethoth-Lochlain said, gesturing to his body, "was a very devout follower. Even while deep in dreaming, I heard his prayers. He was a fascinating human. He didn't ask for glory or riches or any of the other mundane things most humans do.

"He prayed for the thrill, the rush of adrenaline, to never leave him. He always wanted to be excited and intrigued, for his heart to pound, to find spectacular adventure everlasting."

"That... sounds interesting?"

"Try listening to a few centuries of people pleading for money, sex, bigger cocks, and stronger orgasms—"

"Okay, okay!" Sloane interrupted. He doubted the real Lochlain could have gotten out half of that without blushing.

"I listened," Azaethoth-Lochlain went on, idly tracing a finger inside the empty pie pan for errant crumbs. "I often answered his prayers. But last night, there was a problem. A very serious problem. When I went to him, the damage was already done. I found your card in his pocket."

"Damage, what damage?"

"That's what I need you to investigate," he continued impatiently. "That's what your card says you do. Investigations of a private nature, yes?"

"Wait, wait," Sloane snapped, getting frustrated. "If something really serious happened, you need to contact the police. And Lochlain, or… Loch-Thoth, whatever your name is! If this is some super weird way to get out of a date, I swear—"

"No police," Loch-Thoth said firmly. "They'll only get in my way, and they won't allow me to do what I want."

"Which is?"

"Revenge," he replied with a hungry smile, baring all of his teeth. "Now, I will gladly compensate you for your services however you wish. Money is customary?"

"I don't want anything," Sloane protested. "Except maybe some kind of an explanation. What happened to you?"

"You desired this one, yes?" Loch-Thoth turned his head. "Would you like me to pleasure you with his vessel?"

"Wh-what?" Sloane sank down in his chair, scooting back against the wall. "No! Don't do that! That's… that's not right! Whatever you are, you can't just use Lochlain's body like that! He can't consent."

"Of course he can't consent," came the dry reply, eyes rolling dramatically. "He can't consent to anything. He's dead."

"Dead?" Sloane's breath caught in his throat, his stomach dropping violently. "What do you mean, dead?"

"Haven't you been listening to a word I've said?" Loch-Thoth complained loudly. "Sloane Beaumont, I want to hire you. I want you to find out who murdered me."

AMANDA MEUWISSEN is a queer author with a primary focus on M/M romance. She has a Bachelor of Arts in a personally designed Creative Writing major from St. Olaf College and is an avid consumer of fiction through film, prose, and video games. As the author of LGBTQ+ Fantasy #1 Best Seller, *Coming Up for Air*, LGBTQ+ Horror #1 Best Seller and #1 New Release, *A Delicious Descent*, and several other titles through various publishers, Amanda regularly attends local comic conventions for fun and to meet with fans, where she will often be seen in costume as one of her favorite fictional characters. She lives in Minneapolis, Minnesota, with her husband, John, and their cat, Helga, and can be found at https://linktr.ee/amandameuwissen.

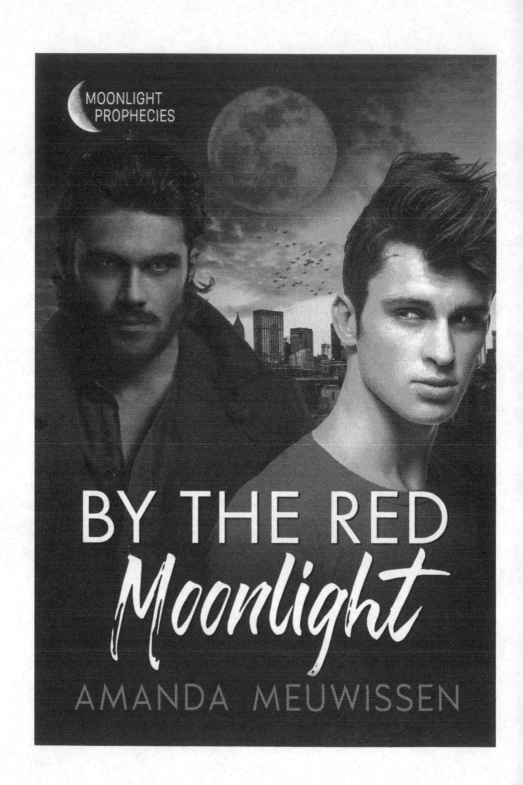

MOONLIGHT
PROPHECIES

BY THE RED
Moonlight

AMANDA MEUWISSEN

Moonlight Prophecies: Book One

Alpha werewolf, crime boss, and secret Seer Bashir Bain is neck-deep in negotiating a marriage of convenience with a neighboring alpha when a tense situation goes from bad to worse. A job applicant at one of Bash's businesses—a guy who was supposed to be a simple ex-cop, ex-con tattoo artist—suddenly turns up undead.

A rogue newborn vampire would have been a big wrench in Bash's plans even without his attraction to the man. After all, new vampires are under their sire's control, and Ethan Lambert doesn't even know who turned him. When Bash spares his life, he opens himself up for mutiny, a broken engagement, and an unexpected—and risky—relationship.

Ethan just wants a fresh start after being released from prison. Before he can get it, he'll need to turn private investigator to find out who sired him and what he wants. And he'd better do it quick, because the moon is full, and according to Bash's prophecy, life and death hang in the balance.

www.dreamspinnerpress.com

MOONLIGHT
PROPHECIES

BLUE MOON
Rising

AMANDA MEUWISSEN

Moonlight Prophecies: Book Two

Alpha Jay Russell's broken engagement may just be the best thing that ever happened to him. His ex-fiancé's twin, Bari, is much more his type and straightforward about his flirting and desire to unite their packs.

Jay returns home after his misadventures in Centrus City to a new prophecy, an unknown enemy, and tribal unrest over a series of racially-driven murders. Furious, Jay is determined to bring whoever's responsible to justice… but the unrest upsets the fragile peace he's been working to achieve, threatens his new lover's life, and undermines his position as Alpha, which makes investigating a challenge.

Can Jay and Bari work together to fight their inner demons—and a strange adversary dead set on returning to the past—or will mistrust and political machinations tear them apart?

Blue Moon Rising is the second book in the Moonlight Prophecies series. Fans of shifters, soothsayers, and shadowy villains will fall under Amanda Meuwissen's spell in this suspenseful, sexy urban fantasy romance.

www.dreamspinnerpress.com

MOONLIGHT
PROPHECIES

WANE ON
Harvest Moon

AMANDA MEUWISSEN

Moonlight Prophecies: Book Three

Cat shifter Luke and rat shifter Preston have had a solid relationship for ten years, but lately, the increasing attacks on their pack and the stress of raising their adopted daughter are highlighting more of their differences than the values they have in common. When they travel to Glenwood to investigate the source of the ancient artifacts tied to the recent violence, tensions in the shifter community—and their relationship—are already running high.

Strangely, this mystery seems tied to the events that brought them together. On their first mission, eighteen-year-old Luke and twenty-one-year-old Preston had to put aside their differences—and back-burner their mutual attraction—to prevent a disaster that would have revealed the existence of shifter kind to humans.

But how does what's happening now connect to their past? And can they find the answers their pack, their species, and their relationship need to survive?

www.dreamspinnerpress.com

THE PRINCE
AND THE
ICE KING

A Tale from the Gemstone Kingdoms

AMANDA MEUWISSEN

A Tale of the Gemstone Kingdoms

Every Winter Solstice, the Emerald Kingdom sends the dreaded Ice King a sacrifice—a corrupt soul, a criminal, a deviant, or someone touched by magic. Prince Reardon has always loathed this tradition, partly because he dreams of love with another man instead of a future queen.

Then Reardon's best friend is discovered as a witch and sent to the Frozen Kingdom as tribute.

Reardon sets out to rescue him, willing to battle and kill the Ice King if that's what it takes. But nothing could prepare him for what he finds in the Frozen Kingdom—a cursed land filled with magic... and a camaraderie Reardon has never known. Over this strange, warm community presides the enigmatic Ice King himself, a man his subjects call Jack. A man with skin made of ice, whose very touch can stop a beating heart.

A man Reardon finds himself inexplicably drawn to.

Jack doesn't trust Reardon. But when Reardon begins spending long days with him, vowing to prove himself and break the curse, Jack begins to hope. Can love and forgiveness melt the ice around Jack's heart?

www.dreamspinnerpress.com

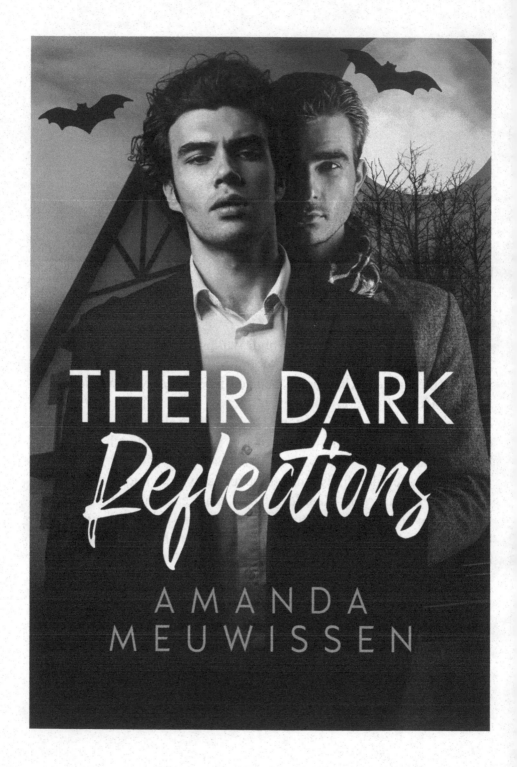

THEIR DARK
Reflections

AMANDA
MEUWISSEN

Personal assistant Sam Coleman can do it all: housekeeping, groundskeeping, bookkeeping. The catch? It's a con.

Ed Simon, his newest millionaire boss, doesn't know Sam Goldman is a Robin Hood for hire who targets rich jerks. Sure, Sam keeps the money for himself, his crew, and his real employers, but at least they only steal from bad people.

Until sweet, fumbling Ed, who doesn't seem to have a single vice. Too bad the people who hired Sam won't let him back out. They want Ed's money, and they'll hurt Sam and his friends to get it.

For years Ed has kept people at arm's length, but Sam's charms wear down his defenses—just as he learns their budding relationship was an act. Sam isn't who Ed thought he was, but Ed has a dark secret too: he's a vampire. And someone is framing him for a series of bloody murders.

When the real villains force their hand, Sam and Ed must choose: work together, trust each other, and give in to the feelings growing between them… or let what might have been bleed out like the victims piling at their feet.

www.dreamspinnerpress.com